IMPIMPI
Traitor/Collaborator

IMPIMPI

BLACK ANGER
WHITE FEAR

By Steve Harris

Quickfox Publishing

PO Box 12028 Mill Street 8010

Cape Town, South Africa

. www.quickfox.co.za

Copyright © 2014 Steve Harris

ISBN 978-0-620-64002-2

First print 2015

Edited by Michelle Bovey-Wood

Cover design by Simon McCausland, Liquid Pixels Design

Typesetting and production by Vanessa Wilson

TABLE OF CONTENTS

PART TWO

PART THREE

FOR THIS IS MY BLOOD

Thursday, 15th November 1976

Mike lay motionless, face-down on the stairs, blood oozing from wounds in his back and head. The red liquid seemed to know its destination as gravity and stairs conspired to forge bloody paths that converged in an expanding crimson pool next his head.

A silver chain and crucifix, the symbol of a covenant to her, hung loosely from his neck. The chain traced a path to the pool, the crucifix submerged like a ship's anchor beneath the bloody depths, unseen.

"For this is my blood of the covenant, which is poured out for many for forgiveness of sin." Matthew 26:28.

If Mike could have looked up, he would have seen the summer sun slowly disappearing behind Devil's Peak into the icy waters of the Atlantic Ocean; its languishing descent ushering in dusk, then night, to the leafy southern suburbs of Cape Town.

He would also have been aware of the world-renowned and critically-needed sanctuary, Groote Schuur Hospital, just a few hundred metres ahead of him, in the foreground of the mountain.

If he could have looked to his left, he would have noticed a bent and broken sign that a few moments before had been mounted to his front door:

Michael James Hanssen – Private Investigator

The official-looking burnished sign, normally associated with a medical or legal practice, lay beside him, like a faithful dog guarding its owner.

The timing of the blast suggested that the perpetrators had chosen to target him when collateral damage would be limited. Having planted many explosives himself, Mike would have admired the bomber's handiwork. The device was selected for purpose, planted with precision and timed to perfection. It had targeted anyone inside the office and would have incinerated all records, while leaving innocent bystanders unaffected and the building intact.

Mike left Dr Solly Goldberg's office at 6pm. His monthly appointment was on a Thursday, always at 5pm.

Driving back to his office, he pondered with some amusement the irony of a so-called jock from the Eastern Cape engaged in protracted therapy to exorcise a shadow government of ghosts that threatened to ruin his life. Most of these ghosts crawled out from the extremely masculine environments that had marked his life; where simply trying harder had been the default solution to every problem.

Some of his spectres harked back to barbaric hunting rituals and the machismo of an Eastern Cape boarding school, where even playing hockey earned the labels of "softie" or "faggot". Others emerged from his time at the country's top Afrikaans university – an institution that produced most of the nationalist government's leaders. The template was clear: Become a male rugby player – and Christian.

Eventually, new ghouls had manifested from his time as a conscript in the government's military, an organisation hell-bent on brainwashing its recruits into hating communism and maintaining white rule at any cost.

There were two groups that planted urban explosives in South Africa. It was safe to assume that both groups kept him under surveillance. Which one had reason to kill him?

The bombers knew enough about Mike's routine to set the trap. Spying 101 would have informed them that, most days, he returned to his office around 6:30pm to catch up on admin work. It was easy to work out that he had a monthly therapy session. He had not tried to hide it.

Had they also discovered his regular, Thursday night, 8pm, clandestine rendezvous? He had been careful to keep it secret. Could he have dropped his guard, become sloppy and been followed?

He entered his office at 6:25pm, welcomed by a blinking light that beckoned him to play new messages on his answering machine. Mike pushed the play button. A beep sounded and a muffled voice called out from the machine: *"They're on to you. Get the fuck out of there – now!"*

His combat training instincts kicked in. The message was not an invitation. It was a command. No time to wait for the second message.

9

The recorded message had sent a signal via his brain stem directly to his amygdala, taking away all contemplation and forcing him into survival mode. Mike raced towards the still-open door, looking to the safety of the road. He had taken one step beyond the door when the blast from within caught up to him, propelling him like a ragdoll through the air before carelessly dumping him on to the grubby stairway. The sign joined him a split second later.

The staff at the Groote Schuur Emergency Unit must have heard the blast. But, a blast does not summon an ambulance. A phone call does. The call was made by Costa; the Portuguese owner of the corner cafeteria, 20m down the road from Mike's now decimated office.

The medical officer on duty couldn't help chuckling at what sounded like a parody of a café owner: "You send ambulance quickly, you understand. There's this big explosion at 26 Bowden Road in Observatory, and my friend's lying on the stairs losing very much blood. I think if you not come quickly, he may be dead already."

Ten minutes later, an ambulance, announced by its familiar *eeeoooeeeooo* modulating siren, rushed along the route to the smouldering office.

The bomb squad, a division appointed to investigate the planting and detonation of terrorist bombs, arrived five minutes after the ambulance had left with its limp load. The group probably included a few of Mike's former colleagues.

PART ONE

1

A Child is Born

30th September 1950

"Oh shit!" Edith exclaimed from the privacy of the small vegetable garden nestled behind their modest, rented home.

"Shit, shit, shit." She was reacting to the tingling sensation around her nipples. Earlier that morning, she had discovered a slight brown-coloured stain in her panties. It was not the bright-red flow of her always-regular period. She was two days late and she knew she was pregnant.

Two weeks earlier, Carl had been discharged from the nursing home. On his first morning home she had been woken up by the unusual, but pleasant, experience of him tickling her back.

"To what do I owe this treat?" she had asked dreamily.

"You'll never guess."

"I won't. Tell me."

"Do you remember how exciting it was for that brief moment eight years ago? When we met in Cairo, got married within a week, had that two-day honeymoon in Alexandria? It was amazing," Carl replied.

"Yes, it was. Want to try again? This time we don't have hurry back after two days to fight Hitler," Edith responded tenderly.

There were two reasons why trying again wasn't the same. By that stage, it was simply sex with a partner whom she no longer loved romantically. Too much had happened since the frenzy of first love. Feelings of passion had gone, wrestled away by the creeping dissonance of a reality that no longer matched up to their dreams. The second was penetration. She gasped as he entered her, not from pleasure, but from pain.

Carl's physical war wounds had healed: The only legacy was a limp in his left leg, courtesy of mortar shell shrapnel. The emotional injuries never healed. His mind had become his jailor, incarcerating him in cynicism and a web of conspiracy theories. If more than two people entered a public washroom at the same time, Carl would sense a conspiracy.

Carl's war service had been with the Special Services Battalion (SSB). Its mission had been to provide vocational military training to youths who, in the wake of the 1929 Great Depression, had not been able to find employment.

The advent of the war saw the SSB integrated into the 11th SA Armoured Brigade. After initial assignments, they had been shipped off to El Alamein to face Desert Fox Field Marshall Erwin Rommel and his Afrika Corps. After that, it was on to the Italian campaign. The unemployable youths from the SSB had become battle-hardened veterans.

Carl was 17 when he enlisted. A scattered array of photographs, medals and infrequent references to the war suggested that Carl had served with distinction in North Africa and Italy. But the devil's always in the detail, and his demons were not apparent in the minutiae of military memorabilia. Instead, their fiendish presence played an endless game of emotional hide-and-seek among the grey folds of Carl's brain.

He was emotionally numb, had difficulty falling asleep, suffered recurring nightmares and was prone to irrational outbursts of extreme anger and violent behaviour.

In a more sophisticated setting, post traumatic stress disorder (PTSD) with intermittent explosive disorder (IED) would have been diagnosed, Carl never acknowledged that he had a problem, so he never rose above it. His condition remained undiagnosed and his symptoms grew progressively worse, culminating in a three-month stint in a nursing home for what the general practitioner diagnosed as a nervous breakdown.

Edith and Carl could not afford the nursing home. Nor could they survive for three months without Carl's income. Fortunately, the M.O.T.H.[1] organisation had stepped in and footed the institution's bill.

Edith felt fortunate to have found temporary employ-

---

1 The Memorable Order of Tin Hats (M.O.T.H.) organisation has been helping fellow military comrades in need, either financially or physically, since 1927.

ment as the housekeeping manager at the Beacon Island Hotel. The job-holder had been given three months' maternity leave. The income was needed, but it had come at a life-changing price.

Carl's convalescence produced no change. The cause remained. When he inevitably found himself in stressful situations, his hyper-anxiety and extreme rage returned.

Edith spent much of their life together shielding Carl from circumstances that might trigger his explosions. She wasn't always successful.

Her war service had been in the British Woman's Royal Navel Services (WRNS); popularly known as the Wrens. In 1942, she had met Carl while on pass in Cairo.

Her military experience had been less traumatic than Carl's, as she had spent most of her service as a radio operator, sending Morse code and decoding messages from relatively safe sites. Although limited, it was her understanding of the war that had made her stoic through the dark and troubled times that had characterised their life together in post-war South Africa.

In 1950, the year Edith fell pregnant, South Africa had begun polarising between white fear and black anger. In an attempt to maintain white supremacy while containing the black liberation struggle, the government had launched widespread apartheid policies with a vengeance. It was during this time that the Immorality Amendment Act; the Group Areas Act; the Suppression of Communism Act and the Population Registration Act effectively divided South

Africans into white, coloured, Asian and native population groups.

During that period, the pernicious H.F. Verwoerd was appointed Minister of Native Affairs and began to implement forced removals of black Africans.

* * *

The couple could not afford to have a child, but Edith's maternal instinct had kicked in and she had rationalised that having a baby might bring them closer again and rekindle the love they had felt so many years before in Egypt.

She had delayed the announcement of the baby until the option of securing a backstreet abortion had expired. So, three months later, while having lunch in the garden, she had informed him that she was in the second trimester of her pregnancy.

"Darling, I went to the clinic this morning and have some sensational news. We're going to have a baby."

He reacted swiftly. "Why bring a child into this world? There's no decent future for a white kid in this country."

He stomped out his cigarette and twisted the butt under his shoe. He was up to 50 a day. His doctor had told him that smoking was medicine for the nerves.

"How the fuck do you think we're going to feed it?"

"He can share my food," she shot back.

"Why did you say: 'He'? You don't know." His tone softened.

"There are many things I know that others don't," she said light-heartedly.

"Mmph, bullshit, you're going to starve when it's born, wench," he said, equally lightly. Any attempt at humour was unusual for Carl. Edith had won round one. In fact, she had won that fight. The issue was never raised again.

For the next six months, Carl behaved tolerably and could even have been described as kind and caring while Edith's girth swelled in anticipation of the birth.

The second and third trimesters passed without a hitch, and Edith worked at their small business until the day her waters broke.

"It's time to go, Carl," she said calmly.

"Okay, okay, I'm ready. You sure you can manage the walk?"

"Sure, I'm sure."

They had decided earlier that they would walk to the nursing home. It was only 180m from their rented two-roomed house.

They actually hadn't had another option. Their old car had broken down a week earlier and was in desperate need of a new gearbox, which they simply couldn't afford. There was no public transport and private taxis were too expensive.

Carl was becoming increasingly apprehensive as they started their slow walk. He held her by her elbow, stopping for breaks every 18m or so. Edith sensed his anxiety, gave him a coquettish glance and said confidently: "Let's hurry Carl; I don't want to give birth to a pavement special."

"Okay, but it's not the right time for that look," he shot back, his mood lifting.

Edith's humour had once more lightened an occasion. I hope that tactic continues to work into the future, she thought.

* * *

Midwife Betsy Loots had the flu, and nurse Beauty Khumalo was her designated replacement for emergency midwifery duties. Beauty was superstitious and God-fearing. She embraced a mixture of African beliefs and the Christian teachings that had once upon a time been brought to her forefathers by European settlers. She always approached healing as a combination of her nursing training learned at college and the traditional healing methods taught to her by her late mother, Nesiwe.

Nesiwe had been a *sangoma*[2] who had served the needs of a small Xhosa[3] community in the Plettenberg Bay area for many years. She had named her daughter Buhle, which directly translated from Xhosa means "beauty". African names were hard for many white people to pronounce or remember, so her "European" name, Beauty, had stuck.

---

2   A *sangoma* is a traditional healer or diviner who uses rituals and natural herbalist medicines for healing.

3   The Xhosa are an ethnic group, classified as black under the Population Registration Act. They live mainly in the southern and central southern parts of South Africa.

Buhle was as beautiful a woman as her name suggested: Beautiful because of her soft, glowing, ebony skin; her almond-shaped eyes and full, shapely lips. Most of all, she was beautiful because of her gentle and caring nature.

* * *

Carl did not stay for the delivery. "Delivering babies is women's work. Making babies is men's work," he had quipped, then regretted his comment almost immediately. Carl was not prone to apologising and his comment hung in the room like a smelly fart.

Mike Hanssen was born on June 15, 1951. It was an uncomplicated labour and delivery, except for one incident, which could perhaps not be called a complication, but a phenomenon.

"Oh my God, Madam!" Beauty exclaimed excitedly as the infant's head presented through the vaginal opening. "Your baby has the sign, the *umhlehlo*!"

Beauty was referring to the shimmery membrane that coated the head and face of the emerging newborn. It was a caul, an omen of good luck in Xhosa culture. Beauty's mother had taught her to assign much value to this rarity.

Seconds later, Beauty cried out: "It's a boy, Mrs Hanssen, a beautiful boy!" She clamped the umbilical cord and rubbed a sheet of paper across the baby's head and face. She pressed the material of the caul on to the paper and presented it to Edith.

Beauty explained: "Madam, oh Madam, this is the most important thing in your boy's life. The spirits say if the mother keeps the caul, the child will experience love's pleasure, the child will be protected from the serpent's evil ways and it will live with fortune and peace.

But madam, if the mother loses the caul or she dies; it must either be passed to another loved one or the child must get in touch with the spirits. If not, the child will experience love's pain, will not be protected from the serpent's evil ways and will live with misfortune and violence."

Ten minutes later, the placenta was expelled and the birth was complete. Beauty's final act was to place the newborn, swaddled in a blue blanket, in the crook of Edith's arm.

The child stopped crying.

Edith uttered a whispered sigh: "I love you already … you and your caul."

The caul was stowed in the safety of a traditionally prepared beaded bag next to Edith's clothes.

Mother and child drifted into a peaceful, bonding sleep. Her final thought before surrendering to sleep: Strange. Carl has a snake tattooed on the inside of his left forearm.

2

THE PROMISED LAND

Few people classified as white ventured into locations[4]. They were considered far too dangerous for the average white person. Edith was no exception. She spent many years living in Plettenberg Bay without ever entering the "no-go" areas. Carl, however, would be duty-bound to enter the locations in later years.

In 1951, the Plettenberg Bay location comprised mostly people classified as coloured, and a minority group of black people, mostly of Xhosa origin.

It was a typical location, characterised by thick clouds of wood smoke hanging overhead; livestock grazing freely among the shacks; chickens pecking at liberally strewn litter, while emaciated, tick-infested dogs, tails perma-

---

4   South Africa's urban areas had outlying locations for people who weren't classified as white. "Location" was the colloquial name given to a township. Resembling squatter camps, most houses were assembled from sheets of corrugated iron and scraps of wood.

nently curled between their legs, engaged in a recursive 24/7 routine with a disinterested abandon.

Roam, then sleep, roam, then sleep.

* * *

16th June 1951

A harsh, cold winter had set in, accompanied by gale-force winds and driving rain. The location was underserviced – it had no electricity, no tarred roads and no piped water. Clean drinking or cooking water was only available from a solitary community tap. Residents queued daily to fill their portable containers or buckets.

On this day, that precious resource flumed down already eroded roads to strategically excavated canals, diverting the torrents away from homes to weirs where residents could capture as much as possible in storage containers.

From there, storm water cascaded into a nearby stream where, in fairer weather, bare-bottomed toddlers played while their mothers did their laundry.

When they built their home, Beauty and her husband, Enoch, had applied indigenous knowledge passed down from their forefathers and had treated the internal walls and floor with *ubulongo*. This mixture of clay and cow dung served the dual purpose of waterproofing and insulating the home against cold and heat.

Enoch was a traditionalist, steeped in Xhosa culture. By age 30, he already had the look of a tribal elder. He always wore a balaclava rolled up into a hat, paired with an old, grey great-coat. His face was unshaven, with a pepper and salt goatee.

That bitter morning, the heavily pregnant Beauty clung to a few moments of additional bed warmth.

"Just five minutes more, Enoch. I'll get up after you bring me some coffee in bed," she said cheekily.

Enoch complied and within the agreed time frame, she had risen from the comfort of their Tokoloshe-proofed[5] bed.

Her first task was to prepare a packed lunch of *rooster-rood*[6] and jam for Enoch's lunch.

Enoch did not have regular employment. He made a living by roaming the village streets, like a door-to-door salesman, selling his labour to do odd jobs – from minor repairs to gardening or car washing.

Beauty looked out the window, shuddered and said: "Enoch, stay at home, just today. It's bitterly cold and wet out there."

Her appeal was appreciated, but he had no intention of staying home. They were going to have a baby and he had to provide for his family.

---

5   A *Tokoloshe* is a mythical dwarf-like, hairy demon. Tokoloshe-proofing is achieved by placing a brick beneath each leg of the bed. This elevation restricted the access of the diminutive demon.

6   *Roosterbrood* is bread made on a grill over an open fire.

"Buhle, I am an *indoda*[7] and soon I will be a *tata*[8]. I must do this."

Enoch would indeed soon leave the house, but not on a mission to provide for his family.

* * *

Outside, in that wintery gruel, the distant sound of engines could be heard. The sounds crept closer as a government passenger vehicle, a bulldozer and a bus approached the location.

Beauty and Enoch were the last of the group to be informed of their imminent eviction.

Hendrik Johannes Coetzee banged on their brittle door, his briefcase tucked under his right arm while battling an inverted umbrella in his left hand.

The wind triumphed and the umbrella remained in the upturned position, with its thin metal stays tearing through the waterproof material. They peeked curiously through the waterproofing, like meerkats emerging from their manor.

The zealous, now-drenched, khaki-uniformed government official had arrived to enact the forcible removal of black people living in areas with other races.

Enoch opened the door.

---

7   *Indoda* is the Xhosa word for "man".
8   *Tata* is the Xhosa word for "father".

Coetzee was a scrawny man; small in stature with a long, sharp nose protruding from a rodent-like, pointy face. The growth above his lips looked more like animal whiskers than the moustache he was desperately trying to cultivate.

This was Coetzee's first eviction assignment and he wanted it to be special. He maintained a stern demeanour as he read out from his script: "Under the authority of the Group Areas Act, No.41 of 1950, I, Hendrik Johannes Coetzee, inform you that you must vacate these premises and that you will be relocated to an area designated to you."

He presented an official-looking document that ordered Beauty and Enoch, along with 24 others, to move to New Brighton.

New Brighton was a black residential area that served as a dormitory township supplying cheap labour to the city of Port Elizabeth. It was a 240km away.

No goodbyes, no ceremony. The official said: "Make your 'X' here, grab your belongings, then get on the bus and go to the Promised Land."

There would be no discussion and no pleas. The law had to be followed. People classified as black were not allowed in the area and had to leave. Plettenberg Bay and its environs were designated for white and coloured people only.

Beauty and Enoch were mortified, but said nothing. The eviction was not unexpected. It had recently been the subject of heated debates at most of the township meetings which had been held in secret. Their anger had been vented. They had come to terms with their impotence, but still their resentment simmered.

"We must hurry, Enoch, before they destroy our house and we lose some of our important things," Beauty urged him anxiously.

She hastily gathered together their important documents: Birth certificates, a post office savings account book and their identity documents, commonly known as the *dompas*[9]. Enoch shook his head in dismay and muttered under his breath while he packed their belongings.

"*Eish, eish, eish!*" he repeated.

Finally, he retrieved their hidden stash. They had accumulated the princely sum of 30 pounds in a Mills cigarette tin they had kept hidden behind the kitchen cupboard. To be safe, Enoch squeezed half of the cash into his wallet and the other half into his trouser pocket.

They had barely exited their home when the bulldozer moved in to raze it. Enoch and Beauty were the last evictees to trudge down the muddy path to the bus, lugging heavy bags and battling the elements. Enoch walked behind Beauty, unaware of a hole that had developed in his greatcoat pocket. It was just large enough for gravity to do eviction work of its own on his wallet.

The wallet first flapped like a fledgling leaving its nest for the first time, then fell noiselessly on to the muddy

---

9   Black people were required to carry a *dompas* at all times.
     Directly translated as "stupid pass", this document was intended
     to restrict the movement of black people to specific areas.

path. Coetzee was following 15 paces behind when it dropped. He instinctively lurched forward to alert Enoch to his potential misfortune.

"Hey, you!" The first attempt was muffled by the storm. He did not try again. Instead, he walked hurriedly towards the slightly submerged wallet, keeping an eye on Enoch's back. He reached the wallet, contemplated for a moment, and then concealed it with his soiled, left *veldskoen*[10].

He maintained his stance as he watched the bus drive off with its 26 passengers.

He called out: "I hear it's quite nice in P.E. Don't know, never been there. At least you won't have to cross the Red Sea to get there, but you might spend 40 years wandering in the desert." He started laughing to himself: "Maybe I should have been a comedian. Probably pays more than working for the bloody government, impounding black strays."

He reached down for the wallet and counted the bounty. Fifteen pounds. Not bad for a day's work. When last did a *boer*[11] get money from a boy?

* * *

---

10 A *veldskoen* is a type of shoe that has been acculturated into the Afrikaans psyche. It is made from soft rawhide uppers attached to leather sole without tacks or nails.

11 The term *boer* was used by black people to refer to Afrikaners or to the government, and "boy" was a demeaning term used by many white people when addressing a black man.

Veronica McCullum witnessed Coetzee's thievery. She had been staring, from the sanctuary of her shack and her colour, at Coetzee's bureaucratic bullying unfolding in front of her. Veronica was in her early 40s and classified coloured.

Veronica's genealogy had its roots in Scotland. It all started with a Scottish officer, Captain Aubrey McCullum. He had come to South Africa with the 1820 settlers, docked in Port Elizabeth and ventured into the Plettenberg Bay area a few years later.

He had not had racial profiling in mind when he had sown his seed and reaped a family of McCullums who, over time, had developed a reputation for their fishing expertise. Aubrey McCullum could not have known that the shoal of McCullums he had spawned would be caught in the net of apartheid under the collective name coloured fishermen.

Coetzee reminded her of a drowning rat. They lived in a township infested by the repulsive rodents, so if she reported him, her action was one small step towards reducing the infestation, she thought.

She did not have the nerve to report the theft to the police, so she explained the incident to the manager at the local bus depot. Hoping to minimise any comeback, she recalled the event with an apparent disinterested use-it-don't-use-it attitude.

The bus depot official recorded Veronica's report in a daily incident book, complying with her request and writing "Anonymous" as the reporter's name.

* * *

The MAN diesel bus bilged smoke as it slowly negotiated the twisting coastal road to Port Elizabeth. Beauty sat two rows behind the driver. Despite the stormy conditions, through the window on her right she caught glimpses of the ragged boundaries where sea met shore on Keurbooms Beach, then Nature's Valley.

To her dismay, she could also see the road pass below her through cracks where rust had won the battle with the metal floorboards. Exhaust fumes snaked through the cracks, filling the interior with the nauseating smell of diesel. Beauty wondered if death by bus fumes was the apartheid government's version of the Nazi's final solution. Were they deliberately being gased with carbon monoxide?

Not this time, she thought. The remedy was simply to open windows and let in fresh air. Everything seemed to come at a price: The icy-cold winter rain buffeting the Eastern Cape shore accompanied the fresh air, soaking its occupants.

Enoch's cough seemed worse, most likely reacting to the fumes, cold and damp. Beauty was concerned that its frequency had increased. Enoch took great care to cough into his handkerchief. When he looked down, he noticed spots of red mucus, like the polka dot pattern on the dresses that so many fancy women wore. Little passed Beauty's notice and this was no exception. She leaned over and put her hand on Enoch's shoulder, whispering in the assuring voice of a caring nurse.

"There's a highly respected hospital in Port Elizabeth. I want you to go there with me and have that cough checked out. Besides, I have to go to hospital soon. Baby's due in three weeks."

Enoch shrugged his shoulders and with eyes downcast, meekly nodded his agreement. He knew. When you cough bloody mucus, lose weight, have pains in your chest and feel unwell, you have a problem.

An hour later, the rusty bus shuddered to a stop. It had broken down while struggling up the steep ascent immediately after the Devil's Elbow. The notorious bend was in the middle of the magnificent, 6.5km-long Bloukrans Pass, which had been built in the late 1800s. It stood as a testament to the engineering prowess of the famous Thomas Bain.

The rain stopped and the sun came out as everyone disembarked. Bus driver Henk van der Merwe gathered his 26 passengers in front of the bus, out of harm's way of any traffic, like a mother hen gathering her chicks.

Henk was in his mid-20s; a classic Afrikaner in name and looks. He was good looking in a rugged sort of way; stocky, deep-voiced, with thick, powerful, hairy arms. He wore shorts that displayed strong legs with large calf muscles. Beauty noticed that he had what was called a boer tan: Lily-white skin under his shorts and shirt, with a rich-brown colour where his skin had been exposed to the African sun. Clean-shaven, his broad face sported deep laugh lines around his eyes and thinning blonde hair on top of his head. But most striking were his eyes. Not only were they an unusual green colour, they had a Jesus-like kindness and a softness that radiated from them.

"Oh heck, I'm so sorry about the breakdown, you guys, but *ag,* don't worry, I will fix it in a jiffy. Or maybe it will take a little more than a jiffy, but fix it, I will." He lovingly tapped the bus on its bonnet during his speech.

"She's a temperamental old girl," he said affectionately, without realising the irony of his relationship with his MAN bus. "This only happens when she's given a tough time, and boy, oh boy, this hill's tough."

While Henk was delivering his speech, a troop of baboons emerged from the dense Tsitsikamma Forest and settled on the road about 50m from them. They maintained a curious, indifferent watch over their recently-arrived human entertainment. Henk continued: "*Ag,* ignore the baboons. It's the elephants and leopards that we must watch out for. No, no, only joking. They're in the forest, wary, and have never attacked anybody."

"Now, the good news is that I planned ahead in case we had a bit of a mechanical problem. There's some *padkos*[12] for you guys."

Henk opened the bus's luggage compartment, revealing three large pockets of oranges, 10 loaves of bread, two jars of Black Cat peanut butter and a large jar of honey. "You guys help yourselves. I don't like what this bloody government's doing, so this is the least I can do, you know."

---

12 *Padkos* is the Afrikaans word for food that is eaten on a journey.

Then, he prised open the bus's squeaky bonnet and secured the metal stay. The top half of his body disappeared into the mechanical maze in front of him. While he was working, the passengers had a banquet. Actually, a feast. Beauty, always the caregiver, made a peanut butter and honey sandwich and handed it to Henk. "You're a noble man, Mr van der Merwe. Thank you," she said gently. "It's nothing," he replied. "Please call me Henk," She added: "I am Beauty."

Henk nodded appreciatively. "Yes, you certainly are."

Two hours later, face smudged with oil and a shifting spanner in his greasy right hand, Henk announced triumphantly: 'You see, a boer makes a plan. She's ready, willing and able to ride." The engine sounded considerably healthier as they shuffled aboard. They all had full stomachs and no left-overs remained for the disappointed troop of baboons.

The rest of the three-hour drive was uneventful, save for the innumerable times Henk glanced in the rear-view mirror, catching Beauty's eye. At first, he looked away immediately. Later, they would lock eyes and he would hold her glance for several moments before refocusing on the road ahead.

Beauty wanted the trip to last forever. The sun was now shining while the passengers spoke animatedly about their future in New Horizons. Enoch and Beauty were offered temporary accommodation in the township, sharing a room with Thandiwe and Seiko. They were fellow refugees and ex-neighbours from Plettenberg Bay.

The room was in their parents' home. Until a month ago, it had been occupied by Thandiwe's brother who, fortunately for Beauty and Enoch, had travelled to the Witwatersrand to seek work on the gold mines

"Stay as long as you need to," Thandiwe volunteered, sensing the couple's apprehension.

"We're beholden. We'll find a place of our own as soon as we get to know the area and can see what's available," Beauty replied.

It would be a temporary arrangement, as Enoch was already visualising a venture inland to get a job as a herder, rather than settling in an urban environment. He had no desire to bring up their child in a city dormitory.

He was in earshot of Henk when he turned to Beauty: "When we get to New Brighton, I am going to contact my uncle, Dumisani. You remember the one who lives near the Sapkamma Railway siding in the Jansensville district? He will help me get a job. If we're lucky, we can find some work for you, too. It's where I was born. It's a worthy place for our child to grow up."

Sapkamma was about 100km inland from Port Elizabeth, on the road to Graaff Reinet.

The New Brighton bus terminus was a hive of activity, with at least 20 buses in the throes of embarking and disembarking. As their bus came to a stop, Beauty was deep in thought, musing about the injustice of their circumstances. There were at least 400 other people milling around the terminus; each with their own unjust circumstances, their own concerns and their own fears.

There were scores of women walking to and from a nearby market with babies strapped to their backs, carrying heavy loads on their heads, from bundles of wood to pails of water. These women were carrying what was necessary to produce everything they were selling at the market next to the bus terminus.

The market was the focal point for the community, a place where they could meet that special person, catch up with news, grab a quick meal or trade produce.

Goods on offer included arts and crafts of beadwork; weaving; woodwork and pottery; plus a range of edibles, like *amasi* (fermented milk); *amathanga* (pumpkins); *umbona* (maize); *unngusho* (samp); and *iimbotyi* (beans).

Enoch's stomach, sated by Henk's generosity just three hours earlier, was now ready for another round. It was the *inyama* (meat) that caught his eye. On display were fly-infested intestines and hideless carcasses draped on hooks, dripping blood on to soiled, wooden tables. The blood-soaked tables were crammed with ox tongues, bulls' brains, pigs' feet, goats' ears, testicles and Enoch's favourite dish, the smiley[13].

Enoch wanted to treat Henk. "Would you like to share a smiley, Mr van der Merwe?'

Before Henk could answer, Enoch thrust his hand into the great-coat pocket to retrieve his wallet, only to discover

---

13 A smiley is a sheep's head, stripped of hair and parboiled before being roasted over hot coals. The smile on the sheep's head emerges as the skin tightens during the roasting process.

the hole and his loss. He frantically felt in the other pockets. No wallet. Without saying a word, he began crawling along the bus floor, searching; it was as barren as his great-coat pocket.

Had he dropped it on the road at Bloukrans Pass? He had a fleeting image of his wallet in the clutches of a baboon basking on the tar road. Dismissing the baboon as a criminal option, he thought further back. Had he dropped it at the location in Plettenberg Bay?

Enoch shared the story of his loss with Henk and the other passengers, once again mentally retracing his steps, this time to an audience of empathetic ears.

Henk put an arm around Enoch's stooped shoulders. "We know it's not on the bus, and I doubt that it's at the Pass. One of the other passengers would have seen it. When I get back, I will check the location and bus terminus. Maybe it was found and handed in. It's possible, you never know. There are many honest people out there. Don't lose hope."

Henk continued: "I overheard you say that you're considering moving to Sapkamma. I drive the P.E. to Jansensville route once a month. Maybe, with your permission, I can drop in at Sapkamma and see how things are going with you guys? Perhaps I'll have your wallet. This time, the smiley's on me. You can buy the next one."

"It will be wonderful to see you, with or without Enoch's wallet and we accept your generous offer to share a smiley," Beauty replied as Enoch nodded his approval. The thought of a free smiley temporarily eased his loss.

After tucking into the smiley, they said their goodbyes, grabbed their bags and followed Thandiwe and Seiko to their temporary accommodation a short distance down a dusty township road.

Henk watched them walk away. His concern for them was outweighed by an outlandish excitement in the pit of his stomach. *What on Earth am I thinking? Married, pregnant and black! Oh man, that's way out – even for me.*

Henk had become a well-read man. Choosing to work as a bus driver was his way of connecting with people, while providing him with ample time for self-study and his books. His reading had stimulated an increasing open-mindedness. He had become more aware of the plight of the disadvantaged and of injustice and inequalities in society. More specifically, he no longer believed that relationships needed to be classified in traditional categories, nor limited by current social boundaries.

Clearly, today's thoughts took him beyond his norm. He was fine with that. So fine that he recalled a Blaise Pascal quote with a sigh: "The heart has its reasons that reason knows naught of."

3

ANOTHER CHILD IS BORN

17th June 1951, 12am

Beauty strolled up to Enoch and calmly announced: "Come, it's time for us to meet our *usana*" (baby). Her waters had broken three weeks premature, yet she was unfazed. Beauty packed a bag of necessities, clasped Enoch's hand, and together they walked to the New Brighton bus stop. Within 10 minutes, they were aboard a bus to Livingstone Hospital's maternity wing.

Arriving at Livingstone Hospital, Beauty couldn't help noticing that the facility was in an advanced stage of disrepair. The once-fetching face-brick building appeared derelict. It stood in spacious grounds that had gone to seed: Unmowed lawns with spindly weeds in abundance lined cracked concrete driveways and pavements. Squeaky doors led to a grimy reception area, which was lined with broken chairs and a stained, threadbare red carpet pocked with holes where the most feet had walked.

She whispered to Enoch: "Another shining tribute of the boere's wilful neglect of black people."

Still, the staff were a tribute to the mantra: "First do no harm". They did not neglect Beauty. On the contrary, she was warmly welcomed upon arrival and whisked into a maternity ward and prepped for childbirth.

To Beauty, the preparation was old hat. She was, after all, a qualified nurse who had assisted with many births. She spared a thought for Edith's little boy whom she had helped deliver just two days earlier. Not just a boy. A boy with a caul. "Oh, it's so important, Mrs Hanssen. I hope you look after it," Beauty thought.

The waiting room offered a wide range of chairs, all excessively worn down on the front edges. Apparently anxious people waiting in the maternity ward sat on the edge of their seats.

Enoch lingered in the waiting room while Beauty went through the initial birth preparations. The normally self-possessed Enoch was anxious. He didn't opt for the seating. Instead, he paced to and fro like a prisoner in a small cell.

To his immense relief, it was not long before an orderly appeared, beckoning him to follow.

Inside the delivery room, Sister Pumla Mjo, assigned to assist with Beauty's childbirth, counted the duration and intervals between Beauty's contractions. They were four every 10 minutes. Beauty's breathing through the contractions was spot-on and she resisted pushing.

Moments later, it was time. Beauty's feet were in stirrups when Enoch joined them. He took great pains to position himself near Beauty's head. The other side looked decidedly too primal for his liking.

Beauty's body was telling her what to do: Breathe and push, breathe and push.

Enoch was quiet during this process, except for several series of "*Eish, eish, eish,*" muttered under his breath.

Then the atmosphere in the delivery room suddenly changed. Beauty knew there was a problem before nurse Pumla said it.

"I am calling Dr Brown, our resident obstetrician. I'm worried that labour isn't progressing and that baby may be distressed."

Enoch was beside himself. Beauty remained calm.

Dr Kyle Brown, a big bear of a man, entered the room and took charge. "Hi Beauty, let's deliver a baby, shall we?" His commanding and composed presence calmed the room and things returned to the former state of peace.

Brown inspected Beauty's baby bump. Satisfied, he donned surgical gloves and conducted an internal examination.

"Beauty we're going to try a little suction to encourage baby to come and say hello to us."

"That's fine, Doctor," Beauty replied.

"Nurse, suction machine, please," Brown requested confidently.

Nurse Mjo set up the vacuum extractor and handed the plastic cup to the doctor. Brown plunged the cup into Beauty's vagina, placing it on the baby's head.

"Now we will create a bit of vacuum persuasion. Nurse, please depress the handle gently."

Nothing happened. The pump was broken – the seals had petrified.

Enoch, ever the odd-job man, offered to attempt a repair and shuffled across to the vacuum extractor. Without realising it, he had moved from the safety of the head of the bed into the line of gynaecological fire. He looked up, and even quicker down again. He did not look up again and focused only on the vacuum machine.

Brown changed tactics: "Right. Plan B, Nurse. Forceps, please."

Brown gently plunged the forceps. Applying light pressure, he tried to coax the baby to make an exit. The effort could not have taken longer than three minutes, when Brown announced: "Beauty, your baby wants its own exit – a short cut. We're moving you to the theatre."

"Nurse, prepare for an emergency caesarean." Brown was less casual, still composed. Apprehension was returning to the room.

If there had been a scale for anxiety, the final turn of events would have been enough to tip Enoch over the edge. He kept his head down and continued to pour over the pump.

Beauty was wheeled out, leaving Enoch to find solace in his broken vacuum pump.

The team worked like clockwork. A nurse put a screen over her chest, and the anaesthetist administered a pain-killer. Brown made a bikini cut into the skin above the pubic hair, parted layers of tissue and muscle, moved the bladder to expose the lower part of uterus and made a small cut.

Beauty felt the surgeon pressing on her belly, and then the whooshing of fluid. Five minutes in all, and a baby boy, Andile Khumalo, was born in the early evening of 17 June 1951.

Two days younger than Mike.

Brown did a quick check on the baby before placing the infant on Beauty's chest.

"Are you always going to be this difficult?" she asked Andile.

Another 30 minutes were spent in surgery; stitching, suturing and stapling. Mission accomplished. Beauty was moved to the recovery room.

"Where's Enoch?" she asked.

Nurse Mjo found Enoch in the delivery room, still pouring over pieces of the vacuum pump. "Enoch, you have a baby boy," Pumla announced joyfully.

"*Eish*," he replied.

Her hospital stay lasted six days. During this time Beauty arranged for Enoch to have chest X-rays. Advanced tuberculosis was diagnosed. The resident intern prescribed streptomycin and explained that the antibiotic could effectively keep the disease at bay. Enoch was to have six-monthly check-ups to monitor the disease.

Enoch, too, had been industrious during Beauty's maternity stay. He had contacted Dumisani and arranged that they move out to Sapkamma when mother and baby were discharged.

Dumisani said there was labourer accommodation on a farm for them and the possibility of a job for Enoch, subject to approval by the farm owner, Geoff Walters.

When Enoch told her, Beauty was hesitant. "That sounds suitable for you and Andile, but what am I going to do? Did you consider that this wife and mother happens to be a qualified nurse who's not going to stay at home and have more babies?"

Enoch gave her a sheepish look. "You're a worthy wife. Yes, I am concerned for you and we will work something out."

They took a train bound for Graaff Reinet and disembarked at the railway station at Sapkamma. The station serviced the needs of a local sheep and goat farming community. It was a typical arid Karoo farming environment: Cactus, aloes, sheep, angora goats and buck in abundance.

The station was linked to a farmhouse, with associated out-buildings and labourer cottages owned by Geoff Walters. Walters also owned a trading store adjacent to the station, which included a post office. He was the postmaster.

His wife, Lucy, was the only teacher at a junior school for pupils up to standard five, which was situated a few hundred metres away. Such institutions were known as farm schools, and hers was for white pupils. A kilometre down the road, there was another reserved for non-whites.

Enoch and family were greeted like royalty at the station by Dumisani and his kin.

4

MIKE'S EARLY YEARS

Edith didn't tell Carl about the caul. She opted instead to hide the secret sack in the back of the bedroom cupboard. No one would ever know her reasons. She probably did not want him to think of her as superstitious. She could rest assured that Carl would never find it. He, after all, never used the cupboard. As his wife, it had become her job to select his clothes and set them out on the bed every morning.

Her other jobs included making his meals, which he ate in solitude while sitting on his bed, and of course she poured his single tot of brandy every night. This, too, was consumed alone on the bed. Edith seldom drank alcohol.

Carl rarely exceeded one drink per night, despite the suspicions of many who had become familiar with his foul moods.

"Are you sure he's not an alcoholic?" they asked.

"Well then, if not, he's a dry drunk," others would speculate.

These assumptions were usually made by people who had alcoholics in their family, so they spent much of their time trying to identify the alcoholic in others'. They played an endless game of spot-the-alcoholic.

After the war, Carl had found unskilled employment with the post office. He had displayed a technical aptitude, and over time he began repairing everything from radios to friends' cars. He was a regular Mr Fix-it.

Edith had encouraged his moonlighting, and by early 1950, he had built a *rondavel*[14] in their back garden, which he had filled with spares and then begun charging for his services.

Carl left the post office in July 1950. His venture into entrepreneurship coincided with his nervous breakdown. When he was discharged, Edith assumed a large role in their repairs business. She managed the administration as well as customer relations, shielding Carl from any unhappy customers or outstanding debts that could drive up his anxiety levels.

Mike knew little about his parents' histories. He was aware that his dad claimed Nordic ancestry, and his mother, British. The thought of being a descendant cocktail of Vikings and Pommies fascinated him. So, when he needed to impress, he would select a spirit ancestor from either source. For physical prowess, he called upon the Viking Ragnar Lodbrok; and for military and intellectual matters, Winston Churchill.

---

14 A *rondavel* is a westernised version of an African-style hut.

Soon after returning from the nursing home, Carl's malicious moods began to dominate the home. Edith learned to read the signs that indicated a change in Carl's mood, and she would try desperately to quell the sparks that could flare the simmering, active volcano that was Carl's temper.

Edith had tried to get Carl to proactively manage his moods. She hoped they were like a light switch over which he could gain control. If he was switched on, he could surely switch his moods off. It was incomprehensible to her that Carl had no control over his moods whatsoever. But Carl lived in a world where one moment the world was in colour and absolutely normal, the next, it was grey.

The image of his mother giving him the "Shh" sign became indelible in Mike's memory. In her case, the sign was her index finger pointing vertically over her lips, accompanied by a stern scowl. It was aimed at unobtrusively instructing Mike to stop talking, or to tone down anything that could disturb Carl.

Memories of his dad's intermittent explosions stretched back to his toddler years. Incidents of rage of variable intensity had occurred several times over the years. He particularly remembered one of the more extreme occasions of 1957.

"There's no future for whites in this country. We might as well be dead; I'll be doing us a favour," Carl roared at Edith.

The warning was followed by the sound of crockery and appliances crashing against walls, then dropping to the floor, accompanied by the inevitable sound of breaking glass.

Mike remembered his mother grabbing his arm and fleeing the house. They had cowered in mortal fear behind a thicket of bushes in the back garden.

He recalled how the moonlight had illuminated a stalking Carl, who had moved like a wolf hunting prey in the garden, a Smith and Wesson 38 in his right hand. Edith's right hand had tightened around Mike's mouth to stifle any sound that may reveal their hiding place.

This scene and several, less perilous, others, ended with Carl returning to his room and falling into a deep sleep, while Edith cleaned up the carnage and repaired what was repairable. There were never any discussions or recriminations after things had calmed down.

On another occasion, Edith had tried to use humour to diffuse one of Carl's tantrums by offering him an alternate jug to smash. The one he had been about to throw was her favourite. Her attempt failed miserably and had escalated the destruction.

In another instance, Carl had sent the portable radio smashing through their bedroom window. It had landed on the ground outside the house and proceeded to play music as the impact of the crash had switched it on. Under different circumstances, the incident may actually have been humorous.

It was times like those that Edith had wondered: Why did I leave England? What do I see in him?

She had decided that her bed had been made and that she was going to sleep in it. Her co-dependency had gone beyond sacrificing her priorities for his. It had extended to simple but significant choices, like never getting a driver's licence. She had become trapped by her own decisions.

South Africans usually assumed that people from England were more liberal than Afrikaners. In Carl's circles, most people bought into this and were circumspect with their racial slurs when Edith was in earshot.

Given the politically conservative hegemony among senior military officers, Mike could certainly conclude that his mother had been more politically liberal in her politics than Carl. It was said that many white people vote for the United Party[15], yet thanked God that the conservative, National Party was in power.

Had Edith's English background made her sympathetic to the political rights of black people? She had definitely lived a life of white privilege and, to a large extent, been a victim of endemic white fear.

There had been a time when his mum had bought ice creams for the pair of them. They had been watched by a group of young coloured children. Mike had said to her: "Shame, they don't have ice-creams," to which she had replied: "Non-white children don't like ice-cream."

Of course it was possible that she simply had not had the money and had hoped that her appalling racist

15 United Party, a political party left of the Nationalist party, had ruled South between 1934 and 1948.

assumptions about non-white preferences had allayed Mike's concerns.

He never asked her about her political views, she never volunteered them, and her views were never again put to the test in front of Mike. The apartheid regime created such an effective separation of races that ignorance ruled.

How could 10 percent of a population have been so ignorant about the 90 percent?

Mike had attended the local primary school similar to a farm school. Boys came to school with no shoes and it had offered no sporting activities, only gardening. After school, Mike fished or surfed, mostly on his own.

He had been blissfully unaware that his school was exclusively for white children. There had been only 20 pupils in total, and he had been alone in his grade, one boy in the grade above, and three in the grade below. He had got on with all of them. Or so he thought.

* * *

Flashes of the rage so typical of his dad started to manifest in Mike's behaviour.

The most significant incident was when he was 11 years old.

He had received a bicycle for Christmas. Upon returning to school in the new year, Kobus Neethling, the boy in the grade above him, had taken his bike for a ride without asking his permission. When he returned, he had announced that he would keep it.

"*Soutie*[16], this bike's now mine."

Mike was livid. He grabbed the bike.

Kobus tugged it back.

This tussle devolved into a tug-of-war with the bike serving as the rope.

Kobus strategically waited until Mike was straining at peak effort before pulling the bike and then suddenly letting go. Mike went sprawling and the bike landed on top of him, lacerating his knees. Kobus stood and watched him, laughing.

Assuming the scuffle was over, Mike leaned the bike against the toilet wall. His back was turned when Kobus lunged at him. The impact propelled him forward, crashing his face into the wall. Blood spurted from his mouth and nose. The pain was excruciating. He fell to the ground, landing on his back, like a boxer who had been felled by a sucker punch.

The older, bigger Kobus jumped on him, sitting with knees astride his chest, raining punches down on his face.

The other boys described what happened next. When his mother quizzed him later, Mike could not remember.

---

16 *Sout* is salt in Afrikaans. Afrikaners often called English speakers the derogatory term "*souties*". It is a derogatory term. Many people claimed that expatriates maintained their English customs without fully embracing their new country. They metaphorically had one foot in South Africa while the other remained firmly planted in England: Their penis immersed in the sea's salt water as they strode the continents.

Mike had apparently given a guttural, primordial scream, heaved the heavier boy off his chest and then attacked.

The prey had become the predator. Mike had transformed into his barbarian warrior. He was Ragnar Lodbrok, and Kobus was his victim. They traded blows like mixed martial arts cagefighters. Mike's aggression had overwhelmed Kobus and the tables turned. Mike lunged, knocking Kobus on to his back. Then, he was on top of Kobus, pounding him mercilessly.

Fortunately, schoolmaster Mr Els had arrived soon after Mike began his barrage of blows. Mike was prised off Kobus, who was still throwing air punches. Kobus had been thrashed by an angry, bleeding, savagely determined younger boy.

Mr Els sent both boys home to get cleaned up.

Edith saw Mike arrive. At first she thought his bloody face was another of his pranks and assumed the red coating to be tomato sauce. The truth hit her when she saw that both of his front teeth were snapped in half and that his jaw was lopsided. The collision with the toilet wall had extracted a hefty price.

Appalled by the state of her broken boy, she attended to his wounds as best she could.

When Carl saw Mike, he shook his head and asked: "Who won?" Mike had not replied.

He was whisked off to the provincial hospital in Port Elizabeth. X-rays revealed a dislocated jaw with multiple fractures.

A wired jaw, weeks of soup and melted ice-cream were followed by endless dental sessions. Kobus's attack had left a permanent lump on Mike's jaw and an indelible mark on his temperament.

Complementing his nascent, volatile temper, Mike grew up in a gun culture that would make an American National Rifle Association (NRA) member's chest swell with pride. A loaded Smith and Wesson revolver was Carl's constant companion. Mike couldn't recall a time when it had not accompanied Carl, whether it was on a fishing trip or to a movie. The handgun was one of a pair, and they were a fraction of an arsenal of 10 weapons in Carl's gun case. Mike loved the entire cache and spent hours stripping, cleaning and assembling pistols, shotguns and rifles.

On several occasions, he had received instruction at the shooting range. By the time he was 11, he was conversant in all of Carl's weapons.

Carl ended each shooting practice session with: "Mark my words, one day you will need these. This country's not safe and it's getting worse."

Like father, like son. When Mike finished school, he always had a weapon handy.

5

Voodoo and Black Magic

Henk returned to Plettenberg Bay's bus depot on 18 June 1951. He didn't know that Beauty had given birth prematurely.

He did know that he had promised to investigate what had happened to Enoch's wallet and he was looking for any reason to renew contact with Beauty.

His bus-driving shifts were five days on and two days off. The two days would be dedicated to Operation Wallet Search.

It was a lot easier than he thought.

The depot manager, Chris Moerdyk, and Henk were close friends. Henk told Chris about the missing wallet.

"Well, I never," came the response. "An incident involving a wallet was reported the day that you left for P.E. It's in the incident report book."

There it was. "Well, we don't know the name of the official, but that shouldn't be difficult. I'll just go to the Department of Native Affairs and ask who conducted the removal," Henk said with confidence.

"Oh yes, and he'll say: 'Of course I stole the wallet. Here it is with all the money intact.' Grow up, Henk!"

"Okay, smart arse. What do we do then?"

"We?"

"You will at least help me make a plan, won't you?"

"Okay, thinking caps on."

After a short discussion, a plan was hatched. It was simple and needed acting skills, but it was worth a try.

The next day, Henk went to the Department of Native Affairs.

"Morning, madam, my name's Henk," he said to the receptionist.

"One of your officials conducted a removal of persons to Port Elizabeth on the June 16. I wonder if you could help me I have something for him."

"You must mean Hennie Coetzee," the receptionist answered in a melodic voice.

"Could I see Mr Coetzee, please?"

"I'm sure that could be arranged. Let's give it a try, shall we?"

She announced over the public address system: "Mr Coetzee, Mr Coetzee, there's a gentleman at reception to see you, Mr Coetzee."

Within five minutes, the mousy midget of a man appeared.

He put out his hand in greeting. "Coetzee, how can I help you?"

"Well it's kind of private. Is there somewhere we can talk, please?"

Coetzee scurried towards a nearby interview room, motioning Henk to follow him.

They entered the privacy of a room decorated with a large, framed picture of a stern Daniel Francois Malan, Prime Minister of South Africa. They took seats on opposite sides of the wooden table as Malan observed their every move.

"Well?" Coetzee asked.

"Mr Coetzee, my name's Henk van der Merwe. I am the bus driver that took the black people to P.E. on June 16."

"Oh, them. Well it's for their own good that they went to P.E. I always say donkeys with donkeys and cows with cows, in a manner of speaking. You know, it's not personal, only business."

"Yes, well, I overheard a group speaking on the bus and I felt you'd like to know what they were saying."

"Indeed?"

"Yes, apparently, one of the passengers lost his wallet. Another claimed he saw someone pick it up from the muddy path at the location. The description he gave fits you."

Coetzee listened intently, his little eyes darting from one side of the room to the other.

"It's what they said then that worried me, and it made me think that if that man found the wallet, he'd like to return it."

Henk changed his tone, trying to sound eerie, as if he were telling a haunted-house story.

"You know, I've heard a lot of stories about blacks and the strange things they can do. One old passenger started talking about black magic and the curses she was going to cast on the person who stole the wallet.

"Another talked about making a voodoo doll, and once they found the name and address of the person who picked up the wallet, they'd get a hair from their hairbrush, or one that had washed down their drain, to complete the spell."

Coetzee's eyes continued to dart. His nose started twitching.

"Another passenger said he had contacts with a gangster organisation that would be willing to cut out the thief's privates to make strong *muti*[17].

You know about *muti* and the uses of genitalia don't you, Mr Coetzee?"

"Us whites, we don't believe in that sort of thing, do we Mr Coetzee?"

At this point, Coetzee's facial movements were at their zenith, his wiry moustache joining in the harmony, animated by the twitching nose. The rodent was complete.

Henk continued: "Now, I was thinking, you being a good Christian and all, if you did pick up the wallet, you must be keen to return it to its owner.

"I could do that for you because in four weeks I am travelling that way again, and I will find them and explain

---

17 Derived from the Zulu word for tree, *muti* is traditional medicine used to protect against evil spirits.

that you were trying to return the wallet. Of course, I will give you a receipt."

"How much money did they say was in the wallet? Just making sure it's the same one, you know," asked Coetzee trying his final move to avoid the set-up.

"Ah, Mr Coetzee, I recall the man saying 15 pounds."

"That's amazing, it is his wallet. I was so concerned about giving it to the rightful owner. Can I bring it to work for you tomorrow?"

The trap was sprung, the victim caught. The next day, Henk received the wallet with 15 recently-drawn pounds inside of it.

6

Onward Christian Soldiers

15ᵗʰ August 1962

There were a number of reasons, mostly the Sharpeville massacre[18] that prompted Carl to rejoin the South African Defence Force (SADF) or, more accurately, the SADF Reserve.

By re-enlisting, Carl found a cause that gave him meaning, purpose and passion. It was as if this act helped him to positively manage his fears and consequent anxiety levels. Although he was still moody, his violent temper appeared restrained.

Carl was also becoming increasingly religious. Having started as a neophyte, he soon developed the zeal of a reborn Christian. Edith observed his transformation from

---

18 The Sharpeville massacre was a bloodbath that occurred on 21 March 1960, after a day of demonstrations against the pass laws. A crowd of 5 000–7 000 black protesters marched on the Sharpeville Police Station. The police opened fire, killing 69 people.

agnostic to rebirth with incredulity. His mantra became: "Onward Christian soldiers." She could not help but remember how he had been opposed to getting married in a church back in 1942, although he had eventually succumbed to pressure and they had had a church service. Since that time, he had not darkened the door of a church. Curiously, though, he had encouraged Mike's presence at Sunday school.

Attending church services, particularly those of the omnipotent Dutch Reformed Church (DRC), was an implicit part of being in the South African military or police services. From the birth of Carl's devotion, the DRC church taught him their theology of apartheid based on the Bible. This delusion made him blissfully unaware that many of the DRC ministers who wielded influence over him had supported the Nazis during World War II, and were, by proxy, co-creators of the torment in which he had lived for the past 17 years.

Carl willingly accepted the notion that God intended people to be structurally apart and organised separately as different races. He supported the claim that black people were the doomed children of Ham.

He accepted the story of the tower of Babel to mean that God wanted people to be divided into separated communities, and he finally concurred with Paul's speech to the Athenians in which he claimed that God had defined the borders of habitation. To Carl, these examples provided conclusive evidence that the church endorsed the good fight. He did not consider that the DRC could have a jaundiced interpretation of Christianity, nor did he see that their views were not shared by most other churches. Many other churches at that time believed that the DRC doctrines of Christianity had become attenuated and distorted.

Carl had a meteoric rise through the military ranks to the position of commandant in a unit curiously known as the Commandos. The origin of the name was in keeping with the legend of Boer commandos from the Anglo Boer War, and was certainly not symbolic of the British commandos that Mike considered to be far more illustrious. Commandant Hanssen would don his uniform every Monday night and attend the local officers' meeting. Of course he did. He was the officer in charge.

The juvenile and impressionable Mike had unconsciously adopted his dad's military, religious and political views. Their infrequent conversations never questioned the legitimacy of the South African government or the influence of the DRC, nor did they refer to the nefarious apartheid system. The euphemism for apartheid was "separate development", and it was as God intended. Conversations fixated on the level of preparedness needed by South Africa to overcome with the twin threats of communism and the *swart gevaar*[19].

---

19 Directly translated from Afrikaans, *swart gevaar* means black threat. This was the security threat that the majority of the black African population, posed to the white minority South African government.

"We must be prepared to fight for our freedom and our land," the commandant would pontificate. "Remember, the communists are crafty. They know how to manipulate our black community. Couple this with the undeniable fact that black people are simple and easily influenced by outside propaganda. Communists already control the African National Congress (ANC).

"Mike, one day you will serve your country, then you will understand the enormity of the challenge we face. It is written that God has given us the job to protect our community from the tyranny of the communist hordes, and we will. When you come of age, I have the right contacts to make sure you will be useful to God and your country."

One of these contacts was Captain Andre van Niekerk, a connection who was destined to cast a long shadow over Mike's future.

Van Niekerk, an ambitious man, was in his mid-30s, approximately six feet tall; slim with short, blonde hair and piercing blue eyes. His grooming was immaculate and his manner efficient, yet affable. His cordiality camouflaged a steely determination to succeed.

Captain Van Niekerk represented the headquarters of Eastern Province Command and was charged with developing regional commando units. Van Niekerk was on an official monitoring visit to the Tsitsikamma Commando. Commandant Hanssen had recently been appointed its commanding officer.

Once they concluded the organisational obligations, Mike's dad invited Van Niekerk to their home for a drink. Carl was unaware that the captain was able to drink copious amounts of alcohol without his judgment becoming impaired. It was one of Van Niekerk's strengths: He could get others to drink in excess and then use their inevitable loss of coherence to gain an upper hand. In so doing, he could manipulate outcomes to suit his agenda. It was not his aim to do so on that occasion.

Even without alcohol, Van Niekerk had a disarming charm and poise that ingratiated him to people. Mike noticed the suave way the self-possessed man held the stem of his glass, the gentle swirl he gave its contents, and his lazy gaze when he held it up to the light to inspect its contents. The man had panache.

Mike listened as the two military men rambled on about the *rooi gevaar*[20] and the level of preparedness needed to meet the looming Russian onslaught.

More remarkably, Van Niekerk shared the news that the police had captured Nelson Mandela on August 5 in Howick. Until then, the name Nelson Mandela had meant nothing to Mike, but the two officers seemed animated and self-congratulatory about his incarceration.

The conversation about Mandela trailed off, and Van Niekerk turned his attention to Mike.

---

20 Translated from Afrikaans, the "red threat" refers to communists and communism.

"The commandant tells me you're already a marksman and can handle almost any weapon. Why don't we see if you can use one in a real situation?"

Mike looked confused.

"No, don't worry, you won't have to shoot a terrorist yet," Van Niekerk continued with a broad grin.

"Let's start with a springbuck. Why don't you two drive up to our family farm across the Karoo next weekend, bag a big springbok and make some nice biltong.[21]"

Mike was delighted. He looked at his dad, and Carl gave a nod of approval that accepted the invitation.

"Thank you, thank you Mr ... Sorry, Captain van Niekerk," Mike said excitedly.

Hunting was to a white South African male what fishing was to a dolphin. That's what men did, and it was time for Mike to join the league of hunters.

During this time, Edith, who was usually sociable and engaging, seemed wary of Van Niekerk and uncomfortable in his company.

Van Niekerk left an hour later. As he left, he reminded the men of the hunting invitation and thanked Edith for being such an excellent hostess. "It was a pleasure to meet you, Mrs Hanssen, You could qualify as an Afrikaner's kind of woman" was his parting and somewhat off-handed compliment.

---

21 Biltong is a type of cured meat that originated in South Africa. It is typically made from raw meat fillets cut into strips, following the grain of the muscle, or flat pieces sliced across the grain.

Edith felt distinctly uncomfortable as he held his gaze on her for slightly too long, then left. She was aware that her pale, English rose skin, long, dark curly hair and curvy figure always presented an attractive package to would-be suitors and lecherous men.

"So what do think of him?" Carl asked Edith as Van Niekerk's dark-green military car disappeared down the winding hill on its way to Port Elizabeth.

"Fine bloke, a real South African," Carl continued, without waiting for a reply.

"Edith, did you know his nickname's *Slang*? That's Afrikaans for what you English call a snake or a serpent. Apparently, he's called Slang because he's like the serpent guardian to the temple of our South African values. But, I think it's because he's always ready to strike with venom."

The description filled Edith with dread. She went cold and alarm bells rang in her head. From the day that Beauty had handed her Mike's caul, it had been embedded in her subconscious that serpents were emissaries of evil. Her unconscious record was recently reinforced by reading Edgar Allen Poe's description of a serpent as "a dangerous symbol for vengefulness".

She felt her apprehension rising and decided to check on the caul. "I may not be superstitious, but why tempt fate?" she muttered under her breath. To her relief, the beaded bag containing the caul was safely stored among her prized possessions at the back of the cupboard, where it had been preserved and arguably working its magic on Mike's welfare for 11 years. The dread caused by encountering

Van Niekerk was moderated by her relief at seeing the caul. I'm being silly, its superstitious nonsense, she thought, berating herself.

7

ANDILE'S EARLY YEARS

19ᵗʰ July 1951

Sapkamma was on the R75, between Uitenhage and Graaff Reinet.

It was not a popular route, yet the government maintained a regular bus service there. Henk was duty-bound to make this run once a month. This time, he was accompanied by five passengers and Enoch's wallet.

With butterflies in his stomach and feeling like a teenager about to see the girl he fancies, he stopped the bus at the Sapkamma Train Station, which also served as the bus stop. He was exactly on time. It was 1pm.

Sapkamma was a lunch-time break stop that gave Henk an hour to catch up with Enoch and Beauty.

He entered the trading store. The facility stocked virtually everything a farmer or peasant could need. The inside looked more like a storeroom than a store. His eye caught two bicycles hanging from the rafters; coils of chewing tobacco on a wooden stick; umpteen jars of boiled sweets;

bully beef; canned fruit; canned vegetables; primus paraffin stoves; and grey blankets.

Geoff Walters was behind the counter. They had met before as this was a regular route for the bus company.

"Good afternoon, Mr Walters, and how are you today?"

"No, fine, Mr van der Merwe; and you? How was the trip from Plettenberg Bay?"

"Very good thank you, Mr Walters, I was wondering … I met a black couple recently. They moved here from Plett. Enoch and Beauty Khumalo. Do you know their whereabouts?"

"Of course, I do. Enoch's helping me as a goat herder and Beauty has many roles. She's a housemaid in the mornings, a babysitter-cum-wet-nurse at lunch time, and then I am told she is training to become a sangoma in the late afternoons and on weekends. Quite a busy lady is our Beauty Khumalo."

"Can I say hello to them?" Henk enquired.

"Finding Enoch will be difficult, as he's somewhere in the hills minding the goats. Beauty will be easy to track down. She's at our house with the little ones. I guess they're fast asleep by this time. You know where the door to the house is. Don't knock, just enter, otherwise you may wake the babies."

Fifty minutes left. Henk was clock-watching, hoping to maximise his time with Beauty.

He opened the door and immediately spotted the beaming Beauty, as she in turn saw him.

Before he could say anything, Beauty gave him a sunny smile, while indicating him to be silent, with a soft "Shhh".

Andile was strapped on her back, fast asleep.

Lloyd, Geoff Walters' two-month-old son, was in his cot, also fast asleep.

Henk tip-toed up to her. Both opened their arms, embracing the other in a huge hug. Henk was careful not to disturb Andile.

"Henk, we have missed you."

"And I, you, Beauty."

A short, awkward silence followed.

Henk cleared his throat and whispered: "I've got the wallet."

With an enormous grin, he extracted Enoch's wallet from his pocket and handed it to her. "That's wonderful, Henk. Enoch will be thrilled. How did you do it?"

Henk gave her the blow-by-blow account, sparing no details. Beauty was riveted.

"Will I see Enoch, or will you tell him the wallet saga?" asked Henk.

"Not this time. If you give me your schedule, I can make sure you meet with him next time."

Henk gave her a knowing look with a cocked eyebrow.

"Henk," she said with a quizzical expression, despite knowing what his look implied.

"Well, maybe we can have exclusive time when you visit," she said. "How long can you stay?"

"I have an hour lunch break. Is that enough?"

"It's what we have, and I look forward to every visit and every minute of that hour, Mr van der Merwe."

The die was cast.

In that short conversation, a depth of feeling was communicated between them. It was their unspoken understanding that Beauty's circumstances were unchangeable. Despite that, they had a connection that would be sustained by one visit per month. For the time being, that was their allocation.

It was one day short of a month since Andile's birth. Beauty had regained the same rubenesque figure she had before her pregnancy: Somewhat plump, yet curvy, with large round hips and ample bosom, her breasts made more than ample by breastfeeding.

Henk found her adorable.

She told him about the calling from her ancestors to become a sangoma. He listened, fascinated.

The hour was over so quickly. A parting hug and Henk reminded her that he'd be back in one month to the day, at lunch time.

He visited every month for the next five years as a driver for the national bus company. In 1956, Henk relocated from Plettenberg Bay to Port Elizabeth and started his own bus service.

His drivers, Johannes and Brian, took all of the shifts, except the one from Port Elizabeth to Graaff Reinet. That was exclusively an owner-driven route. Each visit to Sapkamma grew Beauty and Henk's affections, like a rope strengthened by new strands weaved at regular intervals.

Beauty had always been a sentient being. The training to become a sangoma was another step in this direction. Her learning process had started with purification through steaming, then washing in the blood of sacrificed animals, before she was taught the use of muti. Her lessons had ended with the sacrifice of a goat to appease the ancestors.

Beauty served the Sapkamma community as a healer and counsellor by accessing the wisdom of the ancestors. Where necessary, she added her knowledge of conventional nursing to deliver their babies, cure their ills, broken bones, aches and pains.

During Henk's visits, she would tell him about her work. He heard how she made and used muti, interpreted dreams, threw bones and utilised channelling and possession. He was her most ardent supporter. Over time, she made less and less reference to western religion and God. Her alignment to traditional African beliefs grew stronger. Henk was not a religious man and enjoyed exposure to what he considered to be a more appealing interpretation of spirituality.

* * *

Geoff's son, Lloyd, displayed an academic flair from an early age. It helped that his mum was also his school teacher. His formative years mirrored his dad's life. He helped in the trading store, prepared the mail, played ball games with his dad, and on many a weekend, they went hunting in the hills around the farm.

Andile also showed a flair for school work, but the syllabus for black children that had been enshrined in Bantu education had been designed to keep black people enslaved. It did not cover mathematics. It was a corner-stone of the apartheid philosophy.

Hendrik Verwoerd had been quoted as saying: "There's no place for the Bantu in the European community above the level of certain forms of labour. What's the use of teaching the Bantu child mathematics when it cannot use it in practice? That's quite absurd. Education must train people in accordance with their opportunities in life, according to the sphere in which they live."[22]

Andile and Lloyd became friends and spent a lot of time together. However, their relationship was tainted by the shared awareness of an assumption that whites were superior. Geoff tried his best not to perpetuate this notion, but it was endemic and although not overt, apartheid beliefs crept into their relationship. Andile went on several hunting trips with Geoff and Lloyd, only as an observer. Andile would share their coffee, but not their crockery. He was given his own enamel mug to drink from.

Enoch appreciated the solitude of being in the hills alone with the goats. The salt and pepper goatee on his chin had a pictorial resonance with the herd. He communed with his ancestors as he offered them protection from predators

---

22 Dr Hendrik Verwoerd, South African Minister for Native Affairs (prime minister from 1958 to 66), speaking about his government's education policies in the 1950s. As quoted in *Apartheid – A History* by Brian Lapping, 1987.

mainly jackals. He had often found leopard tracks, but these deadly hunters avoided contact with humans and chose rather to hunt small buck in remote areas.

Enoch had developed a daily routine that differed only when it rained. On those days, he would head for the shelter of a rocky outcrop in the hills, but he would usually guide the herd to grazing areas in the hills, donned in his old grey great-coat and carrying a *knopkierrie*.[23]

At a suitable spot, he would settle the animals by talking to them, much as a horse whisperer communicates with horses. The animals would graze and rest within a 20m circumference of his fire.

He began his watch by making *moer*[24] coffee. A few hours later, he would open the lunch treat prepared by Beauty. He never felt alone. His beliefs ensured that he was always in the presence of all of his significant ancestors.

He had become a trusted ally of Geoff Walters and needed little or no supervision. The reality of the apartheid regime was not apparent on the farm, where they all lived in a bubble of traditional farming life.

Although apartheid was not an issue, stock theft was. Part of Enoch's job was to ward off human predators, too. At least once a year, stock thieves attempted to steal goats.

---

23 A *knopkierrie* is a traditional weapon; it typically has a large knob at one end and can be used to throw at animals during hunting, or to club an enemy's head.
24 Directly translated from Afrikaans as "beaten up" coffee, the coffee is whacked by a log of wood before being brewed in a tin pot over an open fire.

Geoff was tempted to arm Enoch, but decided against it, as stock thieves never carried weapons and Geoff felt that providing arms to his herder could escalate the hazard. He was also not keen on the responsibility of training Enoch in the finer art of weapons handling.

Geoff believed that guns were only useful to those, like his family, who had been brought up with weapons, and to others who had been to the army. Otherwise, guns were a liability to the bearer, not an asset.

Besides, during all of the years that Enoch had been a goat herder, he had successfully chased off thieves. The sight of Enoch wielding a knopkierrie and letting off a blood-curdling scream was a huge deterrent to any would-be thief.

The disease had not left him. Enoch had learned to manage the discomfort and pain in his lungs. After the first month's antibiotic regimen, he had refused to take any more modern medicine. The use of a traditional painkiller had become part of his daily ritual, and he would smoke a *dagga*[25] joint after lunch.

At first, he bought his stash from local farm labourers, but within a year he had a healthy crop of his own cannabis plants growing on the way to the goat's grazing areas. Making marijuana from the dried flowers and leaves was a simple matter of pruning and drying in the Karoo sun.

---

25 *Dagga* is the South African name given to marijuana. Its use as an analgesic in palliative care dates back thousands of years across many cultures, including the Xhosa.

Of course, there were the additional intoxicating benefits derived from smoking the dagga joints, too.

Enoch knew about Henk's monthly visit and was aware of Beauty's feelings for him. He made no attempt to see Henk and accepted that this was something that Beauty wanted. He trusted Beauty's integrity and did not mind their closeness.

After 10 years on the farm, Enoch had aged radically, which could be largely attributed to the creeping tuberculosis. He died peacefully while on watch with the goats. It was probably a heart attack brought on by breathing less, which stressed the heart. Then it stopped.

When he did not arrive back at the trading store with the herd, Geoff drove up to the grazing lands. Enoch's dead body was hunched over his dead fire, knopkierrie at his side. His spirit had already joined his ancestors, attending to their higher calling. The goats milled in mourning close by.

Enoch died with the knowledge that Beauty and Andile were in the safe hands of his benefactor, Geoff Walters. Geoff gently and respectfully retrieved Enoch's body and took him home to prepare for his funeral three days later.

Enoch's Xhosa tradition required that he be returned to the earth at his birthplace. In Enoch's case, the Sapkamma district was his birthplace and now his final resting place. Dumisani and the other elders gathered at his home and spoke to his spirit, telling him that they had come to take him home. This is done to ensure the family does not become concerned that his spirit will be abandoned or wander around. The Xhosa people believe that the departed continue to live a life beyond the physical existence.

Early on the day of the funeral, a goat was slaughtered at his house in preparation for his journey. The men cooked the meat outside in boiling water, without spices. The meat was then eaten outside the house. The ritual's intended to help the spirit to the beyond, so the deceased can return as an ancestral spirit at a later stage.

At the graveside, elders called his name three times as mourners paid their respects. Many wore traditional skins or blankets, and the men carried knopkierries.

Death is a sacred event in Xhosa tradition. Elders' call spirits during the grief period, and any bad spirits that heed the call are cleansed during a ritual the day after the funeral.

Beauty had been expecting Enoch's passing for some time. Her medical training had allowed her to read the signs and symptoms that led up to his dignified demise.

They had not made love for several years. Their relationship had been intimate and loving, but not a sexual one.

Was it because of the disease?

Had her strong feelings for Henk affected this aspect of their relationship?

It mattered not, because they had both been happy.

The relationship was now in the past. Beauty had no regrets, only a profound sense of sadness at the passing of such a fine man. She realised that the government would ensure that her bed was not occupied by the other she loved.

Andile, too, had been prepared for Enoch's passing. Beauty had kept him informed about his father's ill health, as had Enoch. His departure was a matter of when, not if.

The father and son's relationship had been a typical rural, traditional, father-son connection. Enoch had taught Andile Xhosa traditions. They had spent weekends together herding goats. During this time Andile had learned the value of solitude, respect for his elders and an appreciation for culture.

Enoch had spoken to him about the ANC and tried hard not to create an activist in his son, rather a young man who was aware of injustice and of man's potential for inhumanity.

Geoff and Lucy Walters attended the funeral and also covered all costs incurred by Beauty. Despite being well versed in Xhosa tradition, they found the funeral's celebratory atmosphere to be refreshingly different from Christian funerals where, despite a claim that the deceased was going to a better place called Heaven to be with Jesus, there was still such sadness.

Life in Sapkamma returned to a familiar rhythm soon after Enoch's death. Dumisani arranged for another herder, and Andile continued to assist with herding duties on weekends, much as he had when Enoch was the herder.

Geoff reassured Beauty that he would provide for Andile and fill the role of foster father even though the Nationalist government would have viewed such a gesture as heresy. He assured Beauty that Andile would attend a Uitenhage-based high school for black pupils.

Lloyd, Geoff's son, was due to attend Muir College High School in Uitenhage – the same school Geoff had attended as a teenager. Andile could not join him. It was reserved for whites.

Slang van Niekerk visited Geoff Walters a few days after Enoch's funeral. He was in charge of developing regional commando units all the way up to Graaff Reinet. The Sunday's River Valley Commando encompassed the Sapkamma area, and Geoff had been appointed the commanding officer. The amiable and affable Walters, not as enthusiastic as Carl from the Tsitsikamma Commando, was still reliable and steadfast and would discharge his duty to his country.

Slang had not met Enoch, but he knew of Beauty and Andile's presence on the farm. A conversation between Geoff and Slang about traditional funerals had ended with Slang saying: "With the right attitude, young black boys like Andile could come in handy for the country one day."

Lucy, like Edith, did not trust Van Niekerk, and made a point of busying herself with other important matters during his visits.

8

CROSSING THE DESERT

19ᵗʰ August 1962

The weekend of hunting couldn't come too soon for Mike. With what resembled an armoury in the boot of their Fiat 500, they set off on the 484km trip to the Van Niekerk farm, near Hutchinson, early on the Friday morning. The journey took them across the Great Karoo[26]. The drive was punctuated by *koppies*[27] and countless small, round concrete dams and windmills.

Not surprisingly, there was little talk during the six-hour drive. The relative stillness did not bother Mike. He was totally absorbed in his anticipation of the expedition. After all, they had dissimilar personalities: Mike was sanguine and humorous, while his dad was capricious and mostly sullen. To have an animated conversation with his dad, Mike would usually have to open with a subject involving

---

26 A vast desert in the centre of South Africa.
27 *Koppies* is the Afrikaans word to describe pointy hills that are not high enough to be mountains.

the current military situation before conversation could subtly move on to other, more pertinent, matters. Hunting, it seemed, ranked up there with the military, as Carl spoke freely.

"You know Mike, before there were farms with fences, like the Van Niekerks', huge game herds roamed freely through the Karoo. Massive springbuck migrations came from the north, usually going west towards Namaqualand, devouring all plants in their path. These migrations, and of course changes in rainfall patterns, are responsible for the desert-like appearance you see."

Mike sat quietly, enjoying the pearls of wisdom from his father, who was usually so insular and distant.

Carl continued: "During these migrations, the springbuck never ran and were totally unfazed by hunters riding among them, shooting them. Of course, they were also a feast for predators following the herds. Migrations ended some decades ago, leaving a staggering sum of resident springbuck in the area."

The Van Niekerk farm was a beneficiary of the migrations and had thousands of springbuck within its confines.

At 6pm, as the sun was going down, the unusual sound of a stock grid[28] under the car's wheels announced a boundary between public land and Van Niekerk's farm.

---

28 A stock grid is a depression in the road covered by a transverse grid of bars or tubes that are fixed to the ground on either side of the depression. The gaps between them are wide enough for animals' legs to fall through, but sufficiently narrow not to impede a wheeled vehicle or human foot.

The farm gate followed the stock grid. On the gate, the farm's name: *Ons Land*. Afrikaans for "Our Land", the name of the farm was ominously indicative of the strong nationalism that was characteristic of their kin.

Van Niekerk and his parents met the arriving car at the front door of the farmhouse after being timeously notified by the whistle of a delighted gate attendant whose outstretched hand Carl had rewarded with a 2 cent piece as they drove through the entrance.

They received with a hero's welcome. Seven staff members stood at attention in a guard of honour behind Van Niekerk and his parents. Further in the background, enough children to populate a nursery appeared from staff quarters, giving the new arrivals curious looks while pointing and giggling.

Five yelping, barking dogs came charging around the corner from behind the house. First to arrive was a scruffy French poodle. She was probably ahead because of cornering skills. Her prime position was soon usurped by a brindle bull terrier who bowled her over, closely followed by three colossal Rhodesian ridgebacks. The ridgebacks doubled as security-cum-hunting dogs.

Once they had centre stage, the large dogs liberally deposited saliva stalactites from their slobbering gums on to guests' hands and clothing as their contribution to the welcoming ceremony.

Van Niekerk calmed the dogs and introduced his mother and father.

Jannie and Magda were a typical elderly, conservative Afrikaans farming couple. Their house was typical Karoo – a main house; servants' quarters; farm sheds and a wind pump in close proximity.

The design had a European influence within the Karoo style-architecture. It had a facade, flat roof and prominent *stoep* (veranda) that protected humans and domestic animals against the harsh sun. The stoep floor shined with red polish. The roof had been restored using traditional thatch, and shutters covered the windows.

The spacious colonial lounge included a Victorian coal fireplace centrepiece, and the walls were decorated with unmoving animal heads that peered eerily through unblinking teddy bear eyes. The room was replete with old rifles on the walls and animal hides, ranging from springbok to sheep skin, covering the floors.

Carl and Mike spent two nights and a day at the farm, enjoying hospitality rivalling that of a five star hotel.

The Van Niekerks managed their staff with a caring, paternalistic approach that seemed to be much appreciated. There wasn't a hint of the racial tension that was elsewhere tearing the country apart.

Mike was allocated his own room; the large bed covered by an eiderdown. He had never slept under an eiderdown before. The combination of down and feathers made a light yet warm refuge from the freezing Karoo winter nights, where temperatures could plummet to –8 degrees centigrade. He made a mental note to get one for himself when he had his own home one day.

The next day, he awoke to a knock on the door accompanied by a warm cup of moer coffee.

After breakfast, six hunters, each with their own rifle and ammunition, boarded the Land Rover bound for Hunter's Valley. The valley was a triangular stretch of flat land encompassing about five hectares, nestled between three koppies.

The Land Rover driver, *Oom* (uncle) Piet, dropped the hunters in pairs at the different koppies. Mike was accompanied by Captain van Niekerk.

Oom Piet instructed the party on safety standards, clearly indicating the permitted arc of fire to ensure that they did not shoot in each other's directions.

Depending on the amount of springbuck on the farm, there were usually quotas. On this occasion, there were none – it was a season of abundance.

Within the hour, the salivating ridgebacks would be set loose, chasing springbuck and directing them into Hunter's Valley. At that point, if one had a clear shot within their arc of fire, it was allowed.

The hunting culture frowned upon speaking or the making of any noise while in hunting mode. Mike and Van Niekerk sat in silence, waiting for signs of advancing springbuck. Well, relative silence. They chewed noisily on generous sticks of biltong and slurped copious mugs of sweet moer coffee.

Then they appeared: Hundreds of white and tan springbuck in full flight; the males displaying their strength, running stiff-legged, then jumping up into the air with their backs arched, lifting the flaps along their backs.

The herd settled about 150m from Mike's koppie. Van Niekerk nodded to Mike, indicating that he should load the 30 06 Musgrave rifle, select a buck, aim and fire. He whispered with a knowing smile: "Select a ram. The world can do with fewer males. Why do you think we have wars? One ram can cover many ewes."

Mike chose carefully. A magnificent beast looked toward him, unaware what fate had in store for him in the next few seconds.

He stealthily slipped the magazine into the breach, pulled back the bolt, and slid it forward, engaging a bullet.

He shouldered the rifle, aligned the target in the telescope and made a slight adjustment to get the heart into the crosshair.

He breathed out.

Held his breath.

Took up slack in the trigger.

Made a last accuracy check.

Squeezed gently.

A loud gunshot report rang in his ears. A split second later, the beautiful buck fell to the ground.

Van Niekerk fired immediately after Mike, downing a ram about 10m to the left of Mike's quarry.

The herd ran off, deserting their fallen friends.

The hunt was over. Van Niekerk said they should wait for five minutes as a safety precaution, then they could walk down to inspect their victims.

The mandatory five minutes was soon over and the pair went to the killing field.

In addition to his rifle, Van Niekerk carried a large red flag as a further safety precaution.

Van Niekerk's prey was dead; Mike's was still alive, mortally wounded.

The bullet had hit a lung, missing the heart by a few centimetres. "Mike, this is where your mettle's tested, young man," Van Niekerk explained.

He drew his knife from the scabbard on his belt.

"You must slit its throat, like you're working for a halaal butchery."

He passed the knife to Mike.

This wasn't part of the deal, thought Mike.

The springbuck was lying on its side, lifting its head, then dropping it back on to the red earth. As Mike approached, it tried to stand up, but it fell back, too weak to stand.

Mike stared at his ram. Despite its fatal injury, the buck was magnificent.

It had a white face with a dark patch on its forehead. A stripe ran from the eyes to the corner of the mouth; a slender, long, white neck. About 90cm tall, weighing approximately 45kg; its back was tan-coloured, its chest and stomach white, and a dark-brown stripe extended along each side. It had narrow, fragile hooves and thick black horns; the tail was white with a black tip.

A trickle of blood ran from the bullet wound, creating a red stain on the white, woolly chest.

Aerated blood spurted with every breath from its nose, and a rasping sound filled the lungs.

"Mike, do it now. Your animal's suffering," Van Niekerk urged.

The buck gave Mike the most desolate look he had ever seen. The animal knew it was dying and Mike knew he had to act to end the suffering.

The emotions in the animal's eyes burned into Mike's soul. His buck was in agony.

There were no feelings of triumph in Mike, only sorrow.

Does a buck cry? Mike wanted to.

Would that make him feel better?

Would it make his buck feel better?

He stifled a sob, positioned the knife firmly against the snow-white fur of the willowy neck.

He approximated the position of the jugular.

Van Niekerk nodded, knowingly

He applied pressure.

The razor-sharp knife ruptured the skin and blood poured liberally down the blade, creating further red stains on that vulnerable neck.

He plunged it deeper and created a sawing motion until the breathing stopped.

The eyes were finally vacant, lifeless.

Mike was vanquished. But it wasn't over.

Van Niekerk put a hand on Mike's dropping shoulder. "It's your first kill, Mike. There's one rule, or should I say ritual, with your first casualty. It's the price of being a man. There will be many rituals. Wait till you get to the army, they also have one for a first kill – but, I digress. Let me show you. You need to donate a part of the buck to the scavengers of the *veld*[29]. We have many wild cats and jackals. They will appreciate your gift."

"Here, use the knife and slit the stomach." Niekerk indicated a 24cm stretch along the white belly.

Mike followed instructions.

"Right, grab the intestines and remove them. You will need to cut them."

Mike removed the innards, his hands and clothes soiled with vile viscera.

"Great. Those get placed on that rock, and they will be gone before nightfall."

"For the grand finale, you must slip your head into the body cavity and say a silent prayer."

Mike felt he had no choice. He went along with the ritual.

His emerging head was as messy as his hands. "Congratulations, Mike, welcome to the hunting fraternity."

The Land Rover fetched them an hour later, accompanied by a pick-up truck to transport the spoils. Mike was the only new hunter, the only one to undergo an initiation.

The group welcomed him warmly, complimenting him on his kill and congratulating him on becoming one of them. He liked the attention, the idea of community, but not the smell of entrails on his person.

---

29 *Veld* is an Afrikaans word used to refer to certain types of wide open rural spaces in southern Africa.

The one-day, two-night excursion soon came to an end.

In the following years, Mike would go on several hunting trips, but the springbuck's dying eyes remained etched in his memory, somewhat ameliorated by the notion that God had provided animals as food for man and, after all, hunting did produce biltong.

If he had been more perceptive, he would have noticed that the hubristic Van Niekerk had starting to wield as much influence over Carl as the church. In the future, Van Niekerk and the church would work together as co-conspirators in Carl's narrative.

9

HIGH SCHOOL YEARS

Mike, Lloyd and Andile converged on Uitenhage in 1964. Mike and Lloyd were sent to Muir College Boarding School, and Andile went to Xaba High School. Dumisani secured boarding for Andile with a distant relative and Geoff paid the bill.

Mike's lack of worldliness ensured that he was once again unaware of the implication that his school was populated exclusively by white boys. To him, it was simply the norm. He had no idea that race separation was a largely South African issue and that the rest of the world was judging his country harshly.

The hostel accommodated 103 pupils from junior school to school-leaving grade, Standard 10. Mike Hanssen, Lloyd Walters, Bruce Johnson and Trevor McNamee shared a dormitory on the second floor. It was the first time that Mike or Lloyd would spend an extended period with boys their age. It was possibly this shared challenge that sparked an immediate friendship.

Meals were served in a canteen, with eight boys sharing a table. The more senior youths were positioned at the top of the table, with juniors at the other end. It followed that the lion's share of any food considered desirable was consumed at the top end of the table.

Life in a hostel was, in many ways, comparable to life in a prison. They boys were strictly prohibited from leaving the premises. The windows were barred and the doors were locked. The boarders were given a three-hour pass on Saturday mornings – only to access acceptable parts of the town. Many parts were out of bounds, and a pass was subject to admirable behaviour.

Boarders whose homes were close by would get weekend passes twice per school term. Plettenberg Bay was 220km from Uitenhage, which was not considered close.

Mike got to go home four times each year, during school vacations. His favourite holiday was summer break: Six glorious weeks filled to the brim with sun, surf and girls. In the latter part of high school, rum and Coke with Lucky Strike cigarettes were added to these holiday pleasures.

The quality of the food at the boarding school could be described as institutional at best. And, there was always just far too little of it. Mike was constantly hungry, so like most boarders, he filled up on copious slices of bread and jam.

Life in the hostel was rule-bound, managed on a strict schedule that was implemented by bells and policed by prefects. Breaches of rules resulted in corporal punishment executed by prefects. Serious misdemeanours were referred to the hostel master. He, in turn, implemented corporal punishment.

Boys, who had not learned to stay within the confines of the system, or to work the system, were identified by their black-and-blue-striped buttocks, readily displayed in communal showers.

The daily schedule was:

Hostel bell rings – get up, wash, get dressed in school uniform.

Hostel bell rings – go to breakfast.

Hostel bell rings – leave canteen.

Hostel bell rings – go to school.

School bell rings – attend classes.

School bell rings – break.

School bell rings – attend classes.

School bell rings – leave school for hostel.

Hostel bell rings – go to lunch.

Hostel bell rings – leave canteen.

Hostel bell rings – prepare for sport.

Hostel bell rings – go to sport.

Hostel bell rings – have a shower.

Hostel bell rings – go to dinner.

Hostel bell rings – go to study room.

Hostel bell rings – go to rooms to prepare for bed.

Hostel bell rings – say prayers.

Hostel bell rings – lights out – not a word to be said.

Hostel bell rings – get up and get dressed.

Each period between bells was scripted with recurring patterns.

Andile's new environment had routines, too, but his high school experience was unlike Mike's.

His host, Sipho Nayo, was an activist, an angry man. Sipho taught Andile about the history of the African National Congress (ANC). Starting with its beginnings in 1912, he taught Andile about the role of Ghandi in passive resistance; the 1955 launch of the Freedom Charter; the Sharpeville massacre; and the formation of the ANC's military wing, *Umkhonto we Sizwe* (MK), in 1961. Umkhonto we Sizwe meant "Spear of the Nation", he learned.

Nelson Mandela was MK's first leader. Andile learned about Mandela's arrest in 1962; his conviction for sabotage in 1964; and his sentence to life imprisonment on Robben Island, along with Walter Sisulu and other ANC leaders after the Rivonia Trial.

Sipho felt that the armed struggle was the only course of action for blacks to establish their rights. He told Andile: "The boere won't give away any power willingly. We must show them that we're prepared to fight and die for our rights. One day you will heed the call – *Amandla!*[30]"

The unceasing Black Consciousness indoctrination took its toll on Andile, and the moderate views of his father soon became drowned by Sipho's anger.

---

30 *Amandla* is a Xhosa and Zulu word meaning power. The word was a popular rallying cry against apartheid. The leader of a group would call out "*Amandla!*", and the crowd would respond: "*Awethu!*"

Andile also became angry with the government because he was getting an inferior education. Sipho told him that the government spent eight times as much on white education as it did on black children. He told Andile that 66% of white teachers had a degree. The rest had Standard 10. Only 2% of black teachers had a degree and 80% did not have Standard 10.

Andile became angry with black people because they were spineless. In his mind, there were in the region of three million whites and 30 million blacks in South Africa. How could one dictate to 10?

Most of all, he became angry with poverty. His dearly departed dad had been poor, and his relatives were poor. All black people he knew were poor. He did not know one white person who was poor. He vowed to rise above scarcity: If that meant rising up against whites, so be it. But, problems with whites could wait. His first goal was personal prosperity.

Andile's school had a similar routine to Mike's, but extramural time was spent differently. While Mike was being schooled in sport, Andile was being schooled in politics. Being at Sipho's was like living at home, except that he shared a room with Sipho's eight-year-old son, Mveleli.

Andile did not have bells, sport, or weekend passes. He would only go home to Beauty when Lloyd had weekend passes or holidays.

He did not have fagging[31] duties, as Mike and Lloyd did. All newpots (new boys) at Muir College were obliged to provide fagging duties to seniors.

Mike was the allocated fag for Stuart Cooper, an under-sized Grade 12. Mike had heard about short-man syndrome, but this was his first exposure to a near-adult with a chip on his shoulder because of his size. "Cooper's full of shit. He has short-man disease," had been the consensus among the newpots.

Mike bore the brunt of Cooper's wrath. Nothing Mike did was acceptable. Cooper's shoes were never shiny enough; his clothes were never folded properly; his rugby boots never had enough dubbin; and his cadet uniform was never properly ironed. A long litany of complaints resulted in endless beatings with a clothes brush on Mike's posterior. Mike learned to dislike Cooper, the runt of the Standard 10 litter. Given that impulse control had proved to be a significant challenge for Mike, he held no fear for the runt, only contempt.

Within a month of school commencing, the opportunity to vent his latent aggression presented itself through a different outlet. Kobus Neethling, his old adversary, was at Muir in a grade above him. Until that point, they had ignored each other.

---

31 Fagging was a traditional practice in which younger boys would do chores for seniors. It also entailed harsh discipline and corporal punishment as standard practices.

Neethling had been biding his time. At 14, he had undergone a puberty growth spurt and was significantly bigger than Mike. He, too, had matured since their first fracas and already possessed a muscular physique and strength beyond his years.

It was Sunday afternoon and most boarders were playing sport.

"Hey Soutie, we have some unfinished business, you and me," came the call from behind him.

Mike turned to see a menacing Kobus and an entourage of his friends looming from behind. "Piss off," Mike replied.

"Tell you what, when you're finished tossing off Cooper, you can come and do me as well, Soutie."

Mike ignored him. "I think you're shit scared, Soutie. If Mr Els didn't rescue you in Plett, you would have been dead meat, boy."

He walked up to Mike and slapped him across the face with his open hand.

Mike did not need a further invitation.

The rage that lurked within him surfaced. He attacked.

Neethling was in his second year of boxing lessons. He had skills and easily evaded Mike's clumsy attack by weaving to his left.

He counter-punched with a straight right to Mike's solar plexus, winding him. He followed up with a left hook that just missed Mike's vulnerable jaw by millimetres. Neethling's punching sequence wasn't special. It could be found in Boxing 101.

This was an unexpected turn of events. Mike had never been exposed to boxing skills, and the opening salvo made it patently obvious that getting embroiled in a boxing match was out of the question. He would, as Neethling claimed, be dead meat.

Mike knew instinctively he had to turn the fight into a brawl. He charged like an elephant in musth.

Neethling nimbly backed off, avoiding Mike's charge.

He had to be put to the ground, so Mike charged again. Neethling anticipated the move, not the level of animal aggression. The elephant made contact.

Neethling collapsed to the ground and Mike was on top of him. The elephant became an agile hunting lion.

A group of boys formed a protective ring around them as Mike systematically beat Kobus. One of Kobus's friends tried to help him by aiming a swift kick at Mike's back. Although it stung, Mike was undeterred. The opportunist who had kicked him was immediately grabbed and restrained by two fairer-minded boys from the ring.

The neck lock was instinctive. Mike edged behind Neethling and slipped his right arm around his neck. While clasping his left hand around his right wrist, he applied increasing pressure. Within 10 seconds, Neethling started to gasp.

Within 30 seconds, he was weakening.

After one minute, he went limp.

The boys in the protective ring who had been cheering a minute earlier, went quiet. Someone called out: "Leave him, for Christ's sake. Let him go. You're going to kill him."

Mike heard nothing. His right arm increased its pressure as the red in Neethling's face changed to white.

Three group members intervened. With sheer numbers, they forced Mike to let go.

Neethling was still alive, just unconscious.

Cooper was alerted. He arrived on the scene where his charge had committed a serious offence. He asked for help from two seniors to frog-march Mike to Mr Aitken, the hostel master. Cooper was no fool. He was aware that he, the runt, would come off second best in a scuffle with Mike. Calling for reinforcements was a smart move.

"You nearly killed someone," charged the austere Aitken. "He's alive," snapped Mike.

"Don't get stroppy, boy."

"He started it," Mike said defiantly.

"Did that give you permission to strangle him?"

"I did what I had to."

"Well, I am going to do what I have to," said Aitken, selecting his favourite cane and air-whipping it.

"Bend."

Mike obliged and received six of the so-called best.

The cane made a noise like it was breaking the sound barrier as it hurtled towards Mike's posterior. The second hurt more than the first, the third more than the second. By the time the sixth gave its sonic boom, he was in excruciating pain.

"And by the way, you're gated for the rest of the term," Aitken added as Mike left the office.

This meant Mike could not go to town on a Saturday morning pass, nor have a weekend pass to join any friend who might invite him home, as Lloyd often would do in the following years.

Neethling was also caned for his part in the scuffle.

From that day forward, he gave Mike a wide berth and they maintained a frosty relationship through the rest of their school days.

Mike's nickname became Boston, after the notorious Boston Strangler of 1962.

Lloyd and Mike found fagging detestable and vowed to break the cycle when they reached Standard 10. Their view was reinforced by an incident involving John Mortimer, a fag to Clive Russell. Russell was the mega-jock of the hostel. He had represented the school in first team rugby from Standard 8 onwards and had been selected to represent the Eastern Province provincial side in Standard 9.

Mortimer, a soft-spoken, gentle soul, broke into a stress-induced stammer when his anxiety levels increased. The rigors of fagging and the inevitable associated punishments meant that he was constantly under pressure, so his stammering became the rule rather than an exception.

All newpots were obliged to provide a delivery-type service for senior boys, according to a roster compiled by the perfects. They had to take orders for snacks and proceed to Panagi's Takeaways about two kilometres down the road, purchase them and then return.

It was an age-old tradition to which the masters turned a blind eye. Mortimer's turn came on a Friday night during the third week of the first term. He left, but didn't return. An hour later, a search party of prefects went looking for him. He had not gone to Panagi's Takeaway. Two hours later, his parents and the police were called.

His body was found the next morning, near the sewerage works on the outskirts of Uitenhage. He had taken his life by discharging a handgun into the roof of his mouth. There had been no note. Boarding school and fagging were not the cause, but their role as a tipping point had been undeniable.

The hostel master had referred to the tragic news at Saturday lunch. It had been a shock to the boarding community, yet life carried on as usual. As it does.

Mike and Lloyd's attitude toward fagging mellowed over time. History has a way of repeating itself. By the time it was their turn to be serviced by juniors, the objectionable memory had faded and the tradition was upheld.

Mortimer' death had been the second passing to which Mike had been exposed. The first had been a friend who had washed off the rocks in Plettenberg Bay while fishing the previous year. He had drowned.

Mike had taken a religious view on death. Yes, it was sad because the deceased would be missed by loved ones, but if you were a virtuous person, your spirit would go to a better place. It was a comforting belief while it lasted. In later years, he would view death through a pragmatic, military mindset rather than an esoteric, religious one.

Lloyd was an academic who was competent at sport, and Mike was a sportsman who was competent at academics.

Their boarding school life was dominated by schoolwork and sport. Summer sports included cricket and athletics, and winter meant rugby. Hockey was an alternative to rugby, but unless you could offer injury or health reasons not to play rugby, hockey was frowned upon. It was seen as the lesser option, and one would be labelled a *moffie*[32] for choosing the sport ahead of rugby.

There were seemingly no gay boys in boarding school. If there were, and there must have been, they would never have come out of the closet. Most boys, including Mike, were unaware that there was a sexual preference other than heterosexuality.

Mike met Andile in the second term of their first year in Uitenhage. Lloyd had invited him to Sapkamma, and, as usual, Andile, had joined them on the journey home.

It was the first time that Mike had met Beauty – if you exclude his birthday. A brief conversation was all it had taken for her to connect Mike with Edith and her last act in nursing in Plettenberg Bay. She was thrilled to meet him and shared stories about Plettenberg Bay, only leaving out the awful circumstances of her departure. She had not mentioned the caul, which she felt was a personal matter that his mother should communicate to him.

The three boys became inseparable, and when they got together over the next four years in Sapkamma, there was

---

32 *Moffie* is an Afrikaans slang word meaning a guy who dresses and acts like a girl. The word is usually used in a derogatory manner to describe effeminate homosexual men. It also refers to those who display female tendencies in general.

no apartheid, only shared experiences. Lloyd included Andile as an equal in every aspect of their weekend lives including hunting. Andile was a natural with a firearm and was becoming an exceptional marksman. Geoff Walters struggled with this turn of events. His son had armed and skilled a black person with weapons.

The Walters farmhouse had an outside long drop toilet[33]. The toilet room was built around the hole, with a toilet seat carved out of a wooden box. Mike found the long drop particularly intriguing as it had a twin seat facility. One could go to the toilet while sitting next to another person, if you so wished. He wondered if Lloyd's parents sat on the loo together. Despite their friendship, the boys never got around to sharing the toilet. Some boundaries should never be crossed.

Andile remained circumspect about sharing his Sipho-inspired struggle views. It was obvious to him that neither Lloyd nor Mike were overtly racist. They were politically naïve, ignorant of their privilege and unsighted about the plight of black people. Theirs was a typical, so-called liberal, paternalistic approach, and Andile regarded paternalism as watered down racism that tainted their friendship at a deep level.

* * *

---

33 A long drop toilet collects human excrement in a large deep hole dug into the ground.

As boys in the hostel reached puberty, masturbation became a talking point. Most boys accepted it as a natural but private practice, while others regarded it as a taboo, citing religious objections. Most concluded that masturbation was a boy-only thing. That was an obvious conclusion. After all, what could girls do?'

In most instances, it was talked about in joking terms, like: "What a wanker!" Some were more open in their deliberations, and others even had wanking competitions.

In Mike's dormitory, the subject was talked about in light-hearted terms and it didn't reach tournament level. It did, however, provide a few laughs. Mike recalled how one night, a respectable time after lights out, Trevor called out to the other boys, one by one.

"Lloyd, Lloyd, you awake?" No reply.

"Bruce, Bruce?" No reply.

"Mike?" No reply.

A minute later, the *flap-flap-flap* sound of rhythmic masturbation was heard from Trevor's corner of the room. He had been unaware that all of his roommates were, indeed, awake. They burst into laughter, calling out in harmony: "Wanker, wanker!"

Trevor's pleasurable pursuit was interrupted and its conclusion deferred to another time at another place – possibly in the relative safety of a toilet cubicle. Such venues were not totally private, as boys would shimmy up the separating wall in one toilet cubicle and peer down into the neighbouring cubicle.

Mike would ponder: What's worse? A peeping Tom or a wanker?

Jokes about masturbation, wanking, jerking off or one of many other descriptors, took a back seat as the boys matured. Some started telling stories about their sexual experiences. Mike wondered how many were bullshitting. He was still a virgin at 16. His understanding was confusing. Sex was forbidden and fascinating. The view prevailed that it was something deeply scandalous and dangerous.

10

THE MAGICAL OTHER

20th September 1967

Mike assumed that his life fitted into a grand plan. He had been led to believe that his existence had a preordained purpose. If he was noble, the grand plan would become reality.

The role of choice and chance had yet to dawn on him. At 16, he hadn't finely tuned his critical reflection skills. Nor had he engaged in any ontological or philosophical discussions about meaning. So, when Mike met Madelyn, he accepted the meeting as predestination. This was the part of the story where he met his partner – his magical other.

The meeting took place on Central Beach, Plettenberg Bay. It was the September school break, 1967, and Mike, had gone to the beach to meet his friends and do a bit of body surfing.

He immediately noticed Madelyn lying on the beach, soaking up the sun's rays. The perfectly proportioned sun goddess mesmerised him. After what felt like an eternity of staring at her, she stood up, walked into the water and cooled off in the temperate waters of the Indian Ocean.

He had to help the grand plan become reality. He had to meet her.

His way of securing an introduction was somewhat unconventional. After all, God helps those who help themselves.

"Oh my heavens. Sorry – you okay?" Mike asked after bodysurfing into her slight frame.

"You should look where you're going," she replied.

"I'm such a klutz. Sorry, man. Well, not man. I mean lady," Mike was somewhat tongue-tied as he looked her up and down with admiration. Regaining his composure, he continued: "At least let me buy you a cold drink to make up for my clumsy surfing skills."

"That's the least you can do, boy," she replied.

Mike took a closer look at her while they walked to the cold drink stand. You're gorgeous, he thought.

She was petite; around five foot tall, maybe a little less; blonde hair to her shoulders; blue eyes and luscious lips. Her body had curves in all of the right places, accompanied by generous breasts straining against her light-blue bikini top.

"Mike." He volunteered his name and offered a handshake while sipping his Coke.

"Madelyn. Call me Maddy. I prefer it to being called Mad." She paused before continuing: "You would think parents would more careful when choosing names."

Mike smiled in agreement. Madelyn Lance was 16. Her family was on holiday in Plettenberg Bay, from Kimberley.

The pair spent the day on the beach immersed in each other's company. They had chatted about their families, their schools and their shared interest in music. Maddy broke off the conversation when she announced that she needed to get home for dinner. Mike offered to walk her.

Mr Cedric Lance had been waiting at the door. He was a large man, definitely a former rugby forward, with a cauliflower ear to evidence his efforts in the scrum. Maddy introduced them. After some small talk with Mr Lance, Mike had shared a moment alone with Maddy.

"What are you doing tomorrow?" asked Mike.

"I don't know, going to the beach, I suppose. You?"

"Me too, I guess. Want to say hi tomorrow?"

"Okay." "Same place, say 10ish?"

"Sure."

Mike said his goodbyes and walked home.

He was enthralled by her disquieting beauty.

The next day Mike got to the beach at 9:45am and, sure enough, at 10am, she arrived.

If they had been immersed in each other's company the day before, that day they were enthralled and spellbound by each other

Mike suggested a walk along Robberg Beach. By the time they reached the end, they had been walking for an hour. They sat, watching the waves break and rush up the sand.

Dolphins, a regular feature in the Robberg sea, surfed the crest of the waves. Maddy suggested they try to swim with the dolphins. The water was warm, and the experience idyllic. The dolphins welcomed them to their pod with hard-edged squeaks as they playfully swum between and beneath them.

Back on the beach, Mike embraced a dripping Maddy. "Do you think they were trying to tell us something?"

"And what would that be?"

"Maybe they were saying we make a good couple."

"Do you think they're right?" asked Maddy, looking deeply into his eyes.

"Definitely. You know how intelligent dolphins are. We should listen to them and go out tonight."

That evening they went to the lounge at the Beacon Island Hotel. It was bursting with bustling teenagers seeking booze. This required waiters who turned a blind eye to underage drinking. The need was satisfied when they made a correlation between generous tipping and blind-eyed waiters. Beer, rum, Coke and Lucky Strike cigarettes were the order of the evening.

They spent most of the evening staring into one another's eyes, oblivious to the world. The peck on the lips earlier that day upgraded to endless French kissing: Wonderful for the participants, nauseating for the observer.

One day melted into the next. Maddy spent every available moment of her holiday with Mike. They took long walks and even paddled a two-berth canoe up the

Keurbooms River, while fish eagles soared in the clear sky above and mullets jumped from the water over their canoe.

Their evenings included dancing and snogging at the Cave Night Club, and drinking and laughter at the lookout, or at the Beacon Island Hotel.

How soon the second last day arrived. The final night was approaching. Their group of holiday friends agreed that a beach party would provide an appropriate grand finale.

11

YOU SHALL NOT COMMIT ADULTERY

"Tonight's the night. It's my turn, oh shit!' Mike's thoughts were driven by the hormonal frenzy of a male virgin. He was smitten. If he had needed to propose marriage to get into her pants, he would have done so. At 16, marriage was clearly out of the question. He had made up his mind that making love to Maddy could not wait.

When it came to carnal intent, his reservoir of rational thinking was empty. Even his description of "making love" was a bit of a stretch, but a fool in love, well on his way to deifying the object of his ardour, could not demean his intention with words like "sex" or "fucking".

His religious teachings had been sufficiently concretised in his conscience to provide token resistance. In a fleeting moment of Godly guilt, it occurred to him that he had always assumed that he lived according to the Ten Commandments. If so, wasn't sex outside of marriage a mortal sin? Wasn't it adultery?

He had heard that even thinking about the deed was sinful. Was he plunging down the abyss into moral decay?

He made a mental note to dust off his Bible and to reread the commandments. Not today. Today was about Maddy.

Of course, at that time Mike had no way of knowing that over the next six years, he would fall foul of most of the commandments. If the Lord had had a few more in reserve, these too would have been sacrificed in the turmoil of his future.

"Shit, I'm going to need condoms!" he exclaimed as he exited his ecumenical debate. Mike's sex education had been a combination of salacious stories told by his friends, longwinded life skills lectures from his mum, and his own slobbering over semi-nude pictures in *Scope* magazines.

Scope published pictures of nude women with black strips covering their exciting body parts. His futile attempts to remove the black strips decorating the breast and pubic areas had only resulted in a hole being rubbed through the page.

To date, Mike had never seen a female nude on paper or in real life. Even his mother avoided being seen disrobed. Of course, he had heard about the nudes in *Playboy* magazines, but these magazines were banned in South Africa and contraband copies had thus far eluded his eyes.

He was at least aware of the dreaded diseases associated with sexual intercourse. The risk of getting a disease from Maddy? That was just impossible.

Pregnancy, on the other hand, was a bad idea. For the time being, anyway.

"Okay, I've got the money. Now off to the Village Pharmacy." He realised he was talking out loud to himself.

Just get to the pharmacy, he thought. Thank heavens Willkie won't be there. No embarrassment, having to ask him for condoms.

Wilkie, alias Mr Wilkinson, the local pharmacist, was on leave. A locum was standing in for him.

Mike entered with the pharmacy with the confidence of a great cricket batsman stepping up to the crease. He strode down the passage to the small booth at the end of the room that housed the bespectacled, locum pharmacist.

He was two steps away when a melodic voice called out from behind: "Hello, Mike, and what can we do for you today?"

It was Auntie Joy, his mother's best friend. She worked part time as the pharmacist's assistant.

"How can I help you?" she repeated, emphasising the word "you".

Mike was lost for words, something that did not happen too often. He waited for what felt like eternity, hoping that the locum pharmacist would rescue him. No such luck.

"Cat got your tongue, Mike?" asked Auntie Joy.

"No, no, no," Mike stammered.

"Just looking for a new toothbrush."

"Sure. Hard or soft?" she asked.

"Pick one from that shelf," she added.

Mike meekly obliged.

"Anything else?"

The locum looked on with a grin that would have made the Cheshire Cat in *Alice in Wonderland* proud.

"Umm, no. Well, actually, yes," Mike declared with a sheepish look.

"Okay, spit it out," she encouraged.

Mike decided to revert to his confident cricketer approach. "Actually, I want a packet of con …" He stopped mid-word. His voice had climbed an octave. He sounded like a boy of 13 with a breaking voice. A hot flush went up his neck as the crimson shade of embarrassment filled his face.

He cleared his throat and started again. "A packet of con…stipation pills, please," he continued. At least this time, his 16-year-old voice was working.

He glanced at the pharmacist. The bastard knew what was going on. The Cheshire Cat was well and truly in the room. Auntie Joy handed over a packet of Brooklax for constipation. "Tastes great, like chocolate," she added gratuitously.

Mike sighed, paid for his purchases and left the pharmacy. He stopped at a safe distance before looking back, exasperated.

What now? He decided to wait at a discreet spot for Auntie Joy to leave the shop. Part-time people leave early, surely? Mike waited for a half hour before both the locum pharmacist and the assistant left the shop, locking the door behind them.

And now, what do I do now? Think Mike, think! This is the most exciting day of your life and you're already messing it up.

The café, of course. The solution came to him like a proverbial bolt from the blue. The only café in Plettenberg Bay, the Formosa Café, was run by Spiro Hadjedakis, nicknamed Hadj. Mike rushed down the road and into the café. Hadj was alone and the café was empty. Good. Hadj kept contraceptives on the shelf behind him. Good again.

"Yes, Mike, how can I help you?" Hadj asked.

"I want a packet of condoms, please," he responded quickly.

"What you want, Gold Coin or Crepe de Chine?"

"Uh, Gold Coin." Mike had no idea that there would be more than one type.

"What size you want? Small, medium or large?'

"Hadj, you're not serious!" Mike exclaimed in desperation.

"Ah, yes I am, I not got small, no one ask for small. "Be careful, large is gigantic. You don't want to fish for your condom when you're finished your business. Best you take medium."

Mike nodded.

Always the trader, Hadj continued:

"You only want one packet? I don't think so. Next time you come to buy, maybe someone you know is in café. Take three. Tell you what, I give you one packet on the house. It's your first time?"

Mike didn't answer.

"Put it on early," Hadj said. "Dangerous to start then only put on. Remember to practice putting one on. It's not that easy to think straight when blood's drained from the head on your shoulders to the other head."

Mike paid for the two packets and received three.

As he walked home, his excitement straining against the front of his shorts, an afterthought occurred to him: Maybe, I should have taken the Crepe de Chine. What if they were better?

That night, he left home at 6pm to fetch Maddy for the beach party. While walking down the hill to her holiday home, he felt a twinge of guilt about plotting a sexual experience.

He thought momentarily: Surely nice guys don't do that?

The mole hill of guilt soon paled into insignificance next to his mountain of desire.

She was the one.

He selected his biggest jacket – one that would serve the dual purpose of refuge for condoms and a blanket barrier on the sand.

12

THE COVENANT

The beach party started at sundown with the opening of a crate of beer, the ignition of a bonfire and sound of the Beach Boys belting out *Surfing USA*.

The song soon morphed into a local version, with revellers shouting out "Surfing Plettenberg Bay!" Night had fallen by the time Mike and Maddy arrived. The group was 20-strong; ranging in age from 16–19.

All of the kids were gathered in close proximity to the fire. Some stared into its glow, just as humankind had done for thousands of years. The flickering flames and glowing coals seemed to generate a range of possibilities for its young audience. A few seemingly drifted into a hypnotic shamanic-like trance, while others daydreamed in self-enquiry. Most ignored the allure of the flames, opting instead for a cigarette in one hand and a beer in the other while engaging in animated conversation. Mike sipped a beer. The fire wasn't mesmerising him. That was Maddy's job.

"Want to go for a walk?" Mike asked, gazing at Maddy.

"Sure."

Adrenalin surged through Mike. He had hoped they would escape the group surreptitiously, but their exit was met by cries of: "We know where you're going!"

They walked in silence for a while before Maddy quipped: "That was embarrassing."

"Why, we are just going for a walk, aren't we?" Mike wisecracked.

"Of course we are," she retorted.

Their walk took them to the lookout rocks at the end of the beach – a walk they had both come to know well in the time they had known each other.

Mike stopped at a semi-secluded spot, away from the regular route of casual strollers.

"Should we take a break?"

'Mike removed his jacket and placed the improvised bed on the sand. They sat down, according to plan. He was in unchartered territory. He hadn't been educated in the steps he should take and hadn't read any books that could guide him. He only had his instincts to follow.

A full moon was peeking over the horizon, its light illuminating a golden path across the calm sea. Mike looked back towards the beach party. He could see the bonfire flames licking the sky and the pale glow of cigarettes. The group was out of earshot.

He put his arm around Maddy, drawing her closer. Their faces turned towards each other and their eyes met. She bridged the final inches between them. Their lips met and mouths parted. Her tongue searched for his.

Mike's right hand moved slowly down from her shoulder, stopping at her clothed left breast. It felt soft; he could feel the shape of the breast and nipple under her braless tank top. His hands slipped down to her waist, gripping the bottom of the garment and pulling it up towards her head.

Her nipples peered proudly from beneath the upturned top. Maddy completed its journey over her head, laying it next to the jacket. Mike's gaze was transfixed by her magnificent breasts. He marvelled at the shape of the erect nipples silhouetted in the moonlight. He explored what he saw, cupping her breasts with his hand and caressing her nipples.

"Do you like them?" Maddy asked coyly.

"Just a little," Mike answered cheekily. "No, cancel that. A lot."

His hands obeyed instinct, taking a downward journey, pausing to gently trace her belly button before touching the top of her skirt.

Thank heavens she's wearing a skirt, he thought.

Maddy sensed his thoughts and loosened the clip holding the wrap skirt around her waist. It fell away instantly. She reclined on the jacket, her blonde hair parting into two neat coils on either side of her beautiful face.

Mike looked down her body at the final hurdle – white panties, shimmering in the moonlight.

He lay next to her. The right hand that had felt the splendour of her breasts a moment before slipped down the final frontier, his fingers exploring her, like a blind man reading a Braille book.

First, he felt the softness of her delicate pubic hair and stayed for a moment, before his fingers continued their descent down her pubis, discovering places for which he had no name, while navigating her undulating folds of soft, yielding flesh.

"What are you doing?" Maddy whispered, her wide eyes staring into his.

"Honestly? No idea. I know what I would like to do."

"And what's that? If it's what I think it is, you won't need this."

Maddy reached for Mike's T-shirt, tugging it upwards. He reluctantly interrupted his exploration to assist its trajectory over his head, tossing it next to Maddy's top.

His hands returned to their journey of discovery. He slowly moved his index finger further down, disappearing into the succulent, narrow entrance between her legs. The intrusion made Maddy draw a sharp breath of pleasure. Her right hand responded by feeling for the top of his shorts forcing them down to expose him. Her hungry hand found its target and clasped it firmly. Her hand started a slow rhythm, up then down.

Mike's index finger tuned into the rhythm, stroking the wall of her moist passage, as if he were beckoning someone inside her. Then, he used both hands to guide her panties over her feet, on to the rapidly growing pile of clothing next to him.

He remembered Hadj's advice and felt for the condoms in his jacket pocket. The plastic container bore three condoms that looked like the gold coins one would find in a treasure chest. Mike selected one, removing the gold wrapper and revealing the translucent balloon-like item. Maddy watched, fascinated by Mike's progress.

"Have you done this before?" she asked cheekily.

Mike responded with a single syllable laugh.

"I'm pleased you brought them."

Mike laughed again.

Returning to the matter at hand, he tried to slip on the condom.

He was fumbling at the critical moment.

Maddy's hand joined his, saving time, ensuring the condom's smooth passage.

The next thing he knew, Maddy had pulled him on top of her. Once again, he was fumbling; as he thrust forward he failed to locate the desired destination. Maddy grasped his manhood and directed the gold coin into her treasure chest.

As he entered her, she gave a gasp. He wanted to see her face, but his wish was denied by a cloud obscuring the moonlight.

The rhythm her hand had initiated now consumed his entire body. Maddy responded with synchronised pelvic thrusting, her knees lifted and her feet planted in the sand close to her buttocks.

Mike was overwhelmed by the sheer pleasure of the union.

It was over all too soon as Mike spent his passion in a series of throbbing sensations.

"Sorry," he whispered, fearing he had let her down.

Maddy clasped her hands to his temples with soft assurance: "It was great. There will be many more opportunities. If you want to improve your game, I'm volunteering."

It was the most ecstatic moment of his young life. They were in the throes of hysterical first love. At least, he thought they were.

Maddy reached into her jacket pocket for a cigarette.

Lighting it, she commented: "This is like the movies. You know, having a cigarette afterwards."

She puffed on it and offered it to him. Mike drew on the cigarette as he looked up at the full moon hanging over the beach. For the first time since they had left the fire, he heard the roar of the waves and the crashing sound of water colliding against rocks.

Can arousal make you deaf? He wondered.

A drone of voices was getting louder, approaching their lair. Hurriedly, they slipped back into their clothing. There was no need, as the couple walking toward them chose a path of discretion and gave them a wide berth.

Maddy offered Mike a tissue to conceal the used condom and he disposed of it in a nearby litter bin. It was 9:30pm and Maddy had promised her dad she would be home by 10pm.

They returned to her holiday home, bypassing the party revellers on the way. Still, they passed close enough to catch a whiff of weed wafting across the beach. The gentle south-easter wind generously shared its fragrance with anyone 20m downwind.

The long kiss goodnight at her door was interspersed with arrangements for the next day, the final day of their holiday.

"Can I fetch you at 5 tomorrow morning?"

'What will my dad think?" Maddy said, maintaining her cheeky smile.

"I'm not fetching him, so I don't mind what he thinks."

"No, seriously," she said, frowning.

"Okay, okay. What about 10am? Is that respectable?"

"Ten it is, and let's leave your dad out of it," he confirmed as their lips came together for a final kiss.

Mike walked home, repeating out loud: "That was amazing. That was bloody fantastic!"

That amazing and fantastic night on Central Beach signalled a nascent love affair and opened the sluice gates to a flood of future lovemaking – long and short sessions; behind bushes; next to rivers; on mountains; in rooms; in cheap hotels; on floors; while camping; in cars; at drive-in movies; on the back seats at movie theatres; and of course, at the beach, any beach, again and again. They would often spend the night under the stars with a bottle of wine. Maddy would develop only one intimacy rule: Mike could not leave on his socks. Nothing else mattered, no holds barred.

The next day, the last day of the holiday, Mike visited the pharmacy to select a parting gift for Maddy. They exchanged gifts on the beach under a solemn grey sky. He gave her a Gemini Zodiac symbol attached to a silver chain. She gave him a similar chain with a crucifix. Looking into each other's eyes, they declared their love and commitment for one another. It was their lovers' pact. The gifts would serve as a physical reminder of their covenant. They agreed to write to each other every week.

Their final walk was to the river mouth at the end of Lookout Beach. The stated intention was to look for pansy shells, or sand dollars. Mike started to explain that in folklore it was believed these shells represented coins lost by mermaids, or the people of Atlantis, but the conversation petered out. Their minds were elsewhere.

Instead of walking and talking, they were enticed into the dense thicket that served as a boundary between the river and beach, and used it to camouflage their final round of intimacy. They did not have to say a word. Hours later, they emerged from their heavenly haven. This time, Mike had seen her face during her ecstasy and had seized opportunities to gaze appreciatively on many other normally covered parts.

They wrote regularly and maintained their agreed schedule. The next year her family repeated their September holiday, and Mike and Maddy repeated theirs, and reached new levels of intimacy. They were perfect for each other. Maybe it was a match made in heaven.

13

ACTS OF IMMORALITY

After Enoch died, Henk continued to make his scheduled stops at Sapkamma, and added a few more whenever he could. On several occasions, Beauty would accompany him to Graaff Reinet to buy supplies for both the Walters home and her own. At those times, Andile would help in the store or spend time with Lloyd.

Desire was rising between Henk and Beauty, like a river in flood, about to burst its banks. Henk made the first move.

His bus had been fitted with curtains in its back windows and around the back seat. A handy curtain pole and a drape could be suspended in front of the back seat, creating a private space, much like a hospital bed that could be cordoned off or, in this case, a boudoir.

Henk had not accepted any bookings for this trip to Graaff Reinet. Instead, he had directed all potential customers to the national bus service. Beauty was to be the only passenger joining him. She saw through his plan immediately – and liked it.

They rushed through their shopping in Graaff Reinet in order to maximise their time together. Henk parked in a safe spot off the road and invited Beauty to the back of the bus.

"Henk, am I the first to get in the back of the bus?"

"Yes, the first, and you will be the only."

"Then, let's not waste time."

That day, they contravened the Immorality Act[34]. Henk commented afterwards: "No wonder it's illegal. Anything that enjoyable can't be legal."

It would be the first of many, many such violations of the Act.

About eight months later, Henk and Beauty were in their chamber at the back of the bus, curtains drawn and the bus doors locked, when a provincial traffic policeman stopped to investigate the suspicious stationary bus parked off the road.

Henk watched the blue traffic patrol vehicle pull up through a narrow crack in the curtain. He motioned to Beauty to remain quiet.

Traffic officer Albertus Minaar walked around the bus. He approached the driver's side and tried the door. Locked.

The large handwritten sign stuck on the inside of the door read: "Out of petrol – back soon".

---

34 The Immorality Act 1957 (Act No. 23 of 1957) prohibited sexual intercourse or "immoral or indecent acts" between white people and anyone not white. The penalty was to up to seven years imprisonment for both partners

Minaar smiled, walked back to his vehicle and continued his journey.

Henk laughed as he told Beauty: "You know, we will spend just about the rest of our lives in prison if we're caught and charged together."

"If they lock us up together, it will be worth it," Beauty replied.

"Seriously, though," Henk continued, "I don't want to put you at risk. This is dangerous."

"I am willing to take the chance, Henk. What are our other options?"

"We could go and live in Swaziland or Lesotho."

"It's a thought," Beauty replied.

* * *

Mike had applied to study medicine at Stellenbosch University when he finished school. Edith was thrilled at the prospect of her son becoming a doctor. She had only one concern: An article in the local newspaper said that boys might have to complete military service before studying. She wanted her boy to qualify first and then do his military service as a medical doctor.

She wrote to former Captain van Niekerk, now Major van Niekerk. She knew he had a special interest in Mike. He replied, indicating that he would be in the area the following week and that they could look at her options. Carl reassured Edith that Van Niekerk had sufficient sway in the right circles to ensure Mike's deferment. Edith knew it would be heresy to even mention an exemption.

The next week, Van Niekerk popped in while Carl was busy at a regional commando meeting in Knysna. "Well, Major van Niekerk, can you help me? What are Mike's options? Can he get deferment?"

"It's not guaranteed, Mrs Hanssen."

"What happens if he doesn't get deferment?"

"Let me put it this way, it's much more dangerous in the army for an infantryman than a doctor. You know the saying: The good die young."

"Isn't that a bit extreme?" Edith protested.

He did not reply.

"Can you help?" she pushed.

He gave her a knowing look and said: "For the right reason, I can arrange it."

"And what may that be?" she asked apprehensively.

Van Niekerk was prepared for this question. His answer was at the ready and the equipment required was concealed in his pocket. He moved closer and slipped his arm under her dress, pressing the heel of his left hand against her pubic mound.

"This is a worthy reason. I am sure you're not surprised" he said, scanning her with serpent eyes.

Regaining her composure, she gave Van Niekerk a resigned look.

She loved Mike and was not going to rely on caul superstition to protect him. In that moment, she wondered if she was being guided by God to protect Mike from the serpent.

Edith glared at him: "I will do my part, as long as you do yours."

Van Niekerk's left hand expertly pulled down her panties. From a tube he had concealed in his right hand, he smeared a liberal dose of KY Jelly over her vaginal opening. He guided her to turn around and bent her over into downward-facing dog position, her hands planted on the desk.

He was behind her. She heard the rustle of a condom packet and the slightest sound of latex snapping.

He entered her efficiently, the lubricant ensuring no discomfort or pain. It was over quickly. She felt his spasm. Her part of the transaction was complete.

As he zipped his trousers, she said: "That's the last time. Now fulfil your part of the bargain."

Edith said no more. She had capitulated for a virtuous cause.

A few weeks later, Mike received a letter informing him of his deferment of service. He could first go to university, then report to the military upon completion of his studies.

Maddy was one year below him at school and was due to attend Stellenbosch University the following year.

1 4

THE 12 APOSTLES

1968

Soon after his visit to Edith, Van Niekerk was transferred to the Bureau of State Security (BOSS)[35] as officer in charge of a department that gathered intelligence on the growing communist threat. Their mandate was to collect, evaluate and interpret data on communist infiltrations.

His first assignment was to arrange a strategy meeting with relevant stakeholders. The aim of the meeting: To create a network that would gather relevant information on communist infiltration. The plan was christened The 12 Apostles. The 12 Impimpis may have been more appropriate.

---

35 The South African Bureau for State Security (also called Bureau of State Security; Afrikaans: *Buro vir Staatsveiligheid*) was established in 1969 by Prime Minister John Vorster and by 1971 was more powerful than the Ministries of Defence and Foreign Affairs. The Bureau's job was to monitor national security. It was headed by Hendrik van den Bergh. BOSS was replaced by the National Intelligence Service (NIS) in 1980.

Twelve young black men would be targeted to act as conduits for information about activities that were considered to be advancing communism. US Senator Joseph Mc McCarthy could not have thought of a more ingenious plan.

The men would be handpicked. They had to be from remote rural areas, so not well connected in urban areas; they had to be politically inert, with no known affiliations to the ANC or communists; and they had to be able to leave home without raising suspicion.

The 12 apostles would gather at Waterkloof Airforce Base for intelligence training, commencing 20 January 1969. After that, they would be posted into urban communities and given jobs. They would then receive generous salaries in exchange for routine work, including a weekly postal report. They would also receive bonuses for information leading to the exposure of any communist threat.

Van Niekerk would personally recruit two apostles from the rural Eastern Cape. Finding the other 10 were the tasks of the other five members of the strategic committee. He earmarked Andile Khumalo from Sapkamma, and Seiko Mfikili from Mbkweni region as his disciples.

Van Niekerk visited Commandant Geoff Walters during the June school holidays and shared just enough information about the plan to contract his support. Geoff agreed that Andile would be a suitable candidate.

Andile was summoned to the lounge in the farmhouse, where he met with Van Niekerk. The financial inducement was sufficient to remove any doubts from Andile's mind.

He was particularly impressed by the signing-on bonus of R200 presented to him from Van Niekerk's pocket. Andile signed a secrecy document in which the consequence of disclosure was spelled out as 10 years' imprisonment. All South Africans, black or white, feared being imprisoned. In South Africa, it was clearly worse for blacks.

Certainly, no telling Uncle Sipho about this one, he thought.

School drew to an end. It was December 1968 and time for Andile's *Ulwaluko*[36].

Single males, like Andile, who had not undergone initiation were known as *inkenkwe*. A boy among the Xhosa is a "thing", not a person, until he's been through the tribe's rites of passage.

Andile's initiation took place in the hills near the town of Addo, between 19 December and 19 January. His initiation group performed secret manhood rituals that marked their transition from boyhood to manhood. During the process, the initiates were circumcised with a spear and their foreskins attached to their blankets.

The initiates were then painted white with clay from head to foot and wrapped up in new blankets. They were then lectured on how to be honourable Xhosas.

A one-month period of seclusion followed. After that, the boys ran down to the river to wash themselves. Their

36 *Ulwaluko* is the traditional circumcision and initiation into manhood practiced by the Xhosa tribe to prepare young males for the responsibilities of manhood.

hut and possessions were burnt and each initiate received a new blanket. They were finally considered *amakwala* (new men).

Having rejoined society, Andile caught a bus at the Addo Bus Terminus, which took a circuitous route via Port Elizabeth to Graaff Reinet. Andile stayed on board in Port Elizabeth.

A neatly dressed black man inconspicuously boarded the bus and sat down beside him. Turning to Andile, he said softly: "You must come with me." He was about to protest when the stranger continued: "You remember your agreement with Major van Niekerk? It starts now. Let's go."

Andile left the bus. His only possessions were the new clothes he wore, a stick and some money given to him by the tribal elders. The stranger did not introduce himself. He motioned to Andile to get into a waiting cream Passat. Their destination: The Military section of the Port Elizabeth Airport. From there, Andile and the stranger were ushered aboard a military Dakota.

The three-hour flight to Pretoria's Waterkloof Military Airfield went by in silence. Andile spent most of the time reflecting on his decision to accept Van Niekerk's offer. Was he being a traitor to his tribe? Was he an impimpi?

His relationship with Sipho had made him fully aware of the ANC and its role in the struggle for political liberty. He was angry about the lack of opportunity afforded to him as a result of his race. Lloyd had gone to a better school and was already in his first year at Natal University. He had gone to a school for blacks that had provided an apartheid

STEVE HARRIS

education without Maths – an education that was aimed at permanently subjugating black people. He had no hope of a university education.

His decision to accept Van Niekerk's offer had been two-fold. First, he wanted to escape poverty and secondly, he had accepted because of the kindness Geoff Walters had shown his family. Walters had recommended that he listen to Van Niekerk's offer.

"Andile, at the moment, there are limited opportunities for black youths in South Africa. This will provide you with a stepping stone to greater opportunities. I suggest you listen to Major Van Niekerk's proposal and decide if you think it's viable," Walters had said.

It seemed like a decent deal. Too good to miss.

Andile walked tentatively down the aircraft stairs, only to be greeted by the booming voice of Corporal De Wet: "*Klim uit daardie vliegtuig, jou blou gat*[37]."

Andile was totally dumbfounded. He understood Afrikaans, but had no idea why he was being called a blue bottom. Black bottom was an obvious choice for a black person, or even white bottom during their initiation. But, why blue?

Blou gat was a term used for all new recruits into military services in South Africa. As far as he knew, he was not joining the military.

The stranger, his chaperone since Port Elizabeth, exchanged a few words with the vociferous corporal, then

37   Afrikaans for: "Get out of that aircraft, you blue bottom."

returned to the aircraft, presumably to fly back to Port Elizabeth.

The corporal motioned to Andile to climb on to the back of a military Land Rover, and they drove to a bungalow in a secure area on the Waterkloof base. The bungalow was on a piece of land surrounded by security wire and flat-roofed cement towers with glass windows.

Twelve people, including Andile, occupied the large room. Some had been there for several days, waiting for the full complement to be assembled.

"*Aantree, aantree!*" the high-pitched command came from the loudmouthed corporal. The 12 blundered around, until they realised they were supposed to form a straight line outside the bungalow, in front of the corporal. One of the recruits whispered something and received an immediate rebuke.

"When you are in front of an officer, you shut the fuck up. Do you hear me?"

They stood in silence. "Do you fucking hear me?" the bellowing corporal yelled again.

A few of the group replied randomly: "Yes."

"Yes, Corporal!" De Wet continued his tirade. "I want to hear one voice only. Do you hear me?"

"Yes, Corporal," came the loud reply in reasonable unison.

"That's better. I am not here to welcome you. I don't give a shit if you feel welcome or not. I am here to train you. You are now going to wait in silence until Major Van Niekerk comes to address you."

They waited for two hours in the hot sun, not daring to say a word.

"Attention!" Corporal de Wet barked. Van Niekerk had arrived.

The major addressed them in a soft, serious tone.

"You must excuse Corporal De Wet. He only knows one way, and that's the army way. You may not be in the army, but certain military disciplines will be useful to you in your future endeavours. You will stay in this confined section of Waterkloof for the next three months.

"The 12 of you have been handpicked from remote, rural parts of the country. It's most unlikely that you will meet anyone from your youth where you will be deployed. In the event that you do, it's only a three-month gap that needs to be accounted for. You will be trained to handle this type of event.

"You're the first and only group of this kind. There's no intention that you will engage in any combat. In your interview, when you were recruited, that was one of our commitments for your involvement. The only villains in your lives are the communists. You will be well rewarded, and the biggest reward is that you will play an important part in stopping the communists.

"As you know, if they take over, it's not only the whites that will suffer. All South Africans will hurt. You see, the communists couldn't give a rat's arse about your colour. They simply want South Africa's resources. They're like a plague of locusts. They will devour everything, including your culture.

"You will be trained in a range of surveillance and communication skills. While you're training, there must be no contact with your family. Nobody must know where you are. You can contact them afterwards and make a plausible excuse to cover the three months away. Is that clear?

"Is that clear?" he repeated in a higher pitch.

"Yes, Major," came a dozen replies in perfect unison.

"Now, that reply was a military skill," Van Niekerk said smugly.

"After three months, you will be assigned to a community where you will integrate and establish your legitimacy. As far as the rest of the world's concerned, the next three months' training never happened. We will ensure that you get a job and live as ordinary citizens in your designated community. Your acceptance in these societies is vital and may take a long time. We can wait. The stakes are too high to be hurried. The communists are patient. We can also be patient.

"You will report in every month by posting a simple observation report to a private bag address. The nature of the report will be taught to you during your training period. You will not be required to put anyone in danger. Your task is surveillance and reporting so that we can monitor communist and enemy activities in townships."

Andile noted the subtle addition of the word "enemy" into Van Niekerk's speech. No doubt, Van Niekerk meant the ANC or any of its affiliates. He wondered how far Van Niekerk would deviate from the agreement.

"If we need to get hold of you in a hurry, we will send a telegram to your new address. If you need to get hold of me urgently, you can send a telegram to the private bag address. I should get it within two days."

Van Niekerk turned and left. Over the next three months, the dirty dozen – a name they gave to themselves – remained submerged in intensive training along lines sketched by Van Niekerk. A few dirty tricks were added.

At the end of the programme, they were ready to go. Having dutifully served his waiting period, Andile was seconded to the outskirts of Soweto, given a room for accommodation, and sufficient clothing and a bank savings book with enough money to cover his expenses for a month. His job appointment was as a bouncer at a local *shebeen*[38] called the Click Tavern.

It wasn't difficult for government agencies to secure employment opportunities in places like shebeens. If they never offered their co-operation, the shebeen would receive a visit from the authorities and be shut down.

Beauty wasn't overly concerned when Andile did not return to Sapkamma, but she did miss him. She knew nothing terrible had befallen him. That was one of the benefits of being a sangoma. However, she knew little of

---

38 *Shebeens* were located in townships as an alternative to pubs and bars, where under apartheid laws black Africans were barred from entering. The name Click Tavern came from a traditional song which the western world knows as The Click Song, made famous by Miriam Makeba.

what he was actually doing. There's a limit to a Sangoma's knowing.

A few months later, Beauty received a letter from Andile, apologising for his silence and explaining that he was living and working in Soweto.

On one of his frequent visits to Sapkamma, Henk had broached the subject of leaving South Africa.

"Beauty, we mustn't stress about Andile. He's a wise and capable young man who has left home to start a new chapter in his life. We can leave now and start a new life in Maseru. We can live there as a couple without fearing the law. Andile can visit us or even join us there."

Beauty gave her typical, full-faced smile. "I agree about Andile, and leaving sounds romantic, but how will we survive. Can I be your maid?"

"If we go, you will be forbidden from using the 'M' word. I don't want a maid, I want a wife. I want you as my wife. Surviving will be easy. I could run a bus service between South Africa and Maseru. Besides, your healing skills will be as needed there as they are here. With my contacts in their government service, getting residence won't be a problem."

"Then, what are we waiting for?" asked Beauty with predictable optimism.

Three months later, they immigrated to Maseru, Lesotho.

Henk started his business and Beauty worked as a healer-sangoma. Six months later, they were married by a local magistrate. Neither of them had religious leanings and attributed their success to the love they shared. It seemed that nothing could go wrong.

15

OH HAPPY DAYS

Mike enrolled at Stellenbosch University to study medicine in 1969. He became a *Matie*. Stellenbosch University students all get the nickname Matie. It was probably a play on the word "mates". And indeed, Mike made new mates as he immersed himself in a demanding academic and fanatical rugby culture. Of course, there was a drinking culture, too, that competed with both the aforementioned for top priority.

Maties had cunningly renamed Wednesday evening *Klein Saterdag*[39], so Wednesday evenings allowed for additional mid-week revelry. As any seasoned student would reason: "Why wait for the official weekend to party and get trashed?"

By accessing an institution like Stellenbosch University, one paid the tuition price and a separate price through initiation or *ontgroening*[40], as it was called in Afrikaans. Stellenbosch University was, after all, the cradle of Afri-

---

39 Translated from Afrikaans means Little Saturday.
40 The direct translation into English is de-greening.

kanerdom, where one could catch and express pride in Afrikaans culture and conservative Calvinism. It was the spawning ground of most of South Africa's nationalist leaders.

Initiation rites were harsh and downright dangerous. Over the years, they had caused major injuries, several deaths and unfathomable emotional damage. The only saving grace for students was their limited duration. Fortunately, Mike was used to violent and emotional attacks under the guise of initiation rites. The Stellenbosch initiation was merely a continuation of the boarding school culture with which he had become well accustomed. It was simply another degradation ceremony.

The most common initiation methods involved sleep deprivation, accompanied by physical and emotional intimidation. It was standard stuff: Standing on a table in front of a 100 boys and singing your school song was doable. Singing that song in the nude was a little tougher. Attending a *tekkie* party[41] because you, supposedly, sang poorly – was painful.

The least anticipated part of initiation was the punishment metered out to those who were perceived by seniors not to be committed Christians. The small English-speaking contingent fell into the category of not sufficiently Christian.

---

41 A *tekkie* party was the act of crawling on all fours between the legs of a long line of boys – as many as 50 – while they beat your bottom with their running shoes.

Mike suspected that Afrikaans students would additionally use initiation as a cover to extract revenge for old cultural wounds inflicted by the English back in the Boer War of 1899. The zealous dealing out of punishment, accompanied with a ubiquitous use of "Soutie", provided him with all of the evidence he needed.

English students were summoned to prayer meetings, positioned in the middle of the group and subjected to passionate prayers that pleaded with God to make them, heathens, see His light.

Ironically, Mike believed he was already a good Christian. He regularly attended St Mary's Anglican Church in Stellenbosch. This evidence did not change his classification in the eyes of his Afrikaans counterparts. They accused him of righteous indignation. It would seem that going to an Anglican church did not make you a Christian any more than standing in a garage made you a car. To them, he was a miserable sinner and they were going to help him.

Additional help came in the form of a midnight visit, in which he was forcibly removed from his bed, beaten with a range of objects by a group of masked seniors, tied up, blindfolded and driven out of town. He was then dumped in the nude on a far-flung farm road and left to his own devices. Given his nature and temper, Mike's assailants did feel some blows from him in the process.

Two weeks later, initiation was over. It marked the entrance into the Matie fraternity. Everyone was bonded and happy. Adversaries became friends, and they sat next to campfires singing *Kumbaya*, their relationships forged in the fires of initiation.

Or that's what was supposed to have happened. The reality was different. Initiation was mired in controversy. The press had a field day criticising it. If it was intended to bond English-speaking students and Afrikaans-speaking ones, it didn't.

Imagine if black people were allowed to come to Stellenbosch University. That would set the cat among the pigeons, Mike thought.

At last, Mike had become aware of the machinations of apartheid.

Attendance registers were taken at lectures, and the dress code for men was a collar and tie. The ladies usually wore dresses. The late 60s coincided with the zenith of the mini, which made focusing on studies all the more difficult for hot-blooded men. It was rumoured that conservative, theologian Afrikaners were concerned about the level of the skirts because it might result in *wind-bestuiwing* (wind pollination).

All lectures were in Afrikaans. The change in language of instruction from the English of his school days was a much bigger barrier than Mike had anticipated.

Mike wrote to Maddy: "I hear in Afrikaans; translate into English and make notes in English, then fall behind the tempo of the lecturer. After class, I borrow notes from friends and transcribe."

Evolution soon took over, and Mike adapted to a more economical learning style. Eventually, he heard in Afrikaans, thought in Afrikaans and wrote notes in Afrikaans.

The first chemistry lecture produced an unusual motivation. The lecturer opened his presentation by saying: "Look at the person on your left, then on your right. Out of the three of you, only one will pass first year. Good luck."

Mike grinned, thinking: "These two look pretty smart. In future, I had better sit next to people who don't look that clever, or I'm done for."

The smart young man on his left was Peter le Roux. Peter was an erudite Afrikaner, schooled at a private English boarding school in Cape Town. He hailed from a wealthy farming family in the Caledon district. He was handsome, dapper and extremely confident. Some would go as far as to say arrogant and flamboyant. Best of all, he drove a fancy open-top sports car. The wonders of wealth.

They introduced themselves after class and shared a laugh about the negative inspiration provided by the lecturer. Peter showed his form by commiserating with Mike: "You should make the most of this year, seeing it could be your only one!"

Mike and Peter, two doctors in waiting, became constant companions. They worked hard, played hard and spent the occasional weekend at the Le Roux farm. Peter, as was typical of white South African males, was a gun fanatic. His arsenal rivalled Carl's. Bird shooting and clay pigeons shoots, were the default activities on the farm.

Mike's new friends included his roommate, Bertie Steenkamp. At more than two metres in height, Bertie was extremely tall. He, too was enrolled to study law. He, like Peter, had a fancy convertible sports car. His was a Mercedes. They did not spend much time together. Bertie stayed out late virtually every night and slept late. During his first year, his most significant commitment to his studies was his registration for the course. His text books gathered dust on his unused desk.

Initially, Mike and Bertie passed each other like ships in the night. The first time Mike bumped into Bertie during the evening was six weeks after initiation. Mike walked in to find Bertie huddled over his desk. When he turned to greet Mike, he was wearing a jeweller's loop. There were two small piles of bright glass-like stones on the desk.

"Oh, hi, Mike, I didn't expect you back so soon. Don't you have rugby practice on a Monday evening?"

"Yes, we finish at 7pm, and it's already eight. What on earth are you doing?"

"Oh, you mean, what are my *klippies* [42] doing?"

"Yes what are you doing with uncut diamonds – sorry klippies?'

Bertie explained without hesitation that every three months he bought uncut diamonds from a gang in Upington. He would then sell them to a contact in Cape Town, who shipped them to Amsterdam for cutting and integration into the legitimate market.

Mike was incredulous. "Come on, that can't be true. Where did you get the contacts?"

---

42 Directly translated from Afrikaans, *klippies* means little stones.

"Well, I come from Upington. A local coloured gang sources uncut diamonds. They claim they pan for them near the Augrabies Falls. More likely they're stolen from the De Beers Mining Company. I don't care."

"That's IDB, Isn't Illicit Diamond Buying illegal and dangerous?"

"Only if you're caught."

"Shit, Bertie, and if the cops come into our room, what then?"

"The cops are stupid. They won't look in here. Why do you think I enrolled at university? It's the perfect cover. Who needs a degree when you have money?"

"Okay, if you're wrong, I will visit you in jail."

"Thanks, buddy."

A month later, Bertie asked Mike to help him.

"Mike, my Cape Town buyer says it's getting a bit hot. The cops have my description and will set up roadblocks for me or my car between Upington and Cape Town, Can you help? I will hire a car, if you fetch the klippies I will pay you R100."

"R100? You're on!"

Mike's parents struggled to pay his university fees and there was nothing spare for pocket money. He earned money by working as a lifeguard and barman in Plettenberg Bay during the holidays. Ill-gotten gains would come in handy as pocket money. They would also allow him to visit Maddy in Kimberley during mid-year break.

He didn't give a thought to the commandment: "Thou shalt not steal, neither deal falsely".

It wasn't that Mike was indifferent to the law. He rationalised that he was only going to be a courier, not a criminal. No one would get hurt, and it was not stealing, like robbing a bank. The klippies came from the ground. Justifying aside, it was becoming more apparent that in addition to having a fiery temperament, Mike liked to live on the edge.

Similar to most lawbreakers, he felt the risk was worth the reward. He was willing to gamble without calculating its impact. Did he actually know what it would be like to go to jail? Not yet, anyway.

Early that Friday morning, Mike bunked classes. Carrying an envelope of cash and his 9mm pistol in his jacket pocket, he drove the hired Ford Cortina GT to Upington. Bertie had set up the drop with his Upington supplier, Adonis Jacobs, on the corner of Schroder and Rondom streets at 4pm. Adonis would be wearing a red beret. Bertie gave him Adonis's phone number in case of a mishap.

The trip was uneventful. The journey and transaction went according to plan. The exchange occurred in broad daylight.

The drive back with the costly cargo was nerve-racking. Transporting money was fairly easily explainable, but trying to explain why you're transporting diamonds? That was another league altogether. Mike felt like a felon, and he was. He enjoyed the excitement, the adrenalin rush. He imagined what it would be like to lead Bonnie and Clyde-type existence. How would Maddy feel about being Bonnie?

He crashed back down to earth with the sound of a police siren. He saw the police car in his rear-view mirror, lights flashing, so he pulled to the side. The vehicle drew up about 10m behind him.

He wondered if the sickening feeling in the pit of his stomach was universal to all people stopped by police, or if it was reserved only for those who had reason to feel guilty.

Stephanus Roos, the blue-uniformed officer, walked up to the Cortina with the typical swagger of a highway policeman straight out of an American movie.

"Step out of the car, please."

Mike obliged.

"Licence, please."

Mike fumbled in his pocket and handed over his licence.

"What's the aim of your journey, Mr Hanssen?"

"I was visiting a friend in Upington and on my way back to Stellenbosch University."

The policeman peered into the car and noticed the inflated rugby ball on the back seat. "Wait a minute. Didn't I see you playing rugby at Coetzenberg last Saturday?"

"Yes, I played." "Who are you guys playing tomorrow?" "It's a big game, against Villagers." "Well, don't let me stop you, boy. Get back to Matieland."

Mike greeted Officer Roos and drove off, watching the waving policeman in the rear-view mirror.

The klippies remained safe on the back seat, inside the inflated rugby ball.

A few hours later, Mike passed the precious ball to Bertie, who gave him the R100 remuneration, saying: "I guess this is lucrative business for both of us."

Mike calculated that if he made three more Upington trips that year, and a further four trips in 1970, he could earn R300 and R400, respectively. That kind of money would make it a lot easier to keep up with the social pace that Peter set. It would also be handy when Maddy came to Stellenbosch next year.

His mind was racing. Maybe, he thought, I could talk to Bertie about a franchise, rather than a courier service. Then I could pay my tuition. Who knows? I may own a sports car one day. The projections were endless. Rugby and studies filled his time until Peter's birthday bash in Caledon on the Saturday night before mid-year break. Party revellers would stay the night, squeezing into every nook and cranny of the farmhouse.

* * *

Mike left Stellenbosch after the final rugby game of the term against Van der Stel. An hour later, he arrived at the party and became the recipient of a bottle of Red Heart rum with his name and the words "*Drink me – all of me*" inscribed on it. This was the type of challenge Mike couldn't resist.

By 10pm, the bottle was half empty. Everything became a little fuzzy and he was slurring. He didn't care what others were thinking as he indulged bouts of what Afrikaans people call *dronk verdiet*. He melancholically told any sympathetic ear about his deep feelings for Maddy and what a wonderful person she was. The responses ranged from nauseated to avoidance. Any romantic prospects that may have existed for Mike that night evaporated like ether on a hot plate.

By 10:30pm, his only willing listener was Jessie, Peter's border collie. Soon after, even Jessie had reached her limit and had moved off in search of more scintillating company.

By 11pm, his body became numb and his movements appeared to him faster and clumsier as he bumped into doorways and bits of furniture. He felt as if he were having an out of body experience, as if he were watching himself.

By 12pm, the bottle was empty. Mike could not stand without staggering. Peter intervened and dragged him on to a camp bed in his room. Mike kept one foot on the ground in an attempt to stop the room spinning. He lost consciousness at 12:15am.

It was to be the most awful night of his life to date. Half an hour later, he started vomiting. Peter deposited a bucket and aligned it next to Mike's head. Ten minutes after that, Peter heard him choking on his vomit. Fortunately for Mike, Peter placed his head in a recovery position and cleared his throat of vomit particles with his index finger. Neither of the aspirant doctors was aware of the dangers of alcohol poisoning.

The next day, Mike had the mother and father of hangovers: Mental confusion accompanied by the most horrendous headache and ongoing, involuntary retching, although he had no further stomach contents left to expel.

No remedies made Mike feel better. He remained at the farm, in and out of bed for three days. That would be the last time binge drinking entered Mike's realm of possibility. Social drinking was his only option for the future.

On that Friday, he drove to Kimberley to be with Maddy for the mid-year break.

His relationship with Maddy had been sustained by regular letter writing. When he saw her, it continued seamlessly. Maddy's dad had arranged part-time work for him as a barman at a gentleman's club, where he was the chairman. Mike had developed cocktail mixing and typical bar serving skills in Plett. A gentleman's club introduced him to a new skills set. He had to become an accomplished liar, too.

A work shift would include at least three phone calls in which he would be required to relay falsehoods. A typical call would be something like: "Hello, Beaconsfield Club, Mike speaking."

"Is Mr Innes there, please?"

"Hang on, I will check."

With a hand over the telephone receiver, he would whisper,, "Mr Innes, call for you."

"Tell her I left 10 minutes ago," Mr Innes would reply.

"He left 10 minutes ago."

"He had better not be there!"

"Sorry, Mrs Innes, I can't see him."

Another commandment, "Thou shalt not lie to one another" had slipped through Mike's moral net.

Cedric Lance was also the chairman of the Crusaders Rugby Club in Kimberley. It didn't take much persuasion to get Mike to a practice and on to the playing field for his debut game.

In addition to initiation, playing rugby had made Mike increasingly aware of the amount of sectarian praying and proselytising that occurred in his new university environment. He was surprised to find it metastasized to a rugby team in Kimberley. How far does this go? he wondered.

Before rugby games at Stellenbosch, the team would huddle in the change room together, praying to the Lord to prevent injuries and to help them produce a winning performance. Some players extended their evangelical fervour to kneeling on the field before the game and crossing themselves in an act of devotion. The vast majority would also point to the sky in acknowledgement or adulation after they had scored a try.

Do all teams do that? Mike wondered. If I were in the change room next door, would we be asking the Lord to help me win? On what basis would the Lord decide who to favour? If I got injured, would it be as punishment? If we lost, would it be because the Lord preferred the other team?'

Mike's conclusion was that one should play, not pray, sport. He said nothing. The persecution during initiation had ensured his discretion.

Prayer aside, the relationship between girlfriend's father and boyfriend improved immeasurably as Mike's performance on the field helped to produce a rare win for the Crusaders. He graciously accepted praise and thanks.

Cedric leased a shack near Barclay West, on the Orange River. The rustic structure was reminiscent of something out of an Ernest Hemingway novel. It stood alone on the banks of the river. Maddy asked her dad if she and Mike could go there after the rugby game. He searched for an escape clause, but capitulated when Maddy's slightly younger sister, Cloe, volunteered to accompany them.

The shack had one bedroom, an open plan lounge and kitchen, and a caravan parked outside that provided additional accommodation. The unlikely, official plan was that Mike would sleep in the caravan, and Maddy and Cloe would share the bedroom.

Cloe broached the subject on the drive to Barclay West: "Maddy, you and Mike use the bedroom and I'll have the caravan. Please don't be noisy. It's embarrassing."

Maddy responded: "Noisy? Me or Mike? How did you know he snores?"

"You know what I mean."

"You mean I snore."

"Okay, big sister, enough. Or he's back in the caravan."

They arrived at sunset, and the evening started with braai and wine. Stellenbosch, renowned for its wines, was starting to give Mike's cultural development respectability. The scene was set: The wine, meat on the coals, a full moon, and the sound of the Orange River running by. Perfect.

Mike and Maddy chatted to Cloe for a respectable time before bidding her goodnight and promising not to be noisy.

A few hours later, an exhausted Mike lay talking to Maddy. The inevitable cigarette completed the scene.

The conversation flowed with ease from one subject to another. When there was a suitable lull, Maddy gave Mike a somewhat serious look.

"So, Mike, what stories about yourself will you tell our children?"

"I don't know. You go first," he floundered.

She looked up at the ceiling.

"I'll tell them that you were my first and only lover."

"Okay, that's maybe too much information for the children, but I like it. Tell me more stories like that."

"How about: I played first team hockey at my school."

"Ho hum. Boring."

"Okay, I loved my mum and dad and, oh yes, I got an A aggregate in my final school exams."

"But you haven't done them yet."

"So, I will still get an A."

"Oh yes. I will tell them I married the best doctor in South Africa."

"Pressure!"

"Now you," Maddy turned to face him.

"Well, I will tell them I was top of my class in junior school, probably because I was the only one in the class. "Or how about, I got my first pair of shoes at 13.

I never sat at a table for a meal with my parents. "My dad never saw what my high school looked like."

Maddy cried out: "Stop, stop! I can hear violins. They will never believe you. You sound like the old folks telling stories about how tough their childhood was."

"But it's true."

'Well, even if it is, you will need to change it, I don't want our kids rolling their eyes at their dad's stories. I will help you rewrite and sanitise your history until its fit for our children's consumption."

"Oh hell" were the only words Mike could utter as he noticed Maddy's breasts peering over the sheet.

They tried not to be noisy as carnality overrode their conversation.

"Dr and Mrs Hanssen. I like the sound of that," she said, as sleep overcame them.

She liked it. He liked it.

Mike drifted off to sleep to the sound of the mighty Orange River flowing by. In his mind's eye, he pictured alluvial diamonds rolling along the river bed on their journey to the Augrabies Falls, where they would be collected by Adonis.

He made a mental note to try his luck at finding another Star of South Africa[43] along the banks of the river the next day. Before cutting, the original stone, weighed 83.5 carats. That would do nicely.

Mike's dreams did not match his reality. The setting was the Orange River, the context was different.

Maddy and Edith were splashing in the shallows of the river. From the muddy depths in the middle of the waters a creature silently emerged. It sensed the swimmers and

---

43 The Star of South Africa is a 47.69-carat white diamond found in 1869 on the banks of the Orange River.

moved swiftly towards them, creating a wake behind it, like a speedboat. The girls had their backs turned to the oncoming creature. Mike tried to shout a warning, but no sound came from his lips. It was as if his mouth was too full to form words. He tried running down to the women, but his legs were immobilised. They wouldn't move.

The creature had the head of a serpent and a body that constantly morphed and shape-shifted from a large human male to a springbuck. Its forked tongue flicked in and out of its mouth as it moved closer to the unsuspecting women. The serpent's face looked grotesquely reptilian, with hints of human features. Mike recognised the human as someone he knew, but could not put a name to him.

He looked down at his paralysed legs. His feet were trapped in a quicksand-like slurry of uncut diamonds. His mouth was stuffed full of diamonds that he had no way of expelling. He was gagging.

At the critical moment, the girls saw their therianthrope assailant. Edith was the first to fall prey to a vicious attack. The creature grabbed her in its jaws, shook her, and then sank below the surface. A few metres deeper, it broke the surface, with Edith flaying and kicking before going under again. Mike watched in horror, immobilised.

Maddy was screaming as she scrambled towards the river bank. She was within a metre of safety when the creature breached the water behind her, like a killerwhale in pursuit of skyward prey. Mike found his voice and let out a guttural scream.

His scream woke him. Maddy was peering over him.

"Mike, what the hell was that about?"

"You don't want to know."

There was an intimate consolation in store for Mike for waking up in the middle of the night.

He would have recurring nightmares about therian-thropes from that day forward. He would also see something familiar in the serpent's features but never understand why.

The next day, they returned to Kimberley for family time.

The mid-year break ended after a few more shifts at the bar, one more rugby game and further opportunities for familiarity. Mike had developed a love that would sustain him until Maddy came to Stellenbosch the following year. Mike returned to Stellenbosch.

He made the three trips to Upington for Bertie, but got no closer to closing a better franchise deal. The trips were uneventful and money for old rope.

* * *

In February 1970, Maddy enrolled at Stellenbosch University, and Mike moved into private digs that he shared with Peter on the Old Paarl road outside Stellenbosch.

The same month, Carl and Edith moved to Port Elizabeth. Major Van Niekerk's successor at Eastern Province command was not coping with the increase in regional Commando growth and the authorities had decided to create two positions from one. They offered the additional appointment to Carl. His acceptance effectively brought Plettenberg Bay holidays to an end.

Maddy's university initiation was less harsh than Mike had experienced. Her worst experience was being caught by the Wilgenhof Hostel inmates as she cheekily called out *bekfluitjie* (harmonica).

The Wilgenhof Hostel resembled a harmonica, and there was a great deal of sensitivity about this resemblance among its inhabitants. If you dared shout the word "bekfluitjie" in close proximity, the occupants would almost certainly nab you and punish you. In her instance, they dragged her inside and under the showers. Presumably, fully clothed.

The university timetable was once again choked with academia and rugby. Maddy stayed at Mike's digs most weekends. Sometimes they stayed at Peter's farm. In 1970, Mike's university breaks were used to explore Africa with Maddy. The summer holiday was spent in Mozambique skin-diving. Their largess made affordable, thanks to the lucrative courier service that materialised as predicted. There was still no hint of franchising, though. Mike kept this aspect of his life to himself. Both Maddy and his friends assumed he was being funded by his parents and by part-time jobs.

On their way back to university they dropped in to Peter's farm as a final stop before commencing a new academic year. Mike's third and Maddy's second.

Oh, happy days indeed.

PART TWO

16

ASHES TO ASHES

January/February 1971

In a rare meaningful conversation with Carl, Edith expressed sadness about Mike's infrequent visits. She recalled with cold comfort her mother saying: "A son's a son until he takes a wife. A daughter's a daughter for the rest of your life." Carl, thinking it's an old wive's tale, responded with a grunt-like "*Mmph*".

Mike, unaware of his grandmother's wisdom, was indeed feeling remorseful about his rare home visits. He had spent little holiday time with his parents since leaving school. University breaks were invariably spent visiting Maddy and her home.

To appease his growing guilt, that September break he took Maddy on a road trip up the coast, primarily to include a two-day stop-over with his parents. The time passed quickly and the visit was surprisingly pleasant. Despite their agreeable stay, Mike left having drawn the conclusion that he did not regard his parents' house in

Port Elizabeth as his home. He felt like he was visiting a distant relative. The house in Plettenberg Bay had been his home. This one did not have a space allocated to him; it had a spare room. "Is this what happens? You grow up, you leave home, and then your room leaves you?" Mike asked Maddy as they departed his parents' house.

Back on the road, Maddy commented on a different subject: "Mike, your mum's lost a lot of weight. Do you think she's alright?" Mike had noticed, but he didn't think it was out of the ordinary. "You girls obsess about weight," he responded, dismissing it as a typical female preoccupation.

It was a few months later, in December, that his mother's dramatic weight loss was accompanied by abdominal pain and tenderness in the lower abdomen. Blood in her stools was the clincher that convinced Edith to seek medical advice from a general practitioner in Port Elizabeth. He immediately referred her to Dr Susan de Bruyn, an oncologist at the provincial hospital. De Bruyn diagnosed the condition as advanced metastatic colon cancer. It was inoperable and Edith received notice that she, in all probability, had six weeks to live without chemotherapy, and a slim chance at extended life with treatment.

She opted for therapy and asked Carl and their friends not to tell Mike until they knew whether the treatment was working or not. By early February, there had been a sharp deterioration in her condition and it was obvious that treatment was not going to prolong her life.

She was weak and skeletal; her weight had dropped from an average 58 kg to 36 kg. Her head of thick, curly brunette locks had been reduced to a few grey strands, giving her a zombie-like appearance. She was lying at death's door in the provincial hospital when Carl sent a typically impersonal telegram to Mike's digs in Stellenbosch: "*Mum terminally ill. You need to come quickly. Dad*".

Mike was shocked to hear the news and caught the first available flight to Port Elizabeth. For the following week, he stayed in his parents' spare room while keeping a daily vigil at Edith's bedside.

The morphine that made the pain bearable took its toll on her lucidity. She was hardly coherent when Mike arrived. Her rasping voice was difficult to understand and she talked mostly about how much she would miss him. He did not feel it proper to query how missing someone would be possible after death. Nor did he know why she mumbled about the Beacon Island Hotel, a caul and a snake. He assumed she was referring to good times in Plettenberg Bay, and that she meant "call"; possibly referring to contact from the "other side" after death. He could not contextualise her snake reference.

She stopped eating solids two days after he arrived. A few days later, the liquids stopped. She lost consciousness and the life force that used to animate her was sustained solely by an IV drip.

Her appearance became ghoulish as her body gnarled into a foetal position. The medical chart revealed the dying process: Nil solids intake; nil fluid intakes; followed by nil stools and nil urine. Mike correlated the declining fluid level in her catheter bags with the graph at the foot of her bed.

The only other time he had spent so much time alone with his mother was when he was a toddler. It occurred to him that since then, he had learned little about her. He had known what she looked like, but the person lying next to him did not look like his mum anymore.

He knew that she was even tempered and loving towards him anyway.

What was her favourite food? Not sure.

What were her political views? Not sure.

Was she religious? Not sure.

What were her favourite pastimes? Not sure.

Who were her friends? Not sure.

What were her dark secrets? Not sure.

Was this culture of ignorance exclusive to his family, or do all children know so little about their parents? Not sure.

He did know he loved her and that he appreciated her efforts to provide him with sound platforms on which to step as he engaged with life. Many of his friends complained about their mothers being on their back, Mike concluded that his mum hadn't been on his back, but always covering it. He knew she had often protected him from Carl's temper and had provided the motivating force for him to study medicine. She had also supplied most of the funding.

He spent hours sitting next to her bed, his forehead on the blue bedcover, holding her hand, at times, weeping gently.

She gave her final breath with him at her side. The cardiac monitor flatlined; a long continuous tone emanating from the machine that summoned the duty sister. There was no frantic running around of medical personnel; no shout of "Code blue!"; no defibrillator with tightly wound up cords hauled out in an attempt to reconnect the person to life. The end was due. Her lifeless hand flopped from the bed, fingers pointing to the floor. The gold wedding ring that represented her relationship with Carl slipped off her thin, bony finger and fell symbolically on to the linoleum. Mike retrieved it, thinking Edith would have liked Maddy to wear it. He shook his head as he realised he was already referring to her in the past tense.

The medical practitioner on duty confirmed her death and wrote the requisite note:

13/02/1971 16.01 pm: Called to the patient's room by her son, Mike Hanssen; Mrs Edith Hanssen not breathing, no pulse, breath or other auscultated sounds.

Death was pronounced by Dr Harrington at 16.15pm. IV access device in L forearm removed and dressing applied. Belongings checked off on belongings list by Mr Hanssen. Body sent to morgue at 16:45 pm.

Although he was not a demonstrative person, Carl's muted reaction and lack of grief seemed out of place. Mike found it curious, but not noteworthy.

The funeral was held three days later at the St Barnabas Anglican Church in Walmer. A suitably pious priest conducted the service, making, what seemed to Mike, extravagant claims about Edith's religious observance and how she now occupied a perfect, pain-free place with her saviour in eternity. Mike was sure these assertions had been prompted by Carl's worldview and had not reflected Edith's sentiments.

As he moved away from the graveside after throwing the customary handful of earth on to Edith's coffin," he felt a comforting arm coil over his left shoulder. It was Van Niekerk.

"Mike, I am so sorry, she was special. We'll all miss her," he whispered.

"Please stay in touch, and if ever you need help, don't hesitate to call me," he said, passing Mike a card bearing a name and private number in Pretoria.

"Thanks, Major. You have been a good friend to the family. I'll remember your offer."

That night, Mike caught a flight back to Cape Town and drove to his digs in Stellenbosch.

* * *

Carl's personal assistant, Glenda Monk, had been caring and considerate during Edith's stay in hospital. She had provided housekeeping services and had generally gone beyond the call of duty to help Carl and Mike. It was only a while after Edith's death when Mike had begun to suspect that she was possibly more than a staff member.

When did my dad start receiving these superior services?

Carl had asked Glenda to pack up Edith's belongings and to donate them to the Salvation Army. Edith, a typical war-prompted hoarder, had accumulated a wide range of odds and sods. When challenged about being a magpie, she had insisted that she was a collector. Alternatively, she would say: "I keep things just in case they come in handy one day."

Glenda came across the tatty beaded bag containing the caul, looked at it quizzically, and threw it with the other contents for the Salvation Army. "They can decide what to do with this strange stuff," she muttered.

Newly-appointed 18-year-old soldier of the Salvation Army Amanda Macadam fetched Edith's belongings. She had joined the Salvation Army straight after matriculating from Collegiate High School. Her parents, who were devout Methodists, were thrilled by her decision to serve the underprivileged. Mandy, as all knew her, could best be described as a petite natural beauty with an athletic build, shoulder-length auburn hair and big, green eyes.

Edith's effects were duly distributed by the local missionary in the New Brighton Township. But, Mandy felt a moment's hesitation before handing over the beaded bag. She decided to keep it. Instinctively, she felt it had a significance on which she could not put her finger.

The next week, Mandy and the beaded bag boarded the train for Lorenço Marques to take up a new post serving war-torn communities in Mozambique.

Back at Stellenbosch, Mike's recurring nightmares offered up new scenes. He was at his mother's graveside, tossing uncut diamonds, instead of earth, into the grave. He looked down and the coffin lid was off and he saw his mother lying naked inside it. Curled around her like a python, the shape-changing reptile with the familiar face glared back at him. Then he woke up.

17

HAVE NO OTHER GODS BUT ME

13ᵗʰ February 1971

Henk and Beauty made their home on the outskirts of Maseru, near the foothills of the Maluti Mountains. Their community included a host of disaffected ANC exiles, several of whom became their close friends.

Henk's bus service was thriving, as was Beauty's healing practice. As she became known for her holistic approach to wellness, her clients presented with a wide assortment of needs, and her interventions included allopathic, complementary and traditional healing.

Many of her clients consulted her for spiritual well-being, usually aspiring to grow beyond the memes offered by their religions. Some had tried the more popular "I-have-a-personal-relationship-with-God" approach, but sought self-transcendence by accessing spiritual paths that had been untainted by the dogma and ignorance of their religion. In particular, they did not want to be associated with the immoral stance taken on non-believers; the role of women; and the rights of homosexuals that were en-shrined in their holy books.

In these consultations, Beauty became accustomed to hearing words like: Enlightenment; knowing; energy; awakening; higher powers; life force; angels; magic; and the divine. These utterances suggested to her that clients were seeking new ways of spiritual enquiry – that their needs were probably stimulated by some exposure to the Eastern mystical approach popularised by the Beatles and their relationship with the Maharishi Mahesh Yogi.

Beauty responded to these calls by developing know-ledge and skills in transcendental meditation (TM), chant-ing and trance dancing. She also gained proficiency in a potent plant-based means of transcendence.

One of her regular patients, Buang, had been struggling to fall pregnant. She asked Beauty to contact higher spiri-tual dimensions to find out what her options were. Beauty obliged. The psychedelic brew, ayahuasca, enabled her to access these dimensions.

Ayahuasca, first used by natives of Peru, became a common potion to help shamans, witchdoctors and other sages gain access to spiritual insights. The consequent nausea, diarrhoea and hot flushes from taking the brew were accepted as the toll for enlightenment.

That night, Beauty imbibed. Her mind was hurled into a state indistinguishable from psychosis, and she drifted into a clairvoyant trance in which spirits revealed themselves to her. They informed her that Buang needed to wait three years before she could fall pregnant. Her pregnancy would be conditional on her undertaking a strict cleansing process during that time.

To her surprise, the spirits informed her that Edith had passed on. They warned about the dire consequences to the boy and reminded her of her responsibility to her charge. Beauty was informed that they had been sending him warnings about the serpent through his dreams.

When Beauty recovered from her mind-expanding trip, she said: "Henk, oh Henk! She died! We must protect that poor boy."

"Beauty, are you still going on about Edith?"

"Yes, Henk, and I'm not 'going on'. I had a spiritual obligation to her, and now I have one to Mike."

"Okay, what do we do now?"

"We must warn Mike about this grave danger."

"What do you mean by 'grave danger'?"

"The spirits say that if the mother loses the caul or she dies, it must be passed to either another loved one, or the child must get in touch with the spirits. If that does not happen, the child will experience love's pain, will not be protected from the serpent's evil ways, and will live with misfortune and violence."

"Explain what the means, Beauty? Serpents and a caul sound like a lot of gibberish. You know I have learned to respect what you say and do, but so what if he loses a girlfriend? All guys do, and what on Earth's a serpent? The devil?"

"Love's pain means so much more than losing a girl-friend. It means losing trust in life; losing meaning and connection. The serpent could be the devil. Equally, it could be evil in human form, or maybe even the regime, I don't know. I only know that he's a vulnerable young man in love and in danger from dark, malevolent forces."

"Okay, okay, how can we help? The last I heard, they had moved from Plett and Mike had gone to university. I don't know which one."

"We must find him and put him in touch with the spirits so that he can regain their support."

18

Never a Borrower Be

February 17th 1971

That Monday, Mike went to a customary preseason rugby practice. The squad completed an obligatory warm-up before commencing speed training, which consisted of wind sprints: Walking between two beacons; jogging the next section; and taking off at top speed for the final stretch. The finale always proved to be a bit of a jock's race. If testosterone spillage were possible, the groundskeeper would have been able to gather buckets full from the field after the wind sprints.

They were on their third repetition and the group had broken out at maximum speed. Mike had taken five strides when he heard a noise, like a whip cracking. At the same time, a searing pain jabbed his right hamstring. He felt as if he had been stabbed by a sharp knife. He hopped on one leg to the side of the field.

The team physiotherapist, Sean De Wit, checked out Mike's injured leg and shook his head. "You have done it this time, Mike. That hammy's not strained, it's torn. No more rugby for you for at least six weeks, if not more."

"Go home, compress the wounded area with ice, elevate your leg and rest, young man. Come to my rooms tomorrow for an in-depth assessment."

The results of the following day's assessment were bleak: He had ripped his *biceps femoris,* causing severe haemorrhaging. He would be out of rugby for at least three months.

Mike didn't like sitting out because of injury but at the same time, he realised that he had been lucky. Two years of rugby without a major injury was a good record. Yes, he had broken his nose against Hamiltons the previous year, but a broken nose had not stopped him from playing. He had just ended up looking more like a boxer. Besides, it blended well with his already skewed appearance.

"Oh well, at least I'll have more time with Maddy," he thought disconsolately.

The next day, he retrieved a note from his post box at medical school, requesting that he see the financial officer of the medical faculty.

Magda de Vries, the financial assistant, thanked Mike for coming and broke the news immediately: "Mr Hanssen, your 1971 fees are outstanding. As you know, our policy states that fees must be paid by the beginning of the term. What is the problem?"

"I'm not sure. Let me get back to you. My folks pay the fees. I'll call my dad."

He went to the call box and phoned Carl at EP Military Command.

"Mike, I am, so sorry …" Carl began. "Mum's treatment and therapy cleaned us out. I had to use the money set aside for your studies. I will make it up, I swear. There should be enough saved by September."

"Shit, Dad. I must pay now."

"Can you get a student loan? Nedbank advertises one for R400 per year, which should tide you over until September. Not so?"

"I guess."

The next day Mike secured an appointment with the Nedbank manager.

It went smoothly. Mike had heard that a bank was a place that would lend you money if you could prove that you didn't need it. That wasn't his experience. He needed money and they were forthcoming. The only outstanding matter was his father's signature. Mike told the manager he would return the signed loan application forms the following morning.

Forging his dad signature was a piece of cake. The next day, the forms were absorbed into the Nedbank bureaucracy. The manager assured Mike that the finance would be available within a week.

Mike reported the news of the successful loan application to Magda de Vries. She accepted that he would make a delayed first payment, with the balance to be paid in September.

19

SUFFER THE LITTLE CHILDREN

21ˢᵗ February 1971

That weekend, Maddy, arrived at Mike's digs after lectures on Friday afternoon as usual. She had a serious, concerned look on her face, the likes of which he had not seen before.

"I think I'm pregnant." she said, her beautiful, large, round eyes staring straight into his.

"How do you know? Is it good or bad news? Can we get married?" Mike fired off the questions with a big smile, trying to lighten up what appeared to her to be tragic news.

The nubile Maddy may have been physically ready, but she was not emotionally prepared for marriage. "I know because I never miss my period. I'm never late. Now, I'm two weeks late. And yes, it's bad news! We can't have a baby at varsity. I have a career to think about. It's fine for you to say we can marry, but I don't want to married to a student. Our dream was far bigger than that. Besides, I want a qualification. Christ, my dad will kill me. He will kill us both."

"Maddy, let's check it out with a doctor tomorrow. Then we'll know what we're dealing with"

"Okay, but I'm not going have a baby. No way José."

The pregnancy test was positive. The seeds of their happiness had borne unintended fruit. Their child had been conceived in Mozambique.

"Will the baby be eligible for a Portuguese passport?" Mike quipped.

Maddy was not amused. She remained emphatic that having a child was out of the question and insisted that they find a way to abort it. Mike went to see the doctor, who explained that abortions were illegal. The only option left, an illegal abortion, was dangerous and he strongly advised against it.

"Doc, I'm stuffed. Maddy won't have the child and I know her. She'll find a way."

The doctor reluctantly relented and gave Mike the number of an obstetrics nursing sister in Cape Town who could apparently "make a plan".

Mike phoned her.

"Hello, Mrs B here."

"Mrs B, its Mike Hanssen, I need your help please. My girlfriend and I are in trouble. She's pregnant and we're students."

"Yes dearie. I hear that all the time. What's the term?"

"What?"

"How many weeks is she pregnant?"

"About six weeks."

"That's fine. I suggest you come this weekend, which makes it around seven weeks. It's a good time for vacuum aspiration termination. Bring R400. I am two houses from the corner as you turn off De Waal Drive towards Gardens in Cape Town. There's a small brown gate in a low, red-brick fence. Be here on Saturday, 1 March at 2pm."

As he put the phone down, he thought: R400! Is someone messing with me? That's the exact amount Mike was getting from Nedbank to pay his university fees.

Becoming a courier for Bertie once more became a necessity.

Mike spent the rest of the week trying to track down the enigmatic Bertie. He had left the hostel at the end of his first year. From that time onwards, he had met Mike at Tollies Pub for their illicit exchanges, but Bertie had always initiated contact. Mike had the phone number for Adonis in Upington, who may have had Bertie's contact details. He tried it: No reply.

The weekend arrived. Mike and Maddy, filled with fear, drove to Mrs B's home in Cape Town. Her place was relatively easy to find. He knocked on the door and Mrs B opened.

Mrs B possessed the kind of looks that even drinking nine beers would not improve. Probably in her mid-50s, her hair, a stripy-grey, sat on her head like a mop. She had pitted, ruddy skin from years of smoking, and a large, hooked nose. A craggy, turtle-like neck emerged from a stooped body. Mike thought a pointy black hat and broomstick would complete the picture.

Her first words were: "The money?"

He gave her the packet with the R400 he had received the previous day from the Nedbank manager.

She led Mike to a small lounge-cum-waiting room. Maddy followed her through the next door to what she called the procedure room. As she opened the door, Mrs B's cheap perfume blended with the equally strong antiseptic smell, creating an unforgettably nauseating stench.

Fifteen minutes later, an ashen-faced Maddy and Mrs B emerged.

Mrs B explained that some residual material would expel later that evening. Maddy would know when it was coming and should sit in a warm bath to aid the process. She needed to use pushing motions, in the same way that one would deliver a baby.

Mrs B demonstrated the push. To Mike, it seemed basically like going to the toilet. Mrs B instructed them to ensure the bath water was disinfected and to buy several packets of sanitary towels to contain the bleeding.

"What did she do in the procedure room?" Mike asked as they drove back to the digs.

"She used this long, thin syringe; it didn't have a needle, just a suction thing. She inserted it inside me and probed around. Wiggled it, pulled the plunger; and then put in a tampon. She told me most of the foetus had been removed by the suction. Then, she warned me I would still need to eject some remaining material in the bath."

"That's it? Was it sore?"

"No, it just felt strange."

"So, now we wait?"

"Yes, now we wait."

On the way to his digs, Mike stopped at a pharmacy to buy sanitary towels. He thought momentarily of the day he had gone to the pharmacy to buy condoms in Plettenberg Bay. Those had been embarrassing, but much happier times. They seemed so long ago.

Back at the digs, Mike made them each an egg on bread for dinner. They shared a glass of wine and waited. Fortunately, Peter was away at his family's farm.

"Oh!" Maddy cried. "I feel something strange inside me. Something's happening."

"I'll run the bath, come." Mike took her hand and guided her to the bathroom.

The warm bath, combined with her heightened anxiety, made Maddy sweat. She sat in the water looking disconsolate. Her hair needed washing and her black eye makeup ran down her face, giving her a clown-like appearance. To Mike, she still looked gorgeous.

Maddy started pushing. Soon afterwards, fleshy blood clots emerged, followed by a gush of blood, flowing like water from a hose pipe that had been turned on full-ball. Mike was panicked. Although he was a medical student, he felt way out of his depth.

He had never seen so much blood.

His thoughts raced. How much blood can be lost before a situation becomes a medical emergency? Does she need a transfusion? Does she need a drip?

The bath water was crimson and Maddy was crying. It was a dangerous situation. The blood had been flowing too fast and for too long.

Thoughts raced through his mind: What must I do? Call an ambulance? Oh shit.

He climbed into the bath, hugged Maddy and tried to decide on his next move.

Distraught, Maddy was breathing erratically between inconsolable sobs.

"It's going to be fine, Maddy, its going to be fine. I won't let anything happen to you."

He hoped he sounded convincing, because he wasn't at all certain that things would be fine.

After a few more minutes, he said: "Let's get out the bath and try some of those humungous sanitary towels."

"You think so?"

"Yup, I think so."

Mike placed a bath towel around her, passed her panties and helped her slip on the sanitary towel, supported by the panty-hammock.

Within minutes, the sanitary towel was saturated in blood.

Mike put in another. That too, soaked through quickly.

He put in another. He was about to suggest they leave for the hospital when he realised the sanitary towels were finally stemming the red tide.

Maddy looked pallid and said she felt faint, so Mike lay her on a bath towel on the bed.

She settled, and her colour slowly returned, revealing her usually beautiful complexion.

"Would you like a cup of tea?" Mike offered bravely.

Maddy gave an expressionless: "Yes, please."

The bleeding slowed overnight. By morning, the flow was like that of a heavy period.

Mike thought about how often they had made love during her periods. They were simply a time when she bled. They had not been a barrier to intimacy. Their saying had been: "No holds barred". Or was it holes?"

On Tuesday, they returned to classes and nobody knew of their personal trauma. The weeks that followed could best be described as dreadful. Maddy remained on an emotional rollercoaster, talking little and obviously still grieving. She eventually shared her sorrow and its specifics with her digsmate, Hazel Stadler. Mike's grief remained confined to his own mind.

Recurring nightmares tormented him: A sobbing Maddy sitting in a bath brim-filled with blood, clutching a motionless, dead baby. The serpent coiled around the outside of the bath, watching Mike, its tongue flickering. Mike stood rooted to the ground, paralysed.

20

YOU SHALL NOT STEAL

Monday 24ᵗʰ March 1971

University fees were overdue; money was needed – and soon. Mike couldn't think of any honest way to access funds. His only hope was Bertie. The law treated dealing in illicit diamonds as a crime, because it involved stealing government resources. Mike was past caring.

"Where the hell's Bertie?" Then he remembered: The law faculty. He was registered there. They would have a forwarding address.

They did. His address was recorded as 16 Bird Street, Stellenbosch. Mike knocked on the door and, to his relief, Bertie answered.

"Hey Mike, haven't seen you for some time. Tired of making money?" Bertie asked.

"It's a long story. Let's talk about it some other time. Not now."

"It's great to see you. You ready for some driving?"

"You bet I am."

"Well, you're in luck. I need a favour."

"Will you fetch and then drop off the klippies with my contact in Cape Town this time?"

"Sure. Address?"

"103 Son Vida, Hope Street, Gardens. The dude's name's Richard Sutcliffe."

"It'll be next week Friday, 4 April. Fetch at 4pm in Upington, drop off at 12am that night in Gardens. Here's the envelope for that scoundrel, Adonis."

"Done." Mike didn't think to ask why he had called Adonis a "scoundrel".

Weekends with Maddy were proving challenging. She was moody and distant, but Mike accepted her behaviour as normal, given what had happened.

The doctor had prescribed a contraceptive pill, which had helped stop the bleeding two weeks before. That Friday evening, they made love for the first time since the abortion. Maddy, willing as always, went through the motions without any visible signs of emotion. Mike wondered if perhaps it was too soon after their trauma to be intimate. He felt so responsible for what had happened and, indeed, for how she felt.

He thought about the foetus which, in his mind, had been their child. He remembered his mum once trying to explain the unconditional love that a parent felt for a child. It was a concept that he had struggled to understand because he believed everything to be conditional. Her final word on the subject had been: "You won't understand until you're a parent."

"That's rich," thought Mike "Maddy and I killed our child before its birth. So much for the unconditional love of a parent. Or doesn't love factor into right-to-be-born decision-making? Is the love for a child therefore conditional on one meeting it?"

Mike had coffee alone at the Eikestad Café on Monday morning and browsed the complimentary *Cape Times*. On the second page, a headline grabbed his attention.

Monday 31 March 1971

Diamond thief loses his head
Crime reporter

Alleged diamond smuggler Albertus Steenkamp was involved in a high-speed car chase with a police squad car between Cape Town and Stellenbosch during the early hours of Sunday morning. Mr Steenkamp's Mercedes convertible lost control, slewed off the road, and rolled down the embankment at the Klapmuts turn-off. Mr Steenkamp was pronounced dead on the scene. Emergency Services sources say he was decapitated during the accident. He is survived by his mother, Mariekie Steenkamp, of Upington.

Shit. What now? He went to the closest public phone booth and pulled out Adonis's phone number.

Adonis answered.

"Adonis, it's Mike here, Bertie's driver. Did you hear the news about Bertie?"

"Man, it's too bad. He was an Upington brother."

"Yes, it's a tragedy. I have a shipment for next Friday. Is everything still okay?"

"Why not, my brother, why not? It's okay."

"Can we talk about future shipments when I get to Upington?"

"Of course we can talk."

"Okay then, I will see you next Friday, 4pm. Same place?"

"4pm, my brother. See you then."

Mike reckoned that the buyer in Gardens had also heard what had happened and that he should tie up that end, too.

Finding 103 Son Vida in Gardens was easy. Mike rang the apartment bell.

The man who came to the door was clean-shaven with greying temples. Well-dressed, one might say; a distinguished, elegant man in his mid-50s.

"Mr Sutcliffe?" Mike enquired.

"What's your business with Mr Sutcliffe, young man?"

"I have a message from a mutual friend, Bertie Steen-kamp."

"You must be clairvoyant, or some sort of spiritual medium, then."

"Well, no. I know he was killed in a car accident. He spoke to me last week. For the past two years I have been providing a courier service for him. I wanted to ask Mr Sutcliffe if the meeting next Friday at 12am was still on."

"That it is, young man."

"I received instructions and details from Bertie before his tragic accident and I am hoping to continue with his work. Will that be okay? Will the prices be the same?"

Mike fudged it as he did not know what Sutcliffe paid for the transaction. He knew that Bertie paid Adonis R300 per shipment. There was obviously a fixed weight. If only he had thought to weigh the packets on previous trips. Still, he had a rough idea.

"Let's have that discussion next week once you have fulfilled your obligation to the late Mr Steenkamp," the man said, obviously wanting to end the conversation.

"Okay then, I'll see you next Friday." Mike left.

21

YOU SHALL NOT KILL

4th April 1971 (4pm)

Adonis waited, empty-handed, at the intersection of Schroder and Rondom Streets.

"Mr Mike, you have the money?"

"Yes, where are the klippies?"

"At my house. You wanted to talk, that's a good place to talk. Let's use my car. If you drive into the location with your fancy car, they will rob you," Adonis said, laughing at his own humour.

Mike hoped it was humour. He didn't like the idea of going to the location, but what were his options? The diamonds were at the house, and he wanted them. The cold steel of the 9mm inside his jacket pocket made him a little more assured of his personal safety.

"Lead on," Mike said in as deep a voice as he could muster.

Adonis's VW beetle was parked close by. As he climbed into the filthy car, the smell of old cigarettes from Adonis's clothing and an overflowing ashtray hit him, like the smell of a popular bar in the early hours of the morning. The car interior was hot, and the smell of smoke was soon accompanied by the alcohol fumes that emanated from Adonis's breath and pores.

His VW jerked into motion, dislodging an array of empty bottles and a bottle neck strewn on the passenger floor. Adonis turned and gave him a broad grin, revealing his lack of front teeth, flanked by Dracula-like, yellow-stained fangs. His bloodshot eyes revealed clear signs of heavy drinking and excessive use of a dagga pipe.

The location was similar to the ones in Plettenberg Bay or Stellenbosch, or anywhere else in South Africa: Eroded dirt roads, poorly-built shacks and random animals roaming the streets.

Adonis parked in front of his gate. They entered the unoccupied, sparse dwelling. A heavy wooden dining table dominated the small lounge. On the edge of the table squatted a bank bag, similar to the ones Adonis had previously used for the uncut diamonds.

"Mr Mike," Adonis started the conversation, slurring the word "Mister" into "Mishter".

"You know that coloured folks call you whities 'mister' because we must be respectful to our bosses, not so? I'm thinking, now that Mr Bertie has passed on, God rest his soul," Adonis looked up at the ceiling, pointing his finger in a Christian one-way gesture, "we need to respectfully agree to a decent price for the klippies. Not like the stupid one Mr Steenkamp had. Anyway, I told him last time that we needed to increase the price. He was not interested, and you see what happened to him."

Mike started to understand the tag "scoundrel".

"I hadn't prepared for a price change. What were you thinking of?" Mike replied.

"From now on, I want to make big bucks, like you guys. How about double?" He showed two fingers, like a Winston Churchill "V" salute.

"You mean R600 instead of R300?"

"You're smart, Mr Mike, and you probably know that's still cheap. There are many, many people wanting klippies besides Mr Bertie, God rest his soul." This time he made the traditional sign of the cross.

"I see. Can we talk about an increase for the next shipment, I have only got R300 with me this time."

"That's too bad; Mr Mike. How about you give me the R300, and when you have the other R300, you can get the bag?"

"That won't do. How about you give me half the bag in the meantime and I'll give you R300."

"No deal, Mr Mike." He said raising his voice, still slurring "Mishter".

"A dealer never splits a bag. I tell you what: Why don't you just give me the money for all the times I was ripped off and we start again next time at R600. That's a good idea, I think."

"Adonis, that's a bad idea." In that moment, Mike belatedly echoed in his head the wise words of his friend, Peter:

"Do not argue with an idiot. He will drag you down to his level and beat you with experience."

Adonis, the idiot, continued, sounding menacing: "No, that's a good one." As he spoke he drew a large butcher's knife from behind the kitchen table and pointed it at Mike. The blade glinted, reflecting the late afternoon sunlight pouring through the window.

He looked at the knife as he spoke. "My friend, Mac the Knife, agrees with me. It's a good idea. Yes, Mr Mike, that's the deal on the table. You give me the money and piss off back to your rich friends in the Cape."

"I don't agree to the deal, Adonis. Be sensible," Mike answered, thinking: Yes, he's a scoundrel.

"Are you calling me not sensible? Do you think I am stupid, whitey? You think coloureds are stupid, like the blacks, and you can bleed us dry, don't you?"

"No, I don't think that. I think we should honour today's deal, then talk about a new price for the future."

"Well, I think Mac the Knife will explain things a lot better than I can." Adonis moved threateningly toward Mike, his right hand holding the knife low, in a gangster-type fighting pose.

Mike drew his 9mm and pointed it at Adonis's chest.

Adonis stopped. "You think I am scared of your gun? It might as well be a toy. If you dare shoot me, the neighbours will be here before I hit the ground. Do you know what they will do to you? Do you know? Have you heard of necklacing? They will tie your hands, put a tyre around your neck, throw petrol over you and burn your sorry white arse."

Without another word, Adonis lunged at Mike. In that split second, Mike knew he couldn't risk firing a shot. Fortunately the alcohol, which had probably fuelled Adonis's aggression in the first place, also slowed down his movements. Mike side-stepped the charge and the blade caught the edge of his jacket, ripping the pocket.

Adonis turned and attacked again. Mike grabbed the wrist holding the knife. Despite being a lot heavier and stronger than Adonis, the momentum of the charge knocked Mike to the ground. Adonis jumped on top of him while trying to free his hand from Mike's grip so that he could complete the stabbing action.

Mike's right hand still held the pistol. He swung it in an arc aimed at Adonis's head. The impact made a sickening crack as metal collided with the bone of Adonis's jaw. He reeled in agony and Mike released Adonis's wrist while simultaneously thrusting his left knee into his groin.

With knife still in hand, Adonis instinctively clutched at his manhood. Mike, up in an instant, shoulder-charged into Adonis's solar plexus, sending him sprawling backwards against the heavy table. The bag dislodged from the edge of the table, fell to the ground and scattered shiny stones across the floor, like an indoor hailstorm.

The impact with the heavy table caused Adonis to rebound like a rubber ball and fall forward. He hit the ground and called out in pain as his knife cut into him below the sternum. Mike pounced on his assailant's back.

He did not realise at the time that his weight was driving the knife deeper into Adonis's chest cavity.

Adonis did not move. Dark-red blood pooled on both sides of his body. Mike carefully turned him over. No breath. No pulse. The knife had impaled his heart. It had entered his chest cavity under the sternum at precisely the right angle to puncture his right ventricle. Mike's weight did the rest.

Mike's adrenalin spiked, causing a momentary panic, and then he regained his composure. He calmly gathered the diamonds, stuffed them back into the bag, removed the VW keys from Adonis's blood-stained pocket, walked out of the front door and drove to the intersection of Schroder and Rondom Streets before swapping the VW for his hired car. The only witness was the predictable, tick-ridden, mangy, barking dog, owned by no one in particular, outside Adonis's neighbour's gate.

No thoughts were spared on regret for Adonis. As he drove to Cape Town, Mike's main concern was avoiding the familiar flashing blue lights of a police car.

22

EVERYONE IS SUBJECT TO AUTHORITIES

4th April 1971 (11:45pm)

Mike reached Hope Street in Gardens at 11:45pm and waited until two minutes before 12 before approaching Sutcliffe's apartment door.

Had he been better versed in the dark art of surveillance, he might have noticed the black van parked opposite the apartment building. He might have seen the two men lurking under a nearby tree, throwing glances in all directions, waiting for him to arrive.

He rang the bell. No reply. He waited and rang again.

From the shadows of the tree, the two men approached him.

"Excuse me, sir, could you hand over the bag please."

"Why do you want my bag? Who are you?"

"Detective Sergeant Lategan and this is my colleague, Constable van Der Walt. We're arresting you on suspicion of the crime of illicit diamond dealing and we are obliged to inform you of your rights." Lategan pulled out a typed piece of paper and read the standard protocol to Mike.

They had caught him red-handed. He could do nothing about the diamonds and the money on his person. Fortunately, he had a licence for the 9mm. Oh damn, he thought. Will they link the corpse in Upington to him? The charge would then change to murder.

Mike was allowed one phone call from the Caledon Square Police Station. He didn't know who to call. Maddy? Peter? His dad?

As he handed over his personal belongings, including the R300, he noticed a business card in his jacket pocket – the same jacket he had worn to his mother's funeral. The name on the card was Major Andre van Niekerk. He dialled the Pretoria number.

"Van Niekerk."

"Major, it's Mike Hanssen. I am so sorry to call you at this hour."

"You must have a big problem."

"I'm guess so. I've been arrested."

"Where are you?"

"Caledon Square in Cape Town."

"Okay, let's not talk about it on the phone. Can I speak to the arresting officer?"

Mike handed the phone to Lategan.

Lategan and Van Niekerk talked for a few minutes before he handed the phone back to Mike.

Van Niekerk continued: "You're going to spend the night in a cell. I'll get someone to contact you in the morning. Whatever you do, say nothing and don't sign anything, okay?"

"Okay, will do."

"Hang in there. You will hear from me in the morning."

"Don't tell my dad."

"This will be our little secret."

One of the many benefits of apartheid for whites was separate holding cells. Mike didn't see the cells for non-Europeans, but could imagine their level of discomfort to be significantly worse.

That which awaited Mike was by no stretch of the imagination five-star accommodation. It had all of the hallmarks of a prison: A single bed with a straw mattress covered with one blanket; a bucket in the corner that had been provided as a toilet; and a separate container with cold water for washing. The room stank of urine. Sleep did not come easily and when it did, Mike suffered his now recurrent, reptile nightmare – on that occasion involving a decapitated Bertie and a zombie-like Adonis with a dagger embedded in his heart.

Who do the human features on the serpent face remind me of? Mike wondered when he woke up in a cold sweat.

A breakfast of porridge, bread and sweet coffee was shoved through the bars at 6am. The public prosecutor summoned him at 9am.

Public prosecutor Hans Breytenbach was in his mid-40s, replete with a dark suit and funereal demeanour.

"You have got yourself into a great deal of trouble, young man."

Mike decided against apologising. He thought it would sound false. Probably because it was.

"I guess so, sir. What are my options, please?"

"It's not often that someone in trouble can access friends in high places that pay their bail. You're free to go. Your trial date's set for 9am, Thursday 10 April in Court D. Make sure you're not late, and dress nicely. You don't want the magistrate to think you're a corrupt person." Mike thought he saw the hint of a smile on Breytenbach's face.

"Will I need a lawyer?"

"That won't be necessary. You have good contacts."

Confused and relieved, Mike realised that Van Niekerk was his contact.

As he left, his possessions restored, including the 9mm pistol, he wondered what had happened to the money and the diamonds. He decided not to ask. He realised that he actually did not have right to ask, either. He doubted they were in safekeeping. More likely, a few policemen had reaped the benefits of ill-gotten gains.

His first call from the public booth over the road from Caledon Square was to thank Van Niekerk, who warned him that his scenario was bleak and that he would likely have to leave university and fulfil his military obligations. The call ended with Van Niekerk telling Mike to come and see him in Pretoria. A seat on a military aircraft would be booked for him from Wingfield Airforce Base on the Thursday afternoon after the court hearing. Mike marvelled at how well Van Niekerk had been informed. He knows my court hearing date?

The next phone call to Maddy's digs was answered by her housemate, Hazel, who informed him that Maddy was at classes.

Over the next few days, Mike returned to classes while studiously avoiding faculty administration as he mentally fought to find a way out of his monetary quandary.

He saw Maddy frequently over that time. Their relationship seemed to be on an even keel once again. He felt sufficiently comfortable to confide in her about his financial problems and his attempts to secure funding through diamond dealing, which had resulted in his imminent court case. He didn't tell her about Adonis's death. She didn't need to know that her boyfriend might be facing a murder charge.

Finally, he shared his concern that he would probably have to discontinue his studies and, in all likelihood, report for military service. Mike explained about Van Niekerk and the appointment to see him in Pretoria on the Thursday. He told Maddy that he would be back by Sunday night at the earliest.

Maddy listened intently as Mike relayed his saga of monetary morbidity. She was clearly overwhelmed. When he had finished, she spoke somewhat incoherently: "Do you still remember our dream? What you have told me about your life's not in line with our hopes. I haven't tampered with it. You're the one making the changes. I guess you will make a plan. Then, we will see what happens, won't we?"

Mike didn't know what to make of her response. For the first time in their relationship, he felt he couldn't pursue clarification. He concluded: Oh shit, she thinks I am a loser and criminal.

* * *

Thursday 10 April, 9am, a nervous Mike sat on the wooden bench outside Court D. People milled about. They were a completely different subset from what Mike was used to seeing: Men wearing wigs and gowns rushed up and down the corridor, carrying large, brown folders; and policemen accompanied heavily shackled prisoners in orange overalls, guarding against escape.

The court orderly opened the door and beckoned Mike to enter the room. His mind raced as he walked in.

Should I have hired a lawyer? Sure, with what money? Will I end up in jail? If my friend in high places is going to rescue me, how will he do it? He's not here.

The magistrate took centre stage and sat down on an elevated platform in the courtroom. His eyes were glued to the papers on the desk in front of him. Public prosecutor Hans Breytenbach leaned over the desk with his back towards the door. Three others occupied the room: A duty policeman, the court orderly and a stenographer.

Mike stood in the dock, his head bowed to signify humility and reverence. He thought that would be the wisest approach.

A few minutes went by as the magistrate and Breytenbach deliberated. The magistrate looked at Mike and said: "Mr Hanssen, your case is dismissed. You're free to go."

The orderly opened the door and beckoned Mike to exit.

Is that it? No charges? No hand on the Bible to swear to tell the truth? Fat chance of that anyway. No pleading guilty or not guilty; no arguments; no speech about being a first offender and on the wrong track; no plea bargain and no sentence? He almost felt cheated out of his day in court.

Breytenbach exited a minute later and approached him: "You're lucky the arresting officer didn't turn up, so the case was dismissed." He winked at Mike: "Stay out of trouble. Luck has its limits."

The military flight to Pretoria was spartan compared to the flight to his mother's funeral. En route, he once again wondered what had happened to the diamonds and the money.

A military car picked him up from Waterkloof Airforce Base and took him to the Bureau of State Security (BOSS) headquarters in Pretoria.

He dined with Van Niekerk at a steakhouse near Loftus Versveld, the Northern Transvaal Rugby Union's stadium, better known as Fortress Loftus. The restaurant was filled with bearded white men wearing open-necked shirts, some with patchwork leather jackets, shorts and long socks. Their local team was scheduled to play their archrival, Western Province, that weekend, and prematch festivities had begun.

Once again, Mike was astounded at how much Van Niekerk knew about the world, the country, its allies and its enemies. It should have been no surprise. He was, after all, one of the highest ranked intelligence officers in the country. BOSS had jurisdiction over the army and the police. Small wonder an arresting officer could be persuaded to "miss" a court hearing.

They did not speak about Mike's conundrum until their 11:30am appointment the next day at the BOSS offices.

"Mike, you're deep in debt. You don't have the money to continue your studies. You have a dismissed criminal case that can easily be resuscitated if the arresting officer gives a plausible reason for missing the court date. The case could be aggravated by the death of a diamond dealer in Upington."

This took Mike by surprise. How did he know about Upington?

Van Niekerk continued, as if reading Mike's mind.

"You're surely wondering how I know about the unfortunate death of a coloured man in Upington. Was it an accident? Was it gang-related, or was he killed by a courier? These questions would be important if his life was worth investigating. For the time being, he's just another coloured killed in a knife fight. It happens all the time, and neither the police nor state security is interested. As to how we know about his death, you will learn all of that later.

Mike, I feel a sense of responsibility toward you. I told you previously what you could do to make your troubles disappear. You can decide once you're finished with the army whether or not you want to continue studying. Listen, if you enjoy the intrigue of state security as much as I do, you will, in all probability, not continue with medicine.

I will settle your Nedbank debt. Army basic training will be for three months at Diskobolos Military Base in Kimberley. After basics, you will get three months' specialist weapons and explosives training, then six months' frontline border experience. Thereafter, I will arrange intelligence training for three months, and finally you will join us for nine months at BOSS in Pretoria for special assignments. Your two-year compulsory service ends then. Now, I suggest you bring Commandant Hanssen up to speed."

It was clear to Mike that Van Niekerk was kindly disposed towards him. It was equally clear that Van Niekerk had adopted German military theorist Carl von Clausewitz's dictum that war was nothing unusual, just another means of political discourse. Over the next few years, Mike was to learn the opposite. He would learn that war created tragedy, disaster and devastation. War was the outcome of a country trapped by the polar opposites of fear and anger.

Van Niekerk handed Mike a brown envelope marked "Official – Amptelik". This stationery was like a dreaded disease to liberal, young, white males. It contained his conscription notice. He had to report on 1 May 1971 to Diskobolos Military Base.

Mike looked into Van Niekerk's face while he spoke and had an uncanny feeling of recognition. He dismissed it because he had known Van Niekerk for so long.

As he walked down the corridor to exit the BOSS offices, all Mike could think was: What about Maddy?

23

THE FATHER AND THE SON

11ᵗʰ April 1971

By 1971, the Anti-Apartheid Movement (AAM) in London occupied a prime position on BOSS's agenda. Its leader, Peter Hain, emerged as another of South Africa's public enemies. He struck at the heart of white South Africa when he orchestrated protests that came close to sabotaging the South African Springbok rugby tour to the United Kingdom in 1969.

Van Niekerk, a fanatical rugby supporter, was incensed by the way Hain and the British public had drawn politics into sport. Major van Niekerk claimed to have no problem with their right to judge South African politics, but it was not acceptable for them to interfere in international rugby and to deny young South Africans like Johan van Der Merwe the chance to play international sport, simply because they didn't see eye-to-eye with South Africa's attempts to create racial harmony through separate development. It also got up his nose that the British were not grateful for the role South Africa was playing in stopping communist expansion.

BOSS desperately wanted to infiltrate the movement, and Van Niekerk had a plan.

His telegram to Andile read: *Urgent. Meet Van Niekerk. Friday, 7 April 13h00. Office 506, 213 Proes Street. Pretoria.*

Andile arrived on time. As he entered the building, he was surprised to bump into Mike.

"Mike, what the hell are you doing here?"

"Andile, what the …" Mike looked around and rolled his eyes. "Hey, this is not the place to talk. Let's find somewhere a little more comfortable for a drink, then you can tell me what on Earth you're doing here."

"You bet. How about meeting at the corner Proes and Church at 3pm?"

"You're on. See you there."

Van Niekerk sat behind a large wooden desk. Portraits of two government officials gave context to the office. Directly behind him, Prime Minister B.J. Vorster – a man who had spent World War II interned due to his membership of the Ossewa Brandwag, an organisation in sympathy with Nazi Germany. On Vorster's right was the bellicose P.W. Botha, Minister of Defence. His infamous waggling index finger was out of sight in the typical head-and-shoulders representation.

"Andile, welcome. I want to start by telling you how much I appreciate the hard work you have done since moving to Soweto. Your country's proud of you"

"It's my pleasure, Major" The words "your country" rang a hollow note

"I was wondering if you were ready for a new challenge and a change of scenery. Would you like to move to London?"

"That's interesting. Tell me more."

"The work will be similar. We'll set you up with a job as a bouncer in London. This time I want you to join the AntiApartheid Movement, and through them become a member of the ANC external mission. You up for it?"

"It sounds like it's going to be a little more dangerous than the Soweto assignment, Major."

"Certainly. I particularly need you to report on any ANC plans that may result in civilian casualties in South Africa. Rest assured that your participation will be lucrative. We'll give you twice the stipend you received before, and a double bonus scheme paid into a Swiss bank account opened for you. If you agree, I've set up training starting next week. You move to London mid-May."

"No discussion needed, Major; the money's good. I'm your man."

Mike waited for Andile at the corner of Proes and Church. Andile, wearing dark glasses, picked him up in his black 64 Chevy 2, complete with loud township music.

Mike's first comment was: "Shit, Andile, you look and sound like an American pimp in this car."

"Enough of your stereotyping, Mike. Let me show you another side of South Africa. We're off to Soweto."

"Don't be crazy. You want me murdered? Haven't you noticed my white skin?"

"Yes, that's one of the reasons I am taking you. It's time for you to confront your racism."

"Come on, Andile. You know I'm not a racist."

"You're living the life of a racist. I know you don't mean to be one."

"And I must be killed so that you can teach me a lesson in racism?"

"Cut the crap, you won't get killed. The fact that you're saying that indicates the extent to which you have bought into the swart gevaar and the erroneous belief that blacks are savages. Rather tell me about today. What were you doing at BOSS headquarters?"

"Okay, I'll talk first. Then you. I'm damn interested to find out what you're doing there."

Mike told him everything, sparing no details.

Then it was Andile's turn. He took a more economical approach to the truth. He explained that he had met Van Niekerk through Geoff Walters, and on Walters's recommendation, Van Niekerk had offered him an assignment on behalf of BOSS.

"I turned him down, Mike. I could never help this racist regime. In fact, I am planning to go to London soon to get away from the politics."

The rest of the drive was dedicated to small talk reminiscing about the past as Andile gave Mike a tour of Alexander Township and Soweto. It was the first time that Mike had truly seen the squalour and abject poverty of township living. Had he been living in a parallel universe? Was it a case of: None as blind as those that will not see? They arrived at the Click Club Shebeen in Soweto around 8pm.

Mike was the only white face among the 100-odd people in the warehouse-sized club. White plastic tables and chairs were plentiful, along with quarts of Black Label Beer. Mike was astounded at the warm welcome he received, and he was flattered by the number of amorous ladies who sidled up to him. Up until then, he had been unaware that there were good looking black women. He had always had a one-size-fits-all view of black females. Looking at them as prospective romantic partners had been inconceivable. His view changed in an instant quantum leap. Still, he did not act on the impulse caused by seeing black women for the first time as he did white. Some of them were absolutely beautiful, but so was Maddy.

Mike drank the beer, but Andile didn't touch alcohol. His recreational substance of choice was marijuana. The plentiful, tightly-wrapped homemade dagga cigarettes were passed around liberally. Andile was as high as a kite within half an hour. The father's medicinal habit had become the son's pleasure.

Conversation flowed easily, despite the natter of the noisy crowd. Mike found himself the centre of attention, with many questions directed at him. Inevitably, Steve, one of Andile's political activist friends, started quizzing him.

"How many times have you been in a social environment with more black people than white?"

"I guess tonight's the first," Mike replied.

"You see, that's one of the biggest problems in South Africa. The vast majority of the white population's unaware of the inequality between black and white, and they don't take the trouble to find out how bad the situation is for blacks. The government also makes damn sure it stays that way. To make matters worse, young white men join a white army to wage war against black countrymen whom they don't know. Mike, you don't know who you're fighting against."

Mike frowned. "Well, the fact is it's not that simple. I'm not going to the army to fight my black countrymen. I am actually going to combat the threat of communism and terrorists. These present threats to all South Africans. Besides, I don't like to get involved in politics. I am neutral. You don't seem to be. Are you a member of the ANC?"

"No I am not, I am with the Black Consciousness Movement, and as for you being neutral … The real fact is, that's bullshit. There's no such thing as neutral. In this conflict, when you choose neutral, you choose the side of the oppressor. When you join the regime's army, you will mostly be fighting against fellow South Africans who represent the majority in this country. Black people are sick of being in a system that discriminates against them.

"The communists you speak about operate in sympathy with our struggle and don't present a long-term danger to South Africa. They're simply helping us gain legitimacy. We're not terrorists, we're freedom fighters. We do not target or disregard innocent people and non-combatants. So far, it's only been military or state institution targets.

"Mike, at this time in history, your kind are the immoral, momentary masters of our universe. That will change, but not tonight. Tonight will not be spoilt by politics. You're Andile's friend, which makes you my friend, even if you're white. It's time you tried our special weed."

With a wicked smile, Steve passed him a glowing Rizla joint.

Mike had not tried dagga before and reasoned that was a good enough reason to do so. He accepted the joint, sucked on it and inhaled slowly. He felt like he was entering a movie or a dream. He started to see things he'd never noticed before. Suddenly there was more detail, more shapes, more colour around him. He felt happier and content. He was aware of giggling a lot, something that was out of character for him. Time seemed to stand still.

It didn't, though. It came to 5am and Andile took him to his room in Soweto, where he slept the rest of the morning on the floor. That afternoon, Andile dropped him off at Waterkloof Military Airport.

24

THE KISS OF JUDAS

12th April 1971

He left Pretoria on the early evening military flight to Cape Town and arrived at 10pm Saturday night, a full day before he was expected home. The drive to Stellenbosch from the airport became increasingly pleasant as he neared his destination. He wondered if all people felt the feeling of relief when driving to Stellenbosch, or whether it was generally associated with getting nearer to home and to loved ones. The Stellenbosch trip was enhanced by the unmistakable waft of wine processing as he passed the Three Gables Hotel and approached the Stellenbosch Farmers' Winery buildings.

Mike could see Maddy's bedroom window from where he parked outside her digs. The lights were out. Their agreement was no holds barred. If she was asleep, he would slip in beside her. Middle-of-the-night intimacy was one of Maddy's favourites.

The front door was unlocked. Mike entered silently, filled with anticipation as he walked down the dimly-lit corridor to Maddy's room. Her characteristic perfume lingered in the passage. A rusty spring squeaked in the bedroom door handle as he depressed it and slowly pushed the door open.

The passage light illuminated across the room, on to Maddy's bed. In the half-light, someone leaped from her bed. Mike flicked the light switch on the inside left-hand side of her door. Maddy sat bolt upright in bed; pulling up the sheets to cover her nakedness. As her big, round eyes adjusted to the light, they grew even larger as the shock of seeing Mike set in.

The person at the foot of the bed slipped on his jeans. The realisation of who it was shocked Mike to his core.

Mike lunged at him, shouting: "You fucking Judas."

There was no circumstance under which Peter was a physical match for Mike. His current rage made the difference even more pronounced. Mike beat him mercilessly, repeating the words: "Fucking Judas" with every blow. Peter, equipped with a rapier-like wit, had an instant riposte to verbal attacks, but no counter to the ferociousness of Mike's physical attack.

Maddy screamed: "Mike, stop it, stop it, you don't understand." He didn't want to understand. His friend was a traitor. That was all he needed to know. Peter had crossed a line from which he could never step back. In Mike's mind, the betrayal had to be punished. Peter was going to need to apply every bit of his medical training to himself.

The commotion woke Hazel. She entered the room and immediately pleaded with Mike to stop. Her pleas went unheeded. Instead, Mike noticed Maddy. The terror in her eyes and her look of abject horror stopped him. She was frightened of him. He was mortified. His little Maddy was cowering before him. How had he become the antagonist? He was the injured party, wasn't he? Had he crossed over into some parallel universe where infidelity was the norm?

The blow to his cherished myth of exclusivity was the impression of Maddy's breasts straining against the sheets. The breasts that he thought were for his eyes only had been fondled by his best friend.

The thoughts screamed through his mind: This is not happening! He backed off and left the room; his match made in heaven with a magical other set asunder.

He drove to his digs in a daze, as denial and anger jostled for a top emotional ranking in the carnage of his mind.

With his belongings tossed into the boot and on to the back seat of his car, he drove through the night to Kogel Bay. There, he spent the night alone on the beach. A terrible sense of exile caused him to sleep in fits and starts. In his wakening state, Khalil Gibran's words repeated in his mind, like a hamster on a wheel:

"And ever has it been that love knows not its own depth until the hour of separation."

In his sleeping state, nightmares of therianthropes took over. Maddy and Peter took centre stage, having sex in the Stellenbosch University Anatomy Department among an array of corpses as Mike watched hopelessly in a state of paralysis. The serpent was ever present, its face familiar but not recognisable.

Mike knew that if he returned to Stellenbosch, his capacity for revenge would result in dire consequences for Peter. Maddy's horror would be insufficient to save Peter again. He would be dead meat.

He left Stellenbosch in a state of anomie. He left in order to comply with a devil's pact made with a man known as Snake.

He had three weeks before he was required to report for military service. Two weeks were spent camping in Plettenberg Bay, seeking solace from memories of first love and first sex, trying to pacify the pain of parting. His stay deteriorated into alcohol-fueled nostalgia as he tried to plumb a bottomless well of grief. He blurted out his tale of woe to anyone propping up the bar. They gratefully received a free drink in exchange for a sympathetic ear. Some could not resist dispensing agony aunt-style advice about what he should or could do.

Most listened with the knowledge that they were hearing the enduring story of all young men who lost their first love; their understanding most likely forged in similar circumstances. These people appreciated the complexity of love and loss, knowing no amount of advice would make the bereaved feel any better or less unique. If Mike were more attentive, he may have heard many of his drinking partners' muttering: "pussy whipped" and "pity party" under their breath as they shook their heads.

The final days before his military service were spent at his dad's house in Port Elizabeth. More accurately, at his mother's graveside. The time spent at the already unkempt and neglected grave was consumed by reflection. His mum had come to such an undignified end. Cancer had robbed her of her beauty; then she had become the victim of dubious claims in a pious service. He felt it a triple tragedy that her memory was now being sullied by the sloppiness of an unkempt grave.

He muttered, staring at the weeds sprouting from the mound above the grave: "No church service or grave for me when I die. Burn me and toss the ashes into the wind, for all I care."

Despite being at his mum's graveside, his thoughts invariably migrated to Maddy.

If only he hadn't loaded their love with promises and commitments, it may have survived his misfortune.

If only his communication had not been boundaryless and intimate, he may not have been so vulnerable.

If only he hadn't fallen in love with her, he would not have been affected by competition like Peter.

When did the treachery dawn? Was it a sudden thing?

No one told him relationships would be easy, but no one told him they could cause so much pain, either.

The military was just the place for someone who needed to throw away their cup of sorrows and to forget.

25

The Road to Enlightenment

15th April 1971

Beauty could wait no longer. She had been weighed down by ancestor enlightenment since 17 February.

"Henk, I want to see my son and we need to help Mike. He needs to get in touch with the spirits to seek enlightenment. These are good reasons to take a road trip."

Henk didn't need convincing. Work started immediately. He equipped one of his smaller buses with the curtain boudoir they had used a few years previously. This mobile sanctuary would provide accommodation and a place of non-racial sanity, in the same way that Lesotho had been their refuge.

Nights would be spent at caravan parks with Beauty masquerading as Henk's family maid. Henk created a mental picture of her in a frilly black and white outfit, typical of those worn by maids in America's Deep South. Henk and Beauty enjoyed an uninhibited approach to intimacy. It wouldn't take any more than a hint from him and the said maid's outfit would be worn minus underclothes when they were alone. Under these conditions, he thought with amusement, having a maid could be a lot of fun.

He chuckled as he considered how often in South Africa white male bosses had secret liaisons with black maids. Upon immediate reflection, he felt immense guilt for finding it humorous. Racism and the associated abuse of power were not funny under any circumstances. He recalled that many of his male associates in South Africa used to assume they could tell racist jokes in his company just because he, too, was white. Racism was the reason he had left South Africa.

According to his letters, Andile was living in Soweto and would be fairly easy to locate. But, where was Mike?

Henk called his old friend at the Plettenberg Bay Bus Depot, Chris Moerdyk, who informed him that, as far as he knew, Carl Hanssen was stationed at P.E. Command in Port Elizabeth. The Port Elizabeth phone directory supplied the number.

Carl took the call, explaining to Henk that Mike was studying to become a doctor at Stellenbosch University. Henk thought him obviously a proud father as he had emphasised the word "doctor". Carl concluded by giving him Mike's digs address.

"Okay, what do we do now?"

"Is there any doubt? Have you ever been to Stellenbosch? Have you visited a wine farm?"

"No."

"It's decided then."

They left Maseru for Stellenbosch, via Bloemfontein, on 15 April. The intention was to first see Mike, then tour the Cape for a few days. followed by a drive up the N1 to Soweto. They would then make their back home to the outskirts of Maseru.

They arrived in Stellenbosch in the early evening of 16 April. Peter answered the door to the digs that he and Mike had shared until a week previously. His face still bore the yellow and purple discoloration inflicted by Mike's fury. Henk assumed it to be the legacy of a tough rugby game.

"Mike left a week ago. He said he had financial difficulties. I'm not sure where he went. I believe he's going to do his military service." As he explained, Henk and Beauty noticed a petite blonde in the background. They left after requesting that Peter ask Mike to contact Beauty, if he saw him.

Their sightseeing trip around the Western Cape turned out to be idyllic. The ruse of master and maid worked perfectly when they visited wine farms in Stellenbosch, clambered around Cape Point, went up the cable car to the top of Table Mountain and watched whales frolicking in Hermanus. The delight from the intimacy they shared in their bus bedroom at night was equal to, if not greater than, the sightseeing.

Three days later, they were on the road, embarking on the long drive to see Andile in Soweto. This would be a role reversal for Henk, as he would become the odd one out. Andile gave them a similar tour of Soweto that Mike had experienced, excluding the drinking and dagga smoking at the Click Club.

Andile revealed that he was soon bound for London to avoid the political turmoil in the country. Beauty and Henk could only empathise as it was exactly what they had done when they moved to Maseru.

Beauty, thrilled to hear Mike had been in touch with Andile, listened to him retelling Mike's recent misfortunes with a knowing look.

"Mike's having a lot of shit luck lately." Beauty didn't feel it right confiding in Andile about her belief that Mike was suffering his so-called shit luck mainly because of his mum's death and the loss of the caul. Their short stay ended with a request to ask Mike to contact her when Andile saw him again.

26

THE ARMY OF THE LORD

Thursday 1ˢᵗ May 1971

The military had one hairstyle for basic training – short all over. Staff Sergeant Chris "Chopper" van Heerden, the army barber, chuckled with delight as he cut a landing strip from front to back through the middle of Mike's long blonde hair. With an efficiency forged from thousands of heads buzzed, his electrical clippers took a few more swashbuckling shaves to transform Mike's appearance from hippie surfer to American GI.

The next measure of Mike's former identity to be despatched was his clothing. Jeans, T-shirt and slip-slops were replaced at the quarter master stores with ill-fitting browns, a beret and boots. He retained the symbolic silver crucifix, which many mistook for a Christian commitment.

Mike's dad told him that the aim of basic training was to break recruits down, and then rebuild them according to the military's needs. No individualism was tolerated. The renewal process implemented by callous corporals, shouting sergeants and swaggering sergeant majors touting typical military repartee was designed to intimidate. These NCOs' (non-commissioned officers) efforts during basic training left Mike contemptuous, often cursing: "Say or do what you like, I don't give a rat's arse."

But, he did give a rat's arse. He cared about the demographics of his environment. It hadn't mattered at school or university that everyone, except the workers, was white. After his exposure to Andile's Soweto, the lack of diversity in the army was patently obvious.

He cared about racist conversation. This newly-found aversion placed him in an isolated position among the 400 recruits and officers who reported for duty at Diskobolos to fight the "onslaught" popularised by Defence Minister P.W. Botha.

Mike new feelings were that Botha was spin-doctoring. He was trying to make vulnerable white minds buy into a romanticised version of "fighting the good fight." against evil. Evil, in this instance, was represented by communists and their black proxies. The implication was that if you answered the call, you would be a hero in this life, and by rallying under God's banner, you'd accrue eternal benefits.

A media clamp-down ensured that the almost universal condemnation of the South African racist regime was sufficiently muted to manage white concern about isolation from the outside world while still fuelling the fear of being consumed by communism and being butchered by black nationalists.

Mike realised he would profit little by flaunting his new political awareness. When confronted by incidents of bigotry, he bit his tongue, realising that the majority of the 400 doing basic training supported the policies of apartheid.

Instead, he found ruses, other than racist indignation, to engage in bloody brawls with bigots. The spark to ignite a fight was usually trivial – even being called a soutie. He had never been taught to fight dirty. It came naturally. He disabled opponents by ferociously attacking any vulnerable spots. In most instances, they were injured. In turn, Mike received some cuts and bruises. His main penalties for fighting came from the officers in the form of extra guard duties, or he had to hold his rifle at arm's length until muscle failure. When he eventually failed, the entire platoon was punished with running. It did not matter, as his fellow soldiers developed a healthy respect for the Englishman with a crazy edge. Besides, running was common cause during basic training.

By lunch time on the first day, he had short hair and a uniform. An assault rifle, the R17.62mm, was issued after the meal and completed his image transformation into a soldier.

Meal times were reminiscent of the *Oliver Twist* movie, as 400 men jostled for favourable mess queue positions in anticipation of their meagre morsels. There were no plates. Instead, recruits were issued with *vark panne*[44]. Obese

---

44 Literally translated from Afrikaans as pig pans, these are broad
    metal food trays with compartments.

kitchen staff shovelled food from large pots into these pans with total disregard for the integrity of their compartments. Watery stew soaked into several slices of thickly-cut bread, mixing freely with jelly and lumpy custard. It was of no concern to the recipients, who were already behaving like starving dogs waiting for their food – too famished to care. So what if the meal was mush before being consumed? That was a petty detail.

The 20-minute time allocation for eating ended with a siren that signalled that it was time to wash the vark panne. The communal washing tub contained cold, dirty dish washing water resembling pig swill. Mike wondered in amusement if the dish water was the beginnings of the following day's stew.

Later that afternoon, the 400 were exposed to the first of their weekly spiritual enrichment sessions. It came in the form of a one-hour sermon by Colonel J.C. Oosthuizen, the resident NGK[45] chaplain. Mike listened as J.C. (the initials stood for Johannes Cornelius, as opposed to the more obvious in a religious context), preached non-stop for 60 minutes.

He started slowly, like a diesel engine warming up, using measured words at a low pitch. He ended like a motivational speaker in full cry, rousing the crowd as he hit vocal highs sufficient to thrill an audience at an opera.

---

45 The Dutch Reformed Church (Afrikaans: *Nederduitse Gereformeerde Kerk*, abbreviated NGK) is a Reformed Christian denomination in South Africa.

"Almighty and heavenly Father, we stand before you in humility, fully aware that we are sinners and not worthy of your grace. We beseech thee to hear our prayers.

"We know that you're challenging us to carry out your will for a better world. We stand ready to do your work that's assigned to us in the scriptures.

"We ask you to let the Holy Spirit into us so that we can draw the strength and wisdom required for the tasks that lie ahead of us.

"Lord, we are weak and tempted by false prophets. Give us the strength to resist their cunning ways.

"Lord, we are lonely in our battle. The rest of the world stands in judgment of us as we follow your guidance. Give us the fortitude to stay with the task.

"Lord, we stand before you with heads bowed in the knowledge that many are losing their God-given gifts as they weaken to the false gifts of our enemy – the communists.

"Lord, we are losing your gift of democracy when we succumb to the communists' unjust and unholy totalitarian system.

"Lord, we are losing your gift of individuality when we wear the blue jeans that have become the uniform of the communist.

"Lord, we mock your creation of Adam and Eve when we sew symbols of half-eaten apples on to our clothing.

"Lord we ask you to protect us from the Illuminati's evil work. It is aligning our enemies against us and doing Satan's labour."

The sermon went on and on, and to Mike's untrained ear, it just got weirder and weirder.

He looked around the room, noticing the fervour growing among the 400. It was as if a virus had infected them all and indoctrinated them into a hypnotic frenzy. They were reacting like storm troopers at one of Hitler's rallies.

Mike recalled a previous time when he had witnessed rapturous behaviour at a jazz concert in Stellenbosch. In that instance, the audience had ascended into euphoria as they followed the musician's illogical path. To him, it was the same behaviour, fuelled by a different cause. He found himself wondering if people were predisposed to rapture at any cost. He freely acknowledged that he did not have an ear for music. To him, jazz often sounded like a surreal car alarm. He felt that this was a good enough reason to be exempted from jazz rapture. He could not understand why he did not buy into the religious rhapsody.

The room resounded with devout repartee as members of the 400 randomly cried: "Yes, Chaplain, YES. Yes, God, YES. Jesus, help us do thy will.

"Save us from the evil befalling the world and South Africa.

"Rescue us from the temptation of the devil and communism.

"Lord, protect us." Mike was fascinated as the 400 became mesmerised by J.C.'s magnetism. He felt as if he had wandered into some strange religious sect, and found it ironic that J.C. was warning them against losing their individuality to communism while they instead were being seduced into losing their individuality to a messianic minister instead.

Each one was handed a book explaining the wily ways of the Illuminati as they filed out of the makeshift church, before being distributed into four companies. These were then further divided into platoons and finally into sections of 10. Mike was allocated to C Company. Platoon 1, Section 2. C Company occupied Bungalow 3 as their sleeping quarters.

Evening preparations revolved exclusively around readiness for the following day's inspection. The neatness and cleanliness of everything was open to examination, both inside and outside.

Lights out was 10pm. Before that, they scurried around cleaning rifles, polishing boots, burnishing badges, ironing clothes and packing their bedside locker contents in designated spots.

The biggest challenge was making their beds. There was a scrutiny specification for the angles around the mattress; the height of the pillow; the corner folds of the blankets and even the flap of the sheet. Every morning, men kneeled before their beds, some praying, most biting the edges of the blanket to achieve the prescribed requirements.

After passing a bed inspection, several recruits slept on the floor in order to keep their beds perfect for scrutiny the following day. But biting beds and sleeping on the floor was usually to no avail. The examining officer's mood was the main determinant of whether or not the standard was satisfactory.

The bathroom was a short walk from the sleeping quarters and served the 100 men's ablution needs. It was a bathroom in name only; no baths, only 10 showers without dividers. It was serviced by a geyser with enough hot water for 10 showers; the rest endured cold water. The bathrooms were fitted with 10 washbasins minus plugs, and a large urinal trough that, despite being shiny on the outside, stank of old urine. Diagonally opposite the foul-smelling trough were 10 toilets with neither seats covering the porcelain, nor modesty partitioning. Using the bathroom or going to the toilet was a public experience in the army.

Sociologists could have had a field day studying the men walking from bed to ablutions. Those reared exclusively at home donned a dressing gown and clutched a toiletry bag. Those, like Mike, who had been to boarding school, walked to the ablutions in the nude, towels draped over their shoulders with toothbrushes clamped between their teeth.

Reveille (wake-up call) was 3:30am; inspection, 4:30am; breakfast, 5.30am; and they were on parade at 7am.

On the second morning, the 400 recruits were herded on to the parade ground. Mike stood with his hands in his pockets. To an officer, this pose was like a red flag to a bull.

Regimental Seargent Major "Bull" Bezuidenhoudt was so nicknamed because of his low centre of gravity; muscular short neck; broad chest; and wide girth. The picture was completed by a huge handlebar moustache reminiscent of an Afrikaner bull's horns. However, rumour had it that his testicles were not up to a bull's standard. Despite this suspected shortcoming, he retained nickname Bull.

Bull Bezuidenhoudt's keen eye spotted Mike's misdemeanour immediately.

"You there, what the fuck are you playing with?"

Mike ignored him.

"I mean you, numb nuts," bellowed Bull, pointing his swagger stick at Mike.

Mike gave him a quizzical look.

"I am pointing at you. I may be squint, but my fucking stick's not."

Mike responded by pointing at himself.

"Yes, you, you piece of shit. No, actually you are not any piece of shit, you are lower. You are a piece of snake shit. No, you're not a piece of snake shit, you are lower. You are the shadow of snake shit."

Bull barked an order: "Give me 50 on the double."

In military terms, this meant that Mike had to drop to the ground for 50 push-ups. He fell forward on to the parade ground tarmac and obliged. The RSM had developed a liking for hard-arse recruits like Mike. He felt God had sent them to test him, and he was thankful for the challenge. Mike escaped further chastisement courtesy of the hourly smoke break. At least 90% of the recruits were smokers. The pause provided time for a few drags, never enough to finish. Most nipped their cigarettes and stored the smelly stubs in their pockets for the next break.

Section commanders, the tormentors of the army, held the rank of corporal. Mike's dismissive dealing with Bull

Bezuidenhoudt had not gone unnoticed by his section commander. Corporal "Tinkie" Heynes's voice shrieked at Mike, spit spewing freely from his mouth as he closed in on him. Heynes either had no respect for body space, or moving into his quarry's space, until he was toe to toe, eye to eye and nose to nose, was part of his performance. Mike guessed that no one had told him about his horrible halitosis, and he made a mental note to be the first.

"You, troop, Sergeant Major Bull let you get off lightly with your bullshit. I won't. Who the fuck do you think you are?" Mike looked him up and down dismissively, without answering. He was a month shy of 20, and the corporals were 17 or 18. That was just one reason why he refused to bow before them.

"You bloody well answer me, troopie!" The corporal's voice increased in pitch. Mike glared at him. "Okay, so that's the way it's going to be. We will see who is tough after a few days of basics. You see that tree over there? Are you back already?"

Heynes pointed to a tree about two kilometres away. A tree was a rare site in the arid Kimberley environment. When one was pointed out, it was unmistakable. Mike knew the drill. The corporal was ordering him to run to the tree and back. He decided it unwise to disobey an order and obliged. He could do the two kilometre run with consummate ease. His survival instinct kicked in and he pretended it was more difficult than he actually found it to be.

His compliance proved sufficient for the little bantam cock corporal to change focus and to attend to more pressing matters, like marching the section up and down while barking out commands: "Halt, left turn, right turn, about turn."

As could be expected, their efforts were shambolic, and the corporal revelled in the recruits' lack of competence as he broke each movement down into components for practice drills.

"Halt, check, one, two."

"Left turn, check, left."

"Right turn, check, right."

About turn, check, check, one, two, three, four, left."

Parade ground sessions and their drills were repeated again and again and again, until they were executed with military precision three months later.

The army was not for marching only. Many hours were spent on combat training. Mike related well to this and felt at ease with his R1 and its deadly fire power.

Combat sessions included shooting practice on the range, day and night route marches and manoeuvres in which live rounds fired from a Browning .30 calibre belt-fed light machine guns whistled a few inches above their heads as they leopard-crawled across obstacle courses to safety.

The strangest combat practice was the bayonet charge. Mike had no idea why the army still used them. Did they expect him to stab someone with a bayonet? As far as he knew, they were fighting with automatic weapons and explosives.

His views were irrelevant. They were taught to fix bayonets; to charge; to stick them into straw dummies; to twist, and then withdraw by pressing a foot on to the dummy to provide release leverage.

The sergeant in charge of bayonet charge training upped the ante by insisting the trainees give blood-curdling screams as their bayonets stabbed their straw victims. He also required that they name their victims, the most popular being Joe Slovo. Mike had never heard of Joe Slovo.

The better informed knew Slovo to be the leader of the South African Communist party as well as leader of *Umkhonto we Sizwe*.[46] Joe was apparently the military's number one enemy. His misdemeanours were magnified because he was a white man, although this fact was largely

---

46 *Umkhonto we Sizwe* (abbreviated as MK, Zulu for Spear of the Nation) was the armed wing of the African National Congress, co-founded by Nelson Mandela in the wake of the Sharpeville massacre. Its founding represented the conviction in the face of the massacre that the ANC could no longer limit itself to non-violent protest. Its mission was to fight against the South African government. After warning the South African government in June 1961 of its intention to begin retaliatory acts if the government did not take steps toward constitutional reform and increased political rights, MK launched its first guerrilla attacks against government installations on 16 December 1961. It was subsequently classified as a terrorist organisation by the South African government and the United States, and banned.

unknown to the troops, including Mike. Joe Slovo was the ultimate impimpi in the eyes of white nationalist South Africans. Mike thought that if he were ever to meet him, he would apologise for the number of times Joe had been stabbed in mock bayonet charges.

Six weeks passed quickly. Mid-June arrived, the time when universities were on mid-year break. The 400 received their first one-day pass. Many grabbed the opportunity to catch up on sleep. Like a moth to a flame, Mike decided to see if Maddy was at her Kimberley home.

He arrived without prior notice and knocked at the door to her family home. She was home. He didn't have an agenda, only a deep longing to see her. He immediately realised that the visit was a mistake. She was not impressed. Even his uniform failed to impress her. "Doesn't a man in uniform impress the ladies?" Mike asked, grabbing at straws, desperately trying to retain his sense of humour.

The visit lasted 30 minutes. During that time, he made a feckless attempt to rekindle a connection, but it made no difference: Maddy was cold and distant. Mike felt exiled, once again cast as a villain. He was at a loss to understand what awful thing he had done to create such an acrimonious atmosphere. Why had she become so detached?

A malignant ache manifested in the pit of his stomach as he returned to camp. Once again, he reverted to reactive grief. His brain, which had been the seat of his joy, became the seat of his sorrow.

The public address system in the camp was broadcasting the radio programme *Forces' Favourites*. Mike collapsed on to his bunk. He tossed and turned as his thoughts churned like a hamster on a wheel, rehashing, regretting and resenting.

When had her feelings become so out of sync with his?

When had his sacred space become the domain of another?

Was she thinking about him while they were together?

Why had she not told him? Or had she tried to? Where was the "Dear John" letter?

Sleep did not come easy. His ears filled with maudlin messages from soppy soldiers and gushy girlfriends read out by radio announcer Pat Kerr. He eventually dozed off to the sound of Cliff Richard belting out: "I'll give you forty days to get back". The energy of the army would have to do its magic on his sadness. From then on, the only time he would see Maddy would be in his dreams.

A welcome new fixture in the second half of basics was a weekly barbeque with the NCOs. The RSM attended all of them. Bull Bezuidenhoudt had hollow legs. When it came to drinking, he was of the ilk that would spring for a round of drinks at the bar. No one could keep pace with him, particularly when it came to his favourite Klipdrift Brandy and cola. His nose shone brighter, and the little red veins on his cheeks grew broader the more he consumed, and he even occasionally ended the evening with someone in a headlock as he persuaded them to finish the bottle with him.

Bull was the life and soul of the weekly barbeque, providing an endless supply of self-deprecating stories, ranging from whacky tales of wicked women, to the calamities of military mishaps. He dispensed these with the same level of skill with which he managed his parade ground. In the unlikely event that Bull Bezuidenhoudt was to leave the army, the comedy circuit would be a lot richer for it.

He was famous in military circles for his classification of women on a two-dimensional X and Y axis matrix. The X line represented hotness. He explained that women could be classified anywhere between 0 and 10 on a scale of how hot or attractive they were. The Y axis represented how crazy they were. The rating on this axis was from five to 10. He clarified that no woman ever scored below a five rating. Bull concluded: "In the unlikely event you encountered one below five, you should inspect their equipment because you're in for a surprise."

The stories Bull didn't tell were those that made him a legend in the military milieu. These were the folklore of others out of the old rouge's earshot.

Bull was the stereotypical sergeant major. It was generally believed that people in such ranks were always difficult. Bull had learned to be difficult only when it counted.

He was in the army because he valued the military institution and its discipline and camaraderie. The words "bravery" and "valour" were conceived for his kind. On the battlefield, Bull showed a complete disregard for his own life. He never budged an inch from his men while under fire from an advancing enemy. It was said that Bull could spot any fear growing in his men and that he knew how to calm them down without making them feel ashamed. A stickler for discipline, he would even remind the wounded to shave while comforting them.

Mike grew to like and respect Bull. He felt an unexpected pang of affection for the old warrior. The feelings were probably mutual, as during barbeques he often felt Bull's hairy, muscular arm seek him out, tightening around his neck as he coaxed him into consuming copious amounts of brandy straight from the bottle.

Bull had never married. He lived alone and at 58, he could best be described as a "dagga boy". The army was his family during the day, but after hours when his colleagues were with their kin, he was alone. An outcast.

* * *

Slang van Niekerk remained true to his word. When Mike's three-month basic training came to end, he was duly summoned for three months' munitions and explosives training at the premises of a disused mining operation on the outskirts of Vereeniging.

Captain Nicholaas "Nitro" Neethling headed up the Special Task Force (STF) – a secret collaboration between military and police forces under the auspices of BOSS. STF provided training in counter-terrorism, insurgency; weapons; explosives; survival; and the bush skills to execute high-risk counter insurgency (COIN) operations. They shared intelligence with the Israeli Defence Force.

Mike adapted quickly to weapons training. He was a natural – he had been nurtured on his dad's arsenal. Adding an Uzi 9mm sub-machine gun, a Browning .30 calibre belt-fed light machine gun, an 81 mm mortar and fragmentation grenades had been like adding yachting to a wind surfer's skill set.

His new challenge was to learn the intricacies of explosives. Beginning with safe handling, the curriculum went on to cover detecting explosives; deployment and setting explosives; and finally detonating techniques. Within three months, Mike was using C4 explosive and claymore mines on applications ranging from setting or defusing booby traps to blowing up bridges.

November arrived. The training had been powerful, fast and unrelenting. He was Corporal Mike Hanssen: The new rank associated with successfully completing three months' technical training. He received instruction papers seconding him to the South West African Police as an explosives expert. The day of his departure, Andre Slang van Niekerk popped by to bid Mike farewell and spend some time with his old friend, Captain Nicholaas "Nitro" Neethling.

"Mike, you've had a few incidents with the South African police. These guys, the South West African police, aren't like our locals. They're uncompromising. You will find that they shoot first and ask questions later. Their job is to eliminate the South West African People's Organisation's

(SWAPO)[47] military capability in Ovamboland. You will operate as part of their patrols with the specialist task of demolition. This may mean bridges, buildings or captured weapons caches. I envy you."

That was it. Mike shared a few pleasantries, and along with three other graduates, went to Waterkloof Airforce Base, where he boarded a flossie, the C-160Z military transport aircraft, bound for Grootfontein's Military Airfield in South West Africa, just south of Ovamboland.

---

47 The South West Africa People's Organisation (SWAPO) is a political party and former national liberation movement in Namibia.

27

LOVE YOUR ENEMIES, DO GOOD TO THEM

November 1971

Officer in charge of the Ovamboland Police Headquarters Colonel Willie Basson met the three demolition experts at the airport. He immediately deputised them as policemen and explained that a warning order had been issued for a search-and-attack patrol that was to head out the next day, and he asked Mike to accompany them. The patrol leader was Sergeant "Pine" Pienaar.

Basson grabbed the opportunity to bring Mike up to speed, based on his perspective of the situation in South West Africa.

"Mike, our politicians believe that Russia, with its communist doctrine, will try to infiltrate South Africa from Angola, via South West Africa, using the People's Liberation Army of Namibia (PLAN) the military wing of SWAPO. Our brief's to stop them from winning the hearts and minds of the local people and from spreading communism in Ovamboland.

"These people find themselves between a rock and a hard place. When SWAPO cadres arrive at their village, so called 'sell-outs' are victimised, babies are killed and mothers are forced to eat their flesh.

"If villagers claim to be neutral, they are quickly swayed to popular opinion by the public execution of the headman as an example to those who did not toe their line. If this fails to impress, a number of victims are picked at random and the local population is coerced into killing them. If this still did not have the desired effect, the headman's kraal is torched as an example to those who did not agree with their ideology. We often come upon the corpses of these unfortunates, and only wish that those in the outside world, who see South Africa as the only villain, could see SWAPO's victims."

"But, if SWAPO do all that bad stuff, why are we losing the PR war?" asked Mike.

"I guess we're a worse political option, and to crown it, we're also seen as brutal. No right-thinking black person will choose apartheid over communism. Would you?"

"But ... then we're involved in a futile fight. Why do we do it?"

Basson shrugged his shoulders "We are in the armed forces, lad. Ours is not to question why, ours is to do and die. That's from Alfred Lloyd Tennyson, one of the better Englishmen, present company excluded of course."

"That's discouraging," Mike replied. "I doubt if that passage will inspire or motivate the men."

"Don't worry, I try to only tell people who can face the truth. Can you?"

Willie Basson was a sceptic who, over time, had developed reservations about almost everything, particularly about politicians and the role of the military in supporting political doctrine. Paradoxically, it was probably the sceptic in him that drove his interest in science fiction. He spent most of his spare time reading the works of writers like Isaac Asimov, Robert Heinlein and Arthur C. Clarke. When challenged about reading science fiction, he would reply: "At least I know it's bullshit."

Soon afterwards, the patrol gathered for its briefing. A tip-off about PLAN activity in a village 50km north of their camp had been received, along with rumours of a substantial arms cache near the village. Their brief was to make contact with the village headman and to determine the level of infiltration and loyalty towards SWAPO. Most of all, they wanted the location of the arms cache so that it could be destroyed.

Mike had a few hours to prepare his pack with rations for a two-day patrol. He included two tins of corned beef, five dog biscuits[48], his R1 with 10 magazines of 20 rounds each, three M6 fragmentation grenades, two anti-personnel mines and sufficient C4 with detonators for two massive explosions.

Early the next morning, the 15-man patrol set off in their four-wheel-drive Bedford MK. It was the rainy season, the territory was flooded and the roads were poor.

---

48 Hard, tasteless biscuits, high in calories, made especially for the military.

They managed to get within five kilometres of the village before the treacherous conditions forced them to abandon the Bedford and continue on foot.

The tropical landscape in the north of Ovamboland was breathtakingly beautiful and it teemed with wildlife, but this was neither sightseeing nor a hunting patrol. Their mission was dangerous and deadly, and their prey was armed.

Their patrol leader, Pine Pienaar, a rugby-playing lock forward, stood at an imposing two metres; His visible badge of courage was a cauliflower ear the result of years of playing in the scrum. It used to be said that cauliflower ears were a symptom of insanity. People speculated that they were caused by the insane hitting themselves against walls, or being boxed around the ear by asylum staff. Pienaar, while not insane in the strict sense of the word, was often called "fucking crazy" by his patrol members.

He called the patrol members together to pray. It was standard practice before and after a patrol. Mike couldn't help wondering why God would be interested in their patrol, in the same way he used to wonder why God would be interested in Stellenbosch winning a rugby game.

Pienaar's second subject made more sense. He reminded them that they were going to be moving into hostile terrain. It would take two to three hours to reach their destination. He cautioned that a patrol, with clicking and clacking gear, talking and the sloshing of half-empty canteens, could generate a lot of noise.

The patrol formation consisted of a veteran pointman upfront, scanning for an ambush. A heavily armed coverman walked close behind him. Two men operating as flank security walked on either side of the patrol, but a little behind the pointman, providing additional security against an ambush. A tail-end Charlie provided rear security. If the patrol were cut in two, he would take charge of one half. He was also responsible for stopping enemy forces from surprising the patrol from the rear. In front of him was another coverman.

The remainder walked in a scattered formation, maintaining tactical spacing and visual contact with one another. All moved quietly while they followed the premapped zigzag route to the village.

Pine Pienaar stopped the patrol frequently in order to listen to their surroundings, to break for water, or to establish a rally point to which they could evacuate if they came under heavy fire.

They had covered three kilometres when the unmistakable *takka takka* chatter of an AK47 broke the silence. They were under fire. All dropped to the ground, not knowing where the enemy was or how many there were. The patrol responded with an incredible display of unrestrained firepower.

The AK 47 reports went silent. Patrol members lay still for five minutes before each one leopard-crawled for superior shelter.

Having concluded that it was a hit-and-run ambush, Pienaar shouted out for a casualty status. The rear coverman reported that tail-end Charlie, Corporal Niel Ellis, had been hit. Closer inspection revealed three 7.62 bullet wounds in his back, each one fatal.

Pienaar called for a quick debrief from the patrol members.

"Why didn't we spot the sniper?"

"Was there more than one?"

"What action can we take to avoid a repeat situation?"

Based on the sound of the gunfire, the conclusion was that one AK47 was used. There may have been more assailants in back-up positions. Ellis's deadly wounds indicated that the shooter had been on the left of the patrol and slightly elevated; probably camouflaged and hiding in a tree at a height were a small jump returned him to Earth, allowing him to run off to safety. Pienaar decided to use two pointmen for the rest of the patrol. The additional one would be dedicated to scanning the trees.

Before they continued, two patrols members scouted the area to their left. They found cartridge shells below a tree that had obviously been the shooter's sanctuary. Everything felt surreal. It had been Mike's first contact with the enemy and he had not seen them. A faceless foe had killed one in his patrol using hit-and-run tactics.

The radio operator contacted base camp, giving a compass bearing of an Oryx helicopter that would evacuate their fallen comrade. Two heavily armed patrol members stayed with the corpse as the patrol resumed.

An hour later, Pienaar's 12 patrol members entered the impoverished village and approached the kraal of the headman, Chief Tshanika. Pienaar's modus operandi was good cop, bad cop. He usually played the bad cop and Ellis, the good one. There was no back-up plan, which left Pienaar leading with bad cop and probably intending to moderate by turning on his own good cop persona in the absence of the late Ellis. The recent ambush had affected his mood and judgment. He started as bad cop and escalated to worse cop.

"Chief Tshanika, have members of the SWAPO military wing been in touch with you over the past week?"

"No, Sergeant, no SWAPO members have been here. Besides, our village is neutral."

"Well, we were ambushed two kilometres from the village. Do you expect me to believe they just happened to be there?"

"That's unfortunate, Sergeant. I repeat we have had no contact with SWAPO in the past week. Some of their military wing came around two months ago on a recruitment drive. I told them we're neutral, so they left. "

"Bullshit, they would never accept that. I wouldn't be surprised if they're here right now."

"Sergeant, why would I defend them? I am telling you they have not been here and are not here now."

"Fuck you, you're lying. I want to know where they are and where their arms are hidden.'

"Sergeant, you don't do your position any justice by swearing and threatening."

"I am not threatening, I am fucking telling you that if you do not come clean and tell us where the arms are hidden, you are going to be mighty sorry."

"How can I tell you something that I do not know?"

Pienaar ignored him and signalled to two of his men.

"Arrest this man. Cuff him."

As the two men handcuffed Tshanika, the other patrol members took up a threatening stance, pointing their R1s at the villagers who were jabbering to each other while gathering ominously around the kraal.

"Cut off his clothes."

One of the patrol members withdrew a sharp knife from his backpack and proceeded to strip off the headman's clothing. Mike assumed this was the way Pienaar intimidated his victims into giving him the information he wanted.

The headman stood naked, wearing only handcuffs.

The villagers were shocked by the humiliating treatment handed out to their headman. But, faced with an arsenal of R1s, nobody risked acting against the patrol.

"Now, Tshanika, let's see if your memory's improved. Where are the arms hidden?"

Tshanika did not answer.

"Hang him." Pienaar ordered.

His patrol members knew the routine. Rope appeared. They tied his ankles and hung him upside down, dangling from a beam outside his hut.

"You will get enough blood draining into your brain to help you remember. Where are the arms hidden?"

Tshanika face changed colour as gravity drained blood into his head. He still did not answer.

Pienaar smashed the butt of his R1 into Tshanika's stomach.

Tshanika, writhed with pain, regained his composure and gave Pienaar an inverted glare.

Pienaar said nothing, then without warning drove the butt into Tshanika's face. Blood spurted from his nose and poured from a wicked gash on his cheek. He looked like a cow strung up by its hind legs in an abattoir, blood draining on to the ground.

The villagers were outraged. A boy of 16 broke away from the crowd and ran menacingly towards Pienaar, brandishing a machete. Pienaar calmly shot him in the leg, causing him to collapse, like the wounded buck Mike had encountered on his hunting expeditions.

It was the headman's son.

Pienaar called out calmly: "The next shot is to the boy's head."

He looked at the headman intimidatingly: "For the last time, give me the hiding place."

Tshanika spoke: "Please don't shoot him. I will get someone to take you to the arms. Just leave us alone."

"You see, it's much better when you co-operate."

He called out to the patrol's medic: "Attend to the wounded men. While that's being done, let's blow up some weapons."

Mike strategically placed the C4 across the nearby weapons cache. The group withdrew to a safe distance for the detonation. A massive explosion followed as AK47s, hand grenades and anti-personnel mines scattered into millions of pieces.

As the patrol prepared to leave, Mike glanced across at the headman's kraal. The medic had completed his task. The headman's wounds had been cleaned and sutured. His son lay on a mat at the entrance to the hut, his leg strapped, and a lactate drip curled from his arm to a makeshift stand. The father huddled over his son, embracing him. Both men were in tears.

The patrol left. Pienaar turned to Mike: "You're new around here. We don't have any alternative, you know. They're used to violence and it's only by being the biggest bastards and showing the most power that we will get the information we need. I don't like it, but that's war. It's not for sissies. I believe in what General Patton said when he quoted from Psalm 23: "Yea though I walk through the valley of the shadow of death, I shall fear no evil because I am the meanest son of a bitch in the valley."

The return to base camp was uneventful. That night, Mike's nightmares were back with a vengeance. Inevitably, the dream featured the familiar serpent slithering in the background. This time, Mike blew up a bridge, realising as he pressed the detonator that his mother and Maddy were walking across it. He, as usual, was powerless to intervene as his actions destroyed the women that he loved.

28

GREATER LOVE HAS NO ONE

For the next six months, a patrol went out at least once per week. Mike notched up 20 duties during that period. Most of them involved gathering information and destroying arms caches, often using Pienaar's brutal method of getting information from the local population.

Whenever Mike got a chance, he pondered the pointlessness of their military manoeuvres with Colonel Basson.

Mike asserted: "Pienaar's tactics are sure as hell not winning the PR war. We're losing friends and making enemies. Every time he tortures someone, he creates more PLAN recruits."

Basson always had something profound to add. He would seemingly go off on a tangent then link the discussion to their current reality. Mike particularly liked his reference to chaos theory. Basson quoted Edward Lorenz: "We live in uncertainty; behaviour that's initially predictable becomes more random after a while."

He paused then continued: "How does it go? Man proposes and God disposes. What that means and how it applies to us, will make a good discussion." Whatever it meant, Mike liked it.

Several of his 20 patrols involved skirmishes with PLAN soldiers. Over time, PLAN became brazen, varying hit-and-run tactics with exchange of fire. Mike did not keep an exact body count of PLAN corpses. He guessed it close to 50, many falling to his R1. Most bodies were invariably left on the battlefield for the wildlife to feed upon. When some were evacuated, Mike's colleagues referred to them as "floppies". It was a word they chose to describe the flopping of their lifeless bodies as they were transported in the back of a Bedford truck. The use of the name soon became generic to describe live PLAN cadres, too.

In these clashes, five of his patrol members were killed and several were wounded. The kill ratio of 10:1 was regarded as a disaster for the South West African Police Force.

Five-and-a-half months passed. Mike received orders to report for intelligence training within two weeks at BOSS's Pretoria offices. Van Niekerk was obviously still in charge at BOSS, as well as at the helm of Mike's destiny.

His final patrol was different from the others. The brief was to booby-trap the entrance to a PLAN camp four kilometres inside Angola, across the Cunene River. The intention was to strike a blow to enemy morale. They wanted to remind SWAPO that South West African ground forces could get to them wherever they were based. Aerial photo-reconnaissance reports indicated that the camp had around 100 PLAN troops and was equipped with two ZPU-4 14.5mm anti-aircraft guns. Mike assumed the anti-aircraft artillery at the camp swayed the decision in favour of a guerrilla-type attack, rather than an aerial one.

Three men were selected for the mission: Mike, Pienaar and Richard Middleton. It was likely that they would need to move quickly, which meant they had to pack light. Mike didn't prepare rations. One could last for days without food, and water was accessible from the Cunene River. He swapped his R1 for a lighter Uzi 9mm machine gun with three magazines of 20 rounds each, and included two bounding fragmentation mines. The idea was to get to the outskirts of the PLAN camp early in the evening, hole up for the night, set the booby traps at first light (due at 5am), then leave unnoticed. They aimed to be picked up at the original drop-off point at 6.15am. According to the reconnaissance reports, troop movement out of the camp started at 6.30am. Any PLAN member leaving the camp would detonate the hidden anti-personnel mines.

The Cunene River provided a border between South West Africa and Angola, and South Africa helicopters regularly patrolled the South West African side. To eliminate suspicion, flights were increased to five consecutive evenings along the planned drop-off route. On the sixth evening at 6pm, the three men boarded a helicopter.

As he embarked, Mike recalled Basson telling him with distain that senior officers used the helicopters for big game hunting. "They are intoxicated by power. They use automatic rifles as if the game were the enemy. The animals have no chance, and these shameless people are the same ones that complain about rich people abusing their wealth. The law of the echo, Mike, that's what will get them. I can't report a brigadier or a general, but life will find a way."

The trinity and a small rubber dinghy were dropped a kilometre from the Cunene River on the South West African side, in line with the PLAN camp. Pine brought them together in a short prayer as they prepared to walk to the river. "Today, we are faced with an enormous task and with thy help God, we will prevail. Amen."

Their river crossing went undetected by humans, but not by resident reptiles which, alerted by the boat's intrusion, slithered off the banks into the murky water. Recent downpours had swelled the river, transforming it from meandering stream into a fast-flowing river. As a result, the staple crocodile diet of cat fish had become more difficult to catch. They turned to animal prey for survival.

On the other side, the trio secured and camouflaged the dinghy before moving cautiously towards the enemy camp.

They spent an uncomfortable night concealed, but within view of the camp. Despite assigning guard duties, no-one slept. Instead, they shared their silence. In the dim light, Mike could see his mates' faces, all preoccupied with their own thoughts. He wistfully observed the impressive array of stars in the night sky. It prompted him to recall what he had read about William Herschel who, in 1802, told his son that the sky was full of ghosts. Herschel explained that many of the visible stars were already dead. "We still see their light which takes eons to get to us, but their bodies were gone long ago. When we look into space, we're seeing back in time. We see ghosts." A full moon appeared at 10pm, ending the stark darkness that had enabled the clear gazing – ghosts or otherwise.

Accompanied by the chatter of exotic tropical birds, first light came, as predicted, at 5am. The trio moved silently, carefully implanting their lethal load on the path to the camp. One within 10m of the entrance, the other 50m, they would be detonated by pressure plates that were expertly obscured.

The job was done within 15 minutes, leaving 60 minutes to cover the four kilometres and cross the river. Despite the generous time allowance, they jogged along the path through the thick tropical vegetation, with Pienaar leading. When they were within a kilometre of the river, three things seemed to happen simultaneously: They heard the sound of AK47 fire; Pienaar's body began to convulse as the bullets hit him; and they spotted their attackers.

They had expected the return route to be clear, but things had not turned out as they had hoped. They had not anticipated a PLAN patrol returning from a mission in South West Africa. The PLAN members saw them first; their pointman brought up his weapon and opened fire. Rounds rained down on them.

At 100m, it was a lucky shot for the pointman, not for Pienaar. One 7.62 bullet ripped into his throat and another entered his heart. He was dead before he hit the ground. A glance was sufficient to determine that Pienaar was beyond help. Mike and Richard sent a couple of short bursts back before bolting west-bound, off the path, hurtling through the dense bush as bullets followed their hasty escape.

The *bratatat* sound of distant gunfire warranted an immediate response from the PLAN camp. Five un-suspecting victims made what was to be their final run out of the camp. The front runner felt the coil spring depress under his foot, activating a small lifting charge that launched the main body of the first mine out of the ground before it detonated at chest height. Accompanied by a deafening *kaboom* sound, the lethal shrapnel spray covered 200m, killing all in its path. Undeterred, a second group came in hot pursuit, detonating the 50m mine with the same result. Two explosions were enough to discourage the rest. No-one else ventured out of the camp for 30 minutes.

Mike and Richard increased their lead to 150m when they turned south in an attempt to navigate a course to the river. Five minutes later, the Cunene revealed itself 400 metres downstream of their original crossing.

They had been trained to manage fear that induced panic, yet to react quickly to any danger. In a few moments, the patrol pursuing them would clear the undergrowth and they would be trapped in the open. A logical calculation dispensed with the idea of running up the bank to retrieve the dinghy. Without hesitation, they chose what seemed to be the lesser of two evils. They dived into the flowing water and started the 60m swim to the relative safety of the other side.

They were halfway when the PLAN patrol emerged from the shrubs. Bullets sprayed around them, making plopping sounds as they struck the water. Mike and Richard submerged, attempting to swim underwater, hoping to present less of a target to the chattering AK47s. The visibility underwater wasn't just poor, it was zero. They came up for a hasty breath to find they had moved forward 10m, and along the river for 20m

Richard let out a painful cry as a bullet smashed into his back, between the right scapula and his spine. Blood flowed freely and pain overwhelmed him. Mike grabbed the wounded man's left arm, holding him in a wrist lock whilst he side-stroked and kicked towards the South West African river bank.

Richard was losing consciousness when they were spotted from the air. Helicopter pilot Captain James Louw put the chopper into a steep dive in the direction of the PLAN pursuers. His co-pilot tightened his index finger around the trigger of the door-mounted 7.62 belt-fed machine gun, discharging 600 rounds in the next minute.

Mike listened to the *whop whop whop* of the chopper blades and watched as its deadly firepower strafed from the skies.

"They're shooting the shit out of them." he shouted triumphantly at the unhearing, limp body he held in his left hand. The machine gun fire not only decimated the enemy, it ruined the vegetation in their immediate proximity.

Mike sighed with relief as he pulled the unconscious Richard closer, securing him in a lifeguard's hold under his armpits. The relief was short-lived. To his right, the water bubbled in anticipation. A four-metre ferocious crocodile lunged out of the water with lightning speed, like a performing killerwhale at Orlando's SeaWorld. The stealth hunter's earlier movement from land into the river had gone unnoticed in the chaos of escape.

This was no SeaWorld performance. Gigantic jaws crashed down on to Richard's midriff, missing Mike's hand by a few centimetres. Sharp, conical teeth rooted into Richard's ribs with the sickening sound of snapping bones. The reptile's right eye was 15cm from Mike's left eye. Its waterproof membrane parted like the shutter of a camera's lens. For a moment, man and monster's eyes locked.

Mike wanted to pinch himself. Was this one of his nightmares? Where was Maddy? He looked into the reptile's vertical-slit pupil as it revealed 240 million years of the predator's primordial past. The rotting stench from its breath brought a dose of reality and a realisation that he was very much awake. The reptile, unlike the extinct celestial bodies in the sky the previous night, was very much alive.

The crocodile heaved against Mike's hold. They were in a terminal tug of war in which only one result was possible. Mike was dragged underwater as he succumbed to the pulling power of the predator. Within two minutes, his lungs were bursting for air. He reluctantly released Richard. The helicopter had already dropped a ladder for Mike to climb to safety.

A minute later, they were hovering three metres above the path where the initial skirmish had taken place. Pine Pienaar lay on his back in a pool of congealing blood. Flies buzzed around his face, attacking his mucous membranes while crawling insects curiously inspected his wounds. Vultures had started to swirl high above. Pienaar was on the menu.

Mike climbed down the ladder and secured the corpse so that the winch could do its work. Blood flowed freely from Pine's wounds as his body was hoisted into the helicopter. Mike recalled a patrol member saying that Pine had ice in his veins. Mike said aloud: "Sorry, mate. Wrong. It's blood."

Back in the helicopter, he sat in the backseat, Pine's body on the floor in front of him.

Shock was setting in as he addressed Pine.

"So, was all that torture worth it? And the prayer, what was that about? Is it God's will that you're dead? Is it God's will that Richard is being eaten? Or is this just one of the strange fucking ways that God works?

"You quoted Patton, well here's another: "No poor bastard ever won a war by dying for their country. They won the war by making the poor bastards on the other side die."

Pine lay silent, his body animated only by the movement of the helicopter.

29

DO NOT FEAR, FOR I AM
WITH YOU

May 1972

BOSS's official job was to monitor national security, but its actual job was to do whatever was needed to maintain the white Afrikaner government's hold on power in South Africa.

BOSS did this through the clandestine collection of human intelligence and the taking of covert action to disable a range of national security threats. These threats were prioritised as communism and Black Nationalism. A BOSS agent's training curriculum covered propaganda, deception and operational skills.

Propaganda was mostly about how to use the media to win the hearts and minds of the population. Deception training involved 007-like aspects, ranging from disguise to the use of languages and accents.

Operations training covered situations mirroring what the agent might experience in the field. Agents were authorised to carry firearms. Firearm training focused on marksmanship combined with firing under threat. Hitting a target on a shooting range was easy; the challenge was teaching accuracy under fire, when the stress response virtually eliminates precision. Physical training centred on fitness. Finally, the agents were immersed in interrogation techniques and taught how to manage being interrogated and tortured. The final area tested the limits of their pain threshold, both physically and emotionally.

Van Niekerk was always in close proximity, watching over the trainees like an over enthusiastic dad at his son's rugby games.

Their graduation was a festive occasion involving a promotion to lieutenant, excessive drinking, back-slapping and a visit to the movies to see *Diamonds are Forever*, the latest James Bond offering.

* * *

August 1972

As a newly qualified BOSS agent, Lieutenant Mike Hanssen's demolition skills were much-valued by the regime. Most of his operational tasks involved doing forensic work and investigating the origins of bombings on military and state installations.

On two occasions, he was called upon to do the opposite. His assignments required him to set and detonate explosions on sites that were ostensibly civilian targets, while taking care not to inflict injuries. These were clumsy propaganda attempts by BOSS to taint the ANC by blaming them for attacks on innocent civilians. His second explosion was set on the morning he left for Swakopmund. Detonation was set for 5pm that evening with a time mechanism.

* * *

November 1972

An excited Van Niekerk briefed Mike on what he called a top secret mission. He explained that a communiqué from the CIA had alerted them to the possibility of a military coup in Portugal. They felt this could have a ripple effect on countries like Angola, probably culminating in the independence of these countries. This would usher an MPLA[49] government in Angola, headed by Antonio Agostinho Neto.

The CIA speculated that Neto would, in all likelihood, seek economic aid, military training and arms from Cuba.

---

49 The People's Movement for the Liberation of Angola, formerly the People's Movement for the Liberation of Angola Labour Party, is a political party that has ruled Angola since the country's independence from Portugal in 1975. The MPLA fought against the Portuguese army in the Angolan War of Independence of 1961–74, and defeated the National Union for the Total Independence of Angola (UNITA) and the National Liberation Front of Angola (FNLA) in the decolonisation conflict of 1974–75 and the Angolan Civil War of 1975–2002.

Van Niekerk knew that Neto had met Ché Guevara in 1965, and that he had began receiving support from Cuba. Neto had visited Havana many times, and he and Castro shared similar ideological views.

Mike's brief was to clandestinely enter Angola and to gather first-hand information from an Angolan government source in Luanda about the state of the relationship between Angola and Cuba. In addition, he needed to establish an estimate of the timelines leading up to independence. The information was needed for military planning and for financial reasons, as South Africa had a substantial investment in the Angolan Ruacana-Calueque Hydroelectric Scheme.

A fishing boat from Swakopmund passing the coast of Luanda late at night would jettison Mike one kilometre from the shore at a disused mooring buoy outside Luanda harbour. The plan was to swim ashore towing a small waterproof pack containing a false identity, money and travelling clothes. The pick-up was set for three days later at the same time and mooring. In the event of confusion, Mike had a waterproof torch to signal his position.

His new identity was Adam Crowcroft, an Australian political science student who was immersing himself in a different culture as part of his fieldwork. His counterfeit Australian passport contained a false exit stamp from Perth and an entry stamp into Luanda. Via telex, a room had been booked in the Epic Sana Hotel, 103 Rua Da Missao, courtesy of a BOSS contact in Perth. Mike had sufficient escudos to pay for bills and drinks, as well as US$5 000 earmarked for bribery.

According to CIA records, a senior civil servant in the Angolan Ministry of the Interior, José Eduardo Silva, had a reputation for being approachable when it came to leaking information in exchange for US$100 bills. Most evenings, he could be found consuming copious amounts of Cuca beer at the Portuguese Beer House. The bar was in the hotel that had been booked for Mike.

Recent experience with a Cunene crocodile had affected Mike's lifetime enthusiasm for any water that could conceal predators. He concluded that four-metre crocodiles live in some rivers and four-metre sharks live in all seas. The kilometre swim across dark Angolan waters was terrifying, but mercifully shark-free. Luandans were asleep and so were the sharks.

He came ashore a few hundred metres south of the harbour. Nearby vegetation provided cover for a quick change. He hid in a derelict building until later that morning to coincide with the arrival of the Qantas Airlines flight QF 768 from Perth, which was due at Luanda International Airport at 7.05am. He reached his hotel at 10:30am and booked in, for the first time using his broad Aussie accent in a real-life situation.

"G'day, reckon you've got a room for me. Booked in the name of Crowcroft – Adam Crowcroft."

The receptionist asked for his passport and duly noted the number in the hotel register.

"You need to pay the full amount in advance, Mr Crowcroft." Mike obliged in escudos.

He was given room 22, above the bar. That evening at 5pm, he went to the Beer House and asked the barman if he knew a Mr José Eduardo Silva.

"Mr Silva's my best customer and my amigo."

"Will he come in tonight?"

"Not every night, but maybe tonight. What you want to drink, Mr Australia?" The phoney accent had obviously worked on the barman. Mike ordered a Cuca beer.

He was in luck. Silva made an appearance an hour later. The barman greeted him with his usual beer and pointed out Mike. Silva approached him and in excellent English extended his hand in greeting.

"Silva, José Silva, and you are?'

"Adam Crowcroft, Mr Silva, it's a dinkum pleasure to meet you."

"Ah, Mr Crowcroft, what can I do for you?'

"Mr Silva, I am a political science student from New South Wales University in Australia. I have come to do some research on the Angola's political relationships with the outside world."

"Ah, I see, and to what part of the outside world do you refer, Mr Crowcroft?"

Well, my academic supervisor told me Angola's most influential relationships at present are with Russia and Cuba. Can you tell me about these?"

Silva's demeanour changed as he said: "Let's find a private corner to discuss this matter."

They took their beers to a quiet spot in the corner of the room.

Silva didn't waste time: "Mr Crowcroft, that sort of information costs a lot. Can you afford it?"

"I value good information and the best is always expensive." Mike slipped a US$100 bill on to the table.

Silva put his hand over it and pocketed it at the speed of a rattlesnake striking its victim.

"That's a good start, Mr Crowcroft, and worth me confirming that Angola is indeed good friends with Russia and Cuba. I might add that Russia may find it difficult to accept how good a friend Cuba's becoming. But I guess you can't afford to know how good this friendship's becoming, can you?"

"I am keen to know, and yes, although I am a poor student, I have a rich uncle who gave me a few more of these." He put 10 more $100 bills on the table. They disappeared as quickly as the first one. Silva could give rattlesnakes strike speed training.

Both men looked around cautiously. There were eight other people in the room. None took the slightest interest in the government official and the Australian nattering in the corner.

"Okay, you make a persuasive argument, Mr Crowcroft. Ask questions and I will try to answer them."

"Does Russia approve of Angola's relationship with Cuba?"

"As far as I know, they're aware of it. I think it worries them as they cannot control Castro."

"I don't understand. What do you mean?"

"I mean that Russia, to some extent, worries about world politics and protocols, Castro doesn't. He will react on a whim if he can satisfy his yearning to get at imperialists like America and, of course, their surrogates like South Africa."

"What if Portugal changes government through a military coup?"

"What if you put another 10 of those bills on the table?"

"Okay, that's the last I've got. My rich uncle's running out of money."

Mike, as before, repeated the financial transaction.

"I like your uncle and it's not … if Portugal has a military coup, it's when. This means the MPLA takes over in Angola and Neto forms an alliance with Castro. It will annoy the Russians, but there's nothing they can do about it. The Cubans will send troops, and Angola's enemies are in for a shock. The Cubans possess good fighting skills and lots of Russian hardware."

"When's it likely to happen?"

That's difficult to answer, but independence is likely to come to Angola in '74 … '75 is a good bet."

"What's Angola's relationship with communism? I mean, do you think the country will have a communist government after '74?"

"Look, the communists will have a major say. But the nature of the people in Angola is not akin to communism in the long term. They will come and they will go.

I think we have talked enough for one night. Let's have another drink tomorrow and maybe your uncle discovers his wallet overnight."

With that, Silva left. Mike went to his room. Soon afterwards, he succumbed to his nightmares.

At 6am the next morning, Mike woke up to three armed men in his room.

"Mr Crowcroft, please get dressed and come with us."

Keep your cool, Mike, ran through his mind. They don't know anything about you. You're Adam Crowcroft from Australia."

Mike was handcuffed and taken to a cell in a military prison on the coast near Luanda. It had high stone walls resembling a medieval castle, or at least Alcatraz, he thought. History wasn't Mike's strong suit.

He was left alone all day until 5pm, when he heard the clang of the metal door opening. One of the men involved in his arrest entered the cell.

"Mr Crowcroft, I am Eduardo. You can trust that's my name, but we both know that Adam Crowcroft isn't your name, so what is it?'

"Mate, I have no idea what you're talking about. Check my passport."

"Ah, we have checked it, and it's a good one. The only problem is it's false."

"I don't know what you mean, mate. I came in from Perth yesterday. Check the airline, check the bloody passport."

"If only that were true, but you see it's a lie. Let me explain why. The flight you were on from Perth was delayed and only came in last night. By the time it landed, you were already booked into your hotel. Now Mr X, you tell me who you are, how you got into Angola and why you are here. Particularly, why did you spend the early part of yesterday evening with Mr Silva?"

One detail he had not paid enough attention to was a possible fight delay. Mike stalled for time to think.

"I am an Australian political science student. I am here to conduct field work on the political changes in Angola."

"I don't believe you. Try again."

"I am an Australian political science student. I am here to conduct fieldwork on the political changes in Angola."

"I doubt you're Australian. You probably don't even know about the indigenous people of Australia."

"Is this a quiz, mate? We treated our Aborigines a darn side better than your blokes treated your locals. We didn't wipe them out, like you did to the Khoisan."

"I can see this will get boring. I have a friend who will help you remember a different, more accurate version. Mr X, it's time you were introduced to Luis Gonzales. He's more persuasive than I."

Luis could have come out of spy thriller. Better still, a horror movie. He was an antediluvian, knuckle-dragging thug who relished hurting others. His methods were an orgy of brutality. The late Pine Pienaar and BOSS could have learned a lot from him.

Mike passed out after an hour of enduring Luis' persuasive methods. The beatings were brutal. Mike had concluded some time before that life was not fair, but he hadn't expected to be tortured while awake and tormented by dreams when he was asleep.

A bucket of cold water revived him. Eduardo looked at him dispassionately. "Luis is struggling to help you see reason, Mr X.

"Tomorrow, he will have to try more creative means to assist your honesty. It doesn't matter to me how long you take. We know you are not who you say you are. We also know you have a false passport and are obviously trained to withstand pain.

"Oh, and not to mention you had thousands of US dollars in your room, which means you're probably a spy from a country with a problem with us; possibly South Africa, Rhodesia, America or England. You either tell us now or you'll tell us later. I admit, neither presents you with a good scenario. You will, at some point, be tried as a spy and you will be shot. If you rot in jail for a while, so be it."

The next morning Luis came in early for another round. He upped the ante. Mike was blindfolded, a rope attached to his neck and affixed to a rafter above his head. Luis repeatedly struck him with a stick on his head, knees and feet. His nipples and ears were repeatedly twisted and he was assaulted with fists to his face and stomach. Luis threatened that he would be taken out to sea and left to drown. That evening, he was tied to a tree, still blindfolded, and left exposed for the entire night.

It did not achieve the desired result, but Luis had not run out of methods to try. Next, he covered Mike's face with cloth while he was immobilised on his back. Luis poured water on to the cloth over Mike's mouth and nose, causing a gag reflex that made him feel like he was drowning. Again, it did not achieve the desired result.

The attempts continued. The most painful and humiliating were achieved by attaching electrical wires to Mike's testicles and passing an electrical current through them. Still, his torturers did not get the result they wanted.

Many torturous rounds followed, including five days of remaining handcuffed under the ferocious sun, combined with sleep deprivation. Again, Eduardo was denied a satisfactory outcome and he elected to wait for a trial. He concluded that he had many other prisoners to torture, so why waste time on one pseudo-Australian?

The new torture victim was an Angolan who occupied the cell next to Mike. A small grate between them allowed for some secret conversations. Mike was fascinated to learn from him that slavery was commonplace in Angola. His neighbour informed him that approximately a quarter of the population was still in bondage.

* * *

The fishing boat rendezvoused at the mooring buoy for three consecutive days before its captain concluded that their man had either been captured or was dead. When Van Niekerk, who was seldom thrown off his stride, heard the news, he was devastated. Days later, he regained his optimism and was heard saying: "Mike's got a good pedigree. If anyone can get out, he will." He decided not to inform Commandant Hanssen until substantial information was available about his son's whereabouts.

* * *

Mike's body took a month to recover from the beatings. There were no more interrogations and no more poundings.

He spent most of his days exercising in his small cell, waiting for any opportunity to exploit to his advantage. It never came. He was locked up and left alone. The only people he spoke to were the passing population in his neighbouring cell and Pepe, his jailor.

He thought about his food. During his training as a BOSS agent, he had read Dr Atkins's *Diet Revolution*. Based on his diet over the three months in detention, he decided that if he ever got out, he could write a diet book on how to stay lean and fit on a bowl of maize meal per day supplemented by protein provided by a plentiful supply of cockroaches and rats. It wasn't pretty, but it worked. He concluded that the book was unlikely to be a bestseller.

Three months passed and Mike was fetched for his trial. With hands and feet shackled, Pepe guided him into the back of a police van destined for the military court. Pepe had befriended him and kept him informed of his fate. It was predictable, according to Pepe. A short trial followed by a guilty verdict. Moments later, an execution by firing squad would bring matters, and his life, to a close.

Pepe joined him in the back of the van as his guard. Mike deliberately pulled on the foot shackles until they cut into his ankles. His blood flowed freely, pooling on the metal floor. The journey was in its fifth minute when he asked Pepe to slightly loosen his foot shackles as they were causing him extreme pain. The sight of blood convinced Pepe. He leaned over to alleviate his fated friend's distress.

Pepe felt Mike's wrist chains loop around and bite into his neck. It was over quickly. One hard snap and his neck was broken. An abrupt death.

Mike had a moment's remorse before grabbing the keys to free his ankles and wrists. Pepe's keys unlocked the metal door at the back of the van. The vehicle would inevitably slow down, or stop at some point on the journey. It seemed like an eternity before that moment came. When it did, he leaped out of the van, resisting the temptation to break into a run. Instead, he walked confidently to the nearest housing complex.

The driver was unaware of the change of circumstances in the back of his van. He arrived at court 20 minutes later, revealing Pepe's corpse, minus his prisoner, in the back. Eduardo was furious. He still had no idea who the prisoner with the phoney Australian accent was. His hope had been that all would be revealed at the trial, or in the face of death.

Mike stole clothing off washing lines, allowing him to blend into the crowd. He then followed the signs to the Luanda Railway Station.

Two trains were parked at the station. At Platform 1, the train was scheduled for Malanje, and at Platform 2, for Cassinga. Malanje was 350km north and Cassinga was 927km south. It was an obvious choice. His main problems were that he had no money and, of course, no documents. He also had to avoid a possible manhunt for a young Australian who had escaped custody.

The Cassinga train had three passenger cars and six cargo carriages. Mike covertly canvased the cargo carriages. As the train left the station, he hopped aboard an apparently unoccupied one that contained a range of wooden boxes, only to encounter another person in the carriage, also hitching a free ride from Angolan Railways.

His black stowaway companion looked to be in his mid-50s and was unfazed by Mike's presence. He was an escaped slave, unshaven, dressed in threadbare clothing and carrying a hessian bag. Mike, also unshaven, was better dressed, thanks to the range of clothing he had appropriated. He decided to use the story that he was homeless and that he had recently become a wanderer.

They travelled undetected, despite several stops at sidings and various small stations. The vagrant said his name was Miguel. Mike responded with his real name. To Mike's delight, Miguel had an assortment of edibles in his bag, which he generously shared with his fellow itinerant. The trip continued in silence, except for the *clickety-clack* of the train riding on railway joints.

Their freebie ended at the penultimate stop to Cassinga. Two men wearing police-style uniforms adorned with braids and badges peered into the carriage, beckoning them to disembark. They looked like Mexican military bad guys straight out of a Clint Eastwood spaghetti Western.

"What have we here, two bums hitching a free ride?" The bearded officer, who possessed obvious authority, spoke to no one in particular.

"I can see one black slave and a white bum. No, actually, I just see a white oppressor and his black servant about to provide us with a bit of fun," said his typical servile bureaucrat henchman, followed by a manic laugh that threatened to cause his foul-smelling cigarillo to fall from his lower lip.

The bearded officer continued indifferently: "I don't know who you are and what you're doing here, and frankly I don't care. It's hot and you have broken the law."

"Yes, yes, they have broken the law" the obsequious assistant reinforced. Mike couldn't help noticing the man's yellow-stained fingers and teeth. That's the price of years of smoking. I must give it up. If I get out of here alive, he thought.

"Amigos, my friend suggested you could provide some fun. Are you fond of gambling?" The officer continued with a governmental indifference that would match that of an immigration official.

Neither Mike nor Miguel replied.

"Okie dokie, I will answer yes on your behalf. I don't have a casino, but I have a revolver," said the officer as he removed a .38 Smith and Wesson from a holster on his hip.

Mike recognised the revolver immediately. It was the same as Carl's. The one he had fired stationary, fired running and fired while rolling over, literally hundreds of times over a period of six years.

He continued: "The game's Russian roulette. They're our friends, you know, the Russians, so we play their game. I load one bullet and spin the chamber. You hold the gun to your head and pull the trigger. If you hear a click, you're lucky. If you hear a loud bang, you're dead. If you're lucky, you get two more turns. This means you have a 50% chance of living. Good odds, if you ask me."

The manic man burst into another fit of laughter. "Good odds, good odds."

"Who will be first? I think the black man. It's about time us blacks were in the front of the queue."

"You feeling lucky, Sambo?"

"Right, gun loaded, chamber spun. Now my laughing policeman will aim his AK47 at you to stop you getting any ideas of monkey business."

Miguel did not see a viable alternative. With an AK47 at point-blank range, he took the pistol from the officer and pressed it against his forehead.

He squeezed the trigger. The click sound ominous, but it was still a relief.

"You're lucky, Sambo. Now just another two clicks and you can walk away."

He squeezed again. His head exploded as the .38 calibre bullet sent him into oblivion. Bits of brain and bone scattered around them.

The manic man doubled up as he once again descended into a fit of laughter.

The officer was unmoved.

"Now it's your turn, white man. Let see if you're luckier than your black slave."

The manic man pointed the AK47 at Mike. The officer loaded one bullet, spun the chamber and handed the revolver to Mike.

As he took the gun and put it against his head, Mike thought: You have just made a big mistake. It's you who has gambled and you're going to lose."

The officer and his manic companion had no idea of Mike's skills: The endurance; the competitive instinct; and the motivation that a lifetime of handling guns, coupled with army training, had instilled in him. Giving Mike a gun was like giving soccer legend Pele a ball so that he could take a penalty in front of the goals. He wouldn't miss with a soccer ball and Mike wouldn't miss with a revolver.

The holder of the AK47 didn't expect Mike to dive at the officer's legs.

He didn't expect Mike's left hand to fly over the trigger hammer, like a gunslinger in an American Western. The pistol blazed on the third attempt. It was so close to the first that it didn't matter. The manic man hadn't fired a shot by the time the single .38 bullet crashed into his chest, leaving him mortally wounded, twitching in the dust, incapable of using his AK47.

The show wasn't over. Mike was on top of the tumbled officer and wielding his empty revolver. He repeatedly smashed its metal barrel into the officer's temple. The man's skull split open. He crumpled up, also fatally injured.

The commotion attracted the attention of the fallen policemen's two colleagues who had been drinking coffee in the small railway siding building. They ran out, AK47s at the ready. Mike had retrieved the manic man's machine gun and fired a *ratatatat* burst at his new assailants. While deadly at close quarters, the AK47 is not known for accuracy. His burst was wide, but stopped them in their tracks, giving him enough time to reach the sanctuary of nearby undergrowth.

The policemen didn't pursue him. Two mortally wounded comrades were enough to convince them that tending to their colleagues and continuing to drink coffee were better options.

Mike followed the course of the railway line to the outskirts of Cassinga. He took a wide berth around the town and reunited with the line south of it. Fortunately, he came across what South Africans call a farm stall. It was essentially a lean-to with an assortment of local produce for sale.

Once again, he reverted to doing things he would never have dreamed he was capable of doing: He held up the store owner and took sufficient supplies for three days – the time he estimated it would take him to reach the Cunene River.

For the next 18 hours, Mike slogged on and on, following the railway line without spotting anyone. It was hot and a makeshift bandana provided protection against the scorching sun. He was exhausted and about to rest when a single sniper shot rang out. He heard the *p-taff* as he felt the bullet enter his right hamstring. It was a lot more painful than the time he had torn his hamstring while playing rugby two years earlier. He collapsed from exhaustion, pain and shock. The recently acquired AK47 fell at his side.

He had been shot by friendly fire. The sniper was from UNITA, an organization kindly disposed to South Africa. He had mistaken Mike for an MPLA operative. The bandana had concealed his white skin. Carrying an AK47 had sealed his fate. The sniper's shot, aimed to kill, had been off target but still inflicted a serious wound.

Mike felt the jab of a syringe, then blackness. He was taken by truck to a UNITA bush hospital 100km north of Rundu.

UNITA commander Jonas Savimbi contacted the South African forces, who casevaced Mike by helicopter to Rundu the following day. He was in a bad way and spent a week stabilising at the camp before being stretchered onto a flossie bound for Number 2 Military Hospital in Wynberg, Cape Town.

PART THREE

30

My Soul Is Weary

February 1973

Liberal doses of morphine helped to control his pain. The heavy-duty drug acted beyond its mandate. His already high susceptibility to hallucinations escalated. Nightmares featured colossal crocodiles snapping at his bed, while hissing snakes suspended from the ward ceiling flicked their forked tongues. Even when awake, the opiate took its toll, driving up his paranoia levels, encouraging him to believe that hospital staff members were conspiring to poison him.

After 10 days, the physician made the call to take him off the morphine. During that period, he refused to eat and was sustained only by an IV drip that he couldn't remove, thanks to the restraints around his wrists and ankles.

His body ached. Vague memories of a sniper's bullet, a UNITA camp, being casevaced to Rundu, and an airplane journey to Cape Town, drifted in and out of his mind like a net curtain wafting in a light wind on a sultry night.

Newly-promoted Colonel van Niekerk was his first visitor and would witness Mike's more lucid, post-morphine state. Mike noticed that deeply etched lines had appeared on the face of the once-handsome man. The creases folded deeper as he talked, his skin reminiscent of the scaled leather hide of a dead snake.

"Mike, you've had a hard time. I am sorry. Of course, any mission can go pear-shaped, that's the nature of our work," Van Niekerk said, shrugging his shoulders.

"Shit happens," was the best response Mike could think of.

"I'll send one of the local officers to debrief you tomorrow, if you're up to it."

"Sure," Mike confirmed.

"I'm afraid I have sad news, Mike. Commandant Hanssen passed away last month while you were in Angola. It was sudden. He was diagnosed with lung cancer and it took six weeks from knowing until his death. I am so sorry."

The news was a surprise, but yet it wasn't. The most badly kept secret of the '60s and '70s was that smoking causes cancer. Cigarette companies went to great lengths to keep the general public ignorant of the link. If Carl knew, he didn't care and he maintained his 50-a-day habit until death's door.

Carl was dead. The thought continued to hit Mike with deepening sadness. His mind flooded with memories of helping to repair various things in the workshop, and of their fishing and hunting trips. Fleeting memories of tougher times entered his mind, too, but they were diluted by his understanding and empathy for Carl's context. The good recollections prevailed. He made a mental note to catch up with Glenda Monk so that she could bring him up to speed on any logistics or legal matters.

Over the next three months, Van Niekerk stayed in Cape Town and became a frequent visitor to the hospital as Mike's body healed and the emphasis changed to his psychological wounds.

His physician declared: "Good news: Your leg is expected to heal completely, but not so fully that you could play rugby again. You will be transferred to the psychiatric ward so that we can identify any stress concerns. Post traumatic stress disorder's a big challenge among our wounded, and I'd like to make sure you make a full recovery. You will consult with a psychologist twice a week while in hospital and for a considerable time after your discharge. If you feel the person we have appointed is not compatible with you, let me know and we'll find another one."

The following six weeks in the psychiatric ward were set aside to provide a safe place for recuperation. Most people in the ward had trauma associated with military conflict. They arrived stressed and depressed, even suicidal. They were supposed to leave healed, with a fresh perspective on life that would make their time on Earth a more joyful experience. That seldom happened.

Mike met Dr Solly Goldberg at 10am on the first morning. Goldberg was charged with helping him to manage his mental demons.

"Hi, Mike, my name's Solly Goldberg. I've been appointed as your therapist."

"Hi, you're the one that's got a cure for my head?"

Solly replied with a quizzical look: "What do you mean a cure? Do you think I've got an elixir of life – a mystical remedy?"

"No," Mike continued, "I doubt you have magical powers, but you're already asking a lot of questions. I hope you have some answers, too. Otherwise, it's going to become pain and suffering compounded."

"Nobody likes pain, but suffering's optional. Would you like to try something different?"

"Okay, I get it, it's a psychology game. Right, let's start again, as long as you promise not to ask too many questions."

"That's fine. How about you ask the questions?"

"Great, I'll start. Tell me about you and what you do."

"Okay, I am a psychologist. It means I spend a lot of time learning and I devote time to reading."

"That must be boring."

"Only sometimes. If it becomes tedious, I give up on the book, but not on reading. Do you read?"

"Oh no, I am asking the questions. What do you read?"

"I mostly read research on post traumatic stress disorder."

"Have I got post traumatic stress disorder?"

"Possibly. Would you like to find out?"

"There's another question. You can't help yourself, can you?"

"Sorry. It's a little difficult with my job. I even get into trouble when I am doing so-called observational research."

"Explain what that means."

"Well, when something happens, I tend to watch how people react to it so that I can better understand human behaviour."

"You must seem like some sort of weirdo."

"It's true, I get into trouble sometimes. When I started using observation, some women thought I was flirting, not observing. Now they probably think I'm creepy. But that's the price of observing, combined with aging it looks like you're staring. I avoid wearing trench coats, though." Goldberg gave a broad grin.

"Enough for today. Can I see you again in two days' time?"

"Sure. Remember, I'll ask the questions," Mike replied, also grinning.

Goldberg consulted twice a week. The six weeks in the psychiatric ward unearthed Mike's symptoms. He felt that he was consumed by treachery; he had experienced a loss of meaning and emotional deadness; he relentlessly ruminated on things; displayed explosive anger and was not comfortable with making future plans. There was more than enough evidence for a diagnosis of PTSD to be made.

Van Niekerk visited him once a week. He commented on Mike's Angolan debrief. "It's pretty much as I expected, but we needed confirmation before we committed more resources to the conflict in Angola. We are going to kick some MPLA butt, and when the Cuban's enter the war, we will shove their Havana cigars up their arses."

After six weeks in the psychiatric ward, Mike was ready for discharge. Van Niekerk was there.

"Mike, your Jewish psychologist … What's his name again?"

"It's Goldberg … Dr Solly Goldberg." Mike defensively volunteered the correct name.

"Ah yes, Goldberg. He recommended we give you a temporary assignment that won't interfere with your long-term recovery."

"What the hell? I am leaving the hospital, I'm okay."

"I agree. To me, you seem okay – well, okay despite your crazy edge and hair-trigger temper, but that's always been there. Goldberg says people like you don't have brakes, only breakdowns. I guess it means you need an assignment that will help you apply the brakes.

"Think of yourself in this project as a sleeper. When the time comes, you will be woken up for national priorities. We have arranged a cover for you as a private investigator. That should keep your mind sharp while giving you the space to heal. Your BOSS training will help you as a PI, and the PI experience will come in handy for BOSS sometime in the future. What do you think about that? Mike Hanson PI, hey?"

"But Colonel …"

Van Niekerk corrected him with a smile: "No buts, you're still military property. Of course you'll need to find clients to legitimise this special duty. We've placed a Yellow

Pages advertisement for you. Initially, we'll give you a monthly stipend, enough for living expenses, like food and a car. Then, there's an apartment in Rondebosch you can use for the foreseeable future.

"Mike, always remember, I have a special relationship with you and I regard you as a valuable national asset. Don't let me down. Here are two envelopes containing keys and addresses for the office and the apartment. I will contact you every month to arrange a catch-up, either by phone or in person. BOSS will pay for your consultations with the psychologist for as long as it's beneficial."

Without further ado, Van Niekerk, exited the room.

Mike took a taxi from the hospital to 26 Bowden Road, Observatory, the address of the office. A small flight of concrete stairs led to the entrance. The plaque on the door read:

Michael James Hanssen – Private Investigator

The single-roomed office was equipped with a desk; matching chair; a coffee table; three easy chairs; a filing cabinet; golfball typewriter; and an answering machine, along with its first message. Mike pressed the Play button and heard Van Niekerk's voice.

"Hi Mike, it's Colonel Andre van Niekerk. Welcome to your new job. I will be in touch in one month. Now go and find some cases to solve."

31

WALK WITH THE WISE
AND GROW WISE

May 1973

"So, Doc, do I lie on the coach or may I use a chair?" Mike asked lightheartedly at the first of his therapy sessions at Doctor Solly Goldberg's Mowbray practice.

"I realise you're trying to make a joke of your condition, Mike, and that's fine if it promotes talking about your health. By the way, did you know that jesting's a typical male way of avoiding a subject? You realise that PTSD can result in self-harm? It needs to be given serious consideration, not avoided.

"During your convalescence in hospital you spoke of traumatic events you witnessed and experienced in the army. You agreed that these may have compromised your emotional well-being. I want us to explore your beliefs and emotional condition prior to and during these events.

"Can we do that? With the understanding that psychology's not an exact science. Psychology and its models give us insight into problems. The caveat is everything in a context everything nuanced. Nevertheless, we can still learn from these models, so that we get a better understanding of our emotional landscapes and become the master of our minds, not the slaves."

Mike meekly agreed, not daring to risk another joke.

The therapy sessions with Doc Solly developed from a doctor-patient consultation into an enduring, trusting relationship. Solly took the role of confidante and mentor, and Mike occupied a safe space where he could suspend judgment while engaging ideas at deeper levels.

There were no scared cows; everything was subject to review. Counselling and self-reflection put his being under a mental microscope. In this way, he got in touch with and challenged his innermost thoughts and beliefs. Mental health, culture, religion and relationships were treated like dirty laundry in a washing machine of discussion. They were tossed around, cleaned, dried and when ready for re-use, the process started again.

Mike asked the questions. Solly, in response, presented a range of options to generate discussion on how these may be affecting what Mike felt and believed. Interwoven into the deliberations was the effect of Mike's personal exposures and experiences, from early childhood to his military service.

Solly's first line of enquiry lasted several sessions and was around mental health issues, like intermittent explosive disorder (IED) and post traumatic stress and depression (PTSD).

"We have an agreement, Mike, fire away with your questions about mental health."

"Ok, for argument's sake, let say I am affected by IED and PTSD. Did I get these from my dad?"

"We don't as yet know if there's a physiological link. There's certainly a social link. From what you have told me, your dad struggled with IED and PTSD. He also had bouts of depression.

"The research informs us that exposure to IED tends to be stored in the unconscious of the child, available to be repeated under pressured conditions at any time in the future.

"You have had incidents of uncontrolled rage from age 11, and these gradually became more regular as you experienced military-related pressures. During basic training, you were involved in several fisticuffs. An intelligent person knows that there is no good outcome for either party in a brawl. If you win, you still lose."

Mike protested: "Stop there, Doc. Those were all to do with racism. I had a bee in my bonnet about bigots after having a 'Road to Damascus' experience in Soweto with Andile."

"That partially explains it. More likely, your aggression is an unconscious coping behaviour. I said unconscious, because you're probably not aware of the things driving the behaviour, which makes them much harder to address. As Shakespeare wrote: 'No prisons are more confining than those we know not we are in.'"

"Don't mention prisons," Mike quipped in a high voice, a crazed look coming over his face. "Okay, no more jokes. What about depression? Surely our so-called rational brain will tell us that staring at the wall and doing nothing isn't going to solve our problems? It sounds pretty dumb to me."

"Doing nothing's only an option when one's very ill. Before we even developed language, humans had an innate drive to press on. You may know that some of the most brilliant people suffered from depression, such as philosophers William James and Friedrich Nietzsche, and authors Edgar Allen Poe and William Blake. They weren't dumb; they suffered from a serious disease.

"I wouldn't agree with blaming fathers, either. One of the burdens of a father, and it probably applies to all men, is that they suffer emotional wounds. It's only the severity that varies. Most don't even know they have wounds, but they're wounded. Over millennia, men have been socialised into believing they're measured by the 3 'Ws'. These are 'win', 'war' and 'work'. Then they're wounded by their inability to match up to expectations associated with these.

"Take sport: Just one of the ways a male is indoctrinated into believing that his quest is to be competitive and win everything he can. As you know, there are many competitors and only one winner in a sporting contest. These odds start to ingrain a new issue in the male subconscious – the fear of losing. The fear of not measuring up. That's something males seldom, if ever, share with anyone."

Mike responded dismissively: "That's bullshit. I don't fear losing. If my competitor's better than me and I lose, I lose. That's it."

"Really?" Solly countered with a quizzical look. "Think back to the rugby games you lost. Think of athletics, when you stumbled and lost a place. How about exam results, when the guy you always beat got a better mark than you? Think about the many scuffles you have had. Do you mean to say if you lose, you lose? That's it?"

"Okay, okay, I don't like to lose. In fact, I don't know anyone who likes to lose."

"Sure, I don't either, but you may want to consider seeing things differently and taking a leaf out of Rainer Rilke's book when he claimed: "Our quest's to joyfully accept being defeated by ever larger things.""

Mike said pensively: "Don't know him, and not so sure I can accept joyfully."

"Okay, we can work on that one. Then there's war. If you paid attention during history class, you would remember that there are defeats in battle. Every generation has a war, sometimes several, if you're an American. Your dad had his and you're having yours. For us Israelis, war's a way of life, but I digress.

"So, what belief do men take to war? It's kill or be killed. Easy to say the words, but when you're on the battle field and experience it, like you have, these words take on a new meaning with dire psychological consequences."

"Wars are bloody stupid. They seem inevitable, though, because irresponsible politicians start them, but they're still stupid," Mike said.

"You're probably right. The last 'W' is work. The ingrained belief among men is that they must toil and bring in a harvest. In our era, they must get a job and get promoted. As you know, employment is scarce and promotion is rare. Once again, men end up with mental penalties because they simply can't live up to expectations."

"I don't want a promotion in my PI business," Mike added cheekily.

"Wait a few years, then the need for promotion, in one way or another, will get to you. All men are bitches to these beliefs. Your dad was, and you are, too. The beliefs drive both fear and the capacity for terrible violence in men. They are one of the reasons why there are so many bullies."

Talking about violence and bullies led to revisiting these issues in the military. Mike was struggling to come to terms with man's inhumanity to man. He had witnessed horrific, unjust and cruel behaviour. He, too, had killed fellow human beings.

"Doc, are you saying 'win', 'war' and 'work' are the drivers that make men brutal and evil, which in turn makes them capable of torture?"

"To some extent, yes, but it's not that simple."

To clarify what he called this aberration in human behaviour, he referred to Stanley Milgram's experiment with torture: "Milgram measured the willingness of participants to obey an authority figure who instructed them to perform torturous acts, like administering shocks, which conflicted with their personal conscience.

"Participants were led to believe the shocks were real, and to increase authenticity, actors were used to react in a realistic way. He found that, despite hearing an actor crying out in pain at 150 volts, 82.5% of participants continued administering shocks, in line with instruction, to the maximum lethal 450 volts."

"Doc, this Milgram guy sounds like he should be in the Angolan army."

GOD WILL JUDGE THE ADULTEROUS

Mike didn't have to wait long for his first PI inquiry. The phone call came in the second week. The female caller opened the conversation with: "Do you do surveillance?"

"Hi, who am I speaking to?" Mike replied.

"This is Anne Benton-Smith," she said officiously.

"Hello Mrs Benton-Smith. Yes, I do provide a surveillance service. Would you like to come to the office and tell me more about your needs?"

"Oh no, I couldn't possibly come there. You will have to come to my house."

"That'll be fine. What's your address?"

"275 Brommersvlei Road, Constantia. You can come tomorrow at 9:30am"

"With pleasure. See you then."

Anne Benton- Smith lived in an opulent Constantia home. Mike was greeted by two standard white poodles that resembled shaped topiaries, thanks to their Scandinavian haircuts. They cantered down the pathway to the front gate like show horses performing in a dressage competition. He couldn't help comparing them to the mangy mutts from the Upington location.

She was in her mid-40s, still reasonably attractive, largely thanks to a big budget spent on beauty professionals and products. Mike found it hard not to stereotype her, and he put her in the category of ex-private school, rich, grouchy bitch.

From the moment he walked in until the time he left, she didn't stop complaining. Her tedious tirade included the slowness of the workmen renovating her house, to the lazy gardener and the incompetent maid. Her voice was as irritating as the *skrrreeek* sound of fingernails scratching a chalkboard.

"The country's going downhill at a rapid rate, Mr Hanssen. You can't get good help anymore. I may as well do it all myself. But, I ask you, if we don't employ them, what will the poor devils do? I suppose we must do our bit."

Eventually she came to the point of the meeting. Her philandering husband was cheating on her. Mike's brief was to gather photographic evidence of infidelity and, as she put it: "I am going to make him pay. I will sue him for every last penny. That floozy is not going to get a cent." She told Mike that he would be rewarded handsomely for incriminating evidence.

Her husband, Adrian, worked as a director of a large investment broking firm, with head offices in the centre of Cape Town. Anne Benton-Smith gave him a recent photograph of Adrian, and the first assignment began.

It was not exactly the private investigation work Mike had in mind, but he thought ruefully: It's one of the things us PIs do.

He bought the latest model of camera – a Canon F-1 camera with a shooting speed of nine frames per second, apparently ideal for surveillance work.

The next afternoon at 3pm Mike waited a discreet distance from Adrian Benton-Smith's office. He emerged at 3:30pm, got into his car, drove to the southern suburbs and parked outside the Beaurette apartment block in Derby Road, Kenilworth.

Mike watched and took photos as Adrian discreetly knocked on the door of number 13 on the ground floor. A young lady answered, unwisely standing in the doorway and creating a perfect photo opportunity with her caller. Adrian left the apartment at 5pm and drove home to Constantia.

Mike checked the post boxes. The name on 13 Beaurette was listed as Samantha Rhodes. He wondered if he had enough evidence. Did he need shots of them in more compromising positions?

As was to become his habit, he went back to the office and pondered his next move. The following day, he waited outside Benton-Smith's office. Adrian did not appear, so Mike decided to call on Samantha Rhodes.

"Good afternoon, Ms Rhodes. My name's Joe Bartlett. I am from Statistics South Africa. We're surveying demographics in urban areas like Kenilworth. I wonder, could I ask you a few questions please?"

"How do you do, Mr Bartlett, come in, sit down. What do you need to know?"

Mike entered and sat on a modest, comfortable sofa.

"Firstly, how long have you been staying in these premises?"

"It was a year last month."

"One year." he confirmed writing it down on his form.

"What's the occupancy of this apartment? Do you stay here alone?"

"No, I have a four-year-old daughter."

"Two people, you and your daughter?"

"Yes"

"Two" Mike repeated, writing on his form.

"What's your highest education level?"

"I have a matric. I dropped out of university when I fell pregnant with Ruby."

Mike noted the response on his form. It rang a bell inside the emotional compartment of his brain.

"Would you like a cup of tea, Mr Bartlett?"

Mike declined, thanked her for the interview, and left soon afterwards.

That evening, he confronted a new reality relating to his assignment. He waited a week before phoning Anne Benton- Smith.

"Good morning, Mrs Benton-Smith, it's Mike Hanssen."

"Yes, what have you got for me?"

"Not much, I'm afraid. It's been more than a week and I can't report anything untoward, let alone give you any evidence."

"Well, you must be doing something wrong. Adrian's been so distracted and remote recently. I know there's something going on."

"I am so sorry, Mrs Benton-Smith, but I haven't got anything for you."

"You must keep trying."

"I am afraid that won't be possible. I have a very big assignment starting tomorrow that's going to take all of my time. There's no charge for what I have done. I haven't produced a result."

"I should hope not. Goodbye, Mr Hanssen." With that, she ended the call.

Mike spoke to the dead phone receiver: "Goodbye, bitch. I've no doubt that Adrian enjoys his time with Samantha more than his life with you. I'm not going to spoil it for either one of them."

33

YOU OF LITTLE FAITH

"Doc, how can people kill each other in the name of God when they claim to have the same God?"

"I think I know what you mean. Still, explain a bit more." Solly prompted.

"To me, it's illogical that societies in conflict accuse the other side of committing crimes against God, while they claim God's telling them to kill their opponents. These are people who incidentally believe in the same God. I realise that sounds a little convoluted. I'll try to be a little clearer.

"Okay, opponents are usually from different religions, although in South Africa, people with the same beliefs are clashing and still want to corner divine rights for their side. I'm told God works in strange ways, but murder in God's name is outlandish."

"Mike, its mostly religious extremism that drives the killing, and these people do it either in the service of their culture or sometimes to serve their own crazy ideas, not God. Granted, they claim that their culture or their ideology is the word of God. The way they have interpreted

God's needs drives their hate. Killing others who are not like them becomes a consequence. But, religious conflicts are nothing new.

"The clash of Christian and Islam fundamentalism dates back to the Crusades. They allow the past to define their future, and it's going to carry on for a long, long time. My guess is it's going to get a lot worse before it gets better – if it ever does get better.

"But it's not only different religions: It's ideologies and extremists in the same religion that create sub-cultures, as you find with Sunni and Shi'ite Muslims. You find it among Catholic and protestant Christians. Consider the Irish, who are all Christian. They have been fighting for ages about how their religion should be interpreted."

Mike chipped in: "Well, I find it strange. People claim to be good because they obey the Word of God. Their holy books instruct them not to kill. But then extremists find special circumstances which compel and justify them to kill and commit atrocities in the name of God."

Solly picked up the conversation: "The problem is humans have generally not learned to tolerate cultural differences. In many instances, these differences have been used by extremists to wage war with both sides, believing they are right and doing God's work. Of course it's strange, if you view it rationally, but religion isn't about rationality. It's about faith. To survive, you need to appreciate the sheer strength of some people's irrationality and beliefs. But, mostly it's the extremists with good leadership skills that launch dreadful deeds against people holding a different idea."

"I know, but even if you exclude the role of extremists, it still won't make sense. Religious people, probably without meaning to, contribute by providing a fertile environment that births these extremist monsters."

"Mike, it's not supposed to make sense. Most of us are born into a religion that provides a framework for our culture. If you were born in Israel, you'd probably be Jewish. If born in Bagdad, undoubtedly Muslim. If born in Bloemfontein, you would likely be Christian. Our formative years provide exposure to religion, its structures and holy books. These ingrain a set of beliefs in us. That's usually why we have a willingness to accept things, like God, that cannot be objectively demonstrated."

"You mentioned holy books. Examining the Christian teachings, I find so many instances where they are way out of line with the realities of this day and age. I've written a few down. How about:

"God made everything; is omnipotent and omniscient therefore deeply involved in daily life seeing and hearing everything. God can intervene any time he wants." [50]

"God created man in his likeness, therefore man has dominion over all other life forms. The husband is the head of the wife who will serve and obey him." [51]

---

50 John 4:24
51 Genesis 1:27

"God forbids you lie with a man, as with a woman. That's detestable." [52]

"You may have male and female slaves, but buy them from the nations around you." [53]

"Mike, people need a manual. I am not a Christian. I can't defend their teachings and the sense, or lack of sense, in their writings. I remind you to look at it in a faith context."

"Doc, how come some people are atheists? Why don't they buy into religious faith?"

"I guess these people have taken an exclusively rational approach and aren't satisfied with the evidence that God exists. It doesn't make them right. It's entirely possible that people on both ends of the spectrum, from theist to atheist, offer explanations for the mysteries of life that are too simplistic."

"Doc, you're Jewish. What the hell do you believe? Sorry, *what the hell* sounds a bit extreme. What the heaven? That doesn't sound right either, does it?"

"That's fine, Mike, our concepts of heaven and hell are different from Christians. I believe in the Jewish God, Yahweh. It's a faith-based belief and yes, it's the same God as the Christian and Islamic religions."

"Doc, surely in this era we need a better reason than faith to believe in God and to follow a religion? I realise our knowledge is not complete and possibly never will be,

---

52 Leviticus 18:22
53 Leviticus 25:44

but wouldn't it be sensible to at least accept that many of the claims in holy books have been superseded by new knowledge, and that several others may still be clarified over time? Like, the world certainly didn't start 6 000 years ago. Just think how recently we accepted that dinosaurs roamed the planet long before that.

And I can understand people creating an image of a higher power, like God, before they knew what's known today. They thought the Earth was flat; we were the centre of the universe; the sun revolved around the Earth, and so many other things that in their knowledge-limited context, would lead them to believe it's all organised by a higher power."

"Mike, you realise humans believed in other Gods before this one. Gods like Zeus and Ra served the same purposes as our current God. Over time, people became atheists towards these Gods and dispensed them to the realms of myths before they developed a belief in our more modern one."

"Exactly, then how come they don't consider: 'Oops we were wrong about Ra. Maybe we're wrong again?'"

"Mike, when you're in trouble, you cry out for somebody – whether it's God, your parent or your spouse. I think humans need to believe in something or someone that they can rely on. They need that something to give lasting fulfilment, despite the inevitability of change. Once again, I must remind you that religion's not a logic-based pursuit. If it were, you may as well use Pascal's wager."

"What's that?"

"Pascal's wager is a proposition around the existence of God. Seventeenth century French philosopher Blaise Pascal suggested that humans bet with their lives on whether or not God exists. He went on to argue that if God actually exists, and assuming the infinite gain or loss associated with belief in God or with unbelief, a rational person should live as though God exists and seek to believe in God. If God does not actually exist, such a person will have only a finite loss in this life."

"Doc, that's a blow to sense-making. Pascal aside, my revelation is that I have been living in a bubble – call it a faith bubble, if you like. From inside this bubble, I haven't been able to weigh up whether or not there's a God in the first place. How can you have faith and at the same time question faith? The only way that can be done is to observe from outside the bubble. From this position, I can decide if I'm willing to accept a claim that there's an all-seeing, all-knowing God, and that this God says there's a connecting relationship between good conduct and grace.

"In addition, from outside the bubble, I can ask: Is it plausible that this God watches the violence and atrocities occurring in the world indifferently and that He does not intervene to re-establish the values enshrined in the holy books?

"And ... from outside the bubble I can ask: 'Is it reasonable ... no, is it moral, that people can present an ancient book, claiming it's the word of God, and use this as justification to judge others and at times to condemn others to death?' Others who, incidentally, claim to believe in the same God?

"Doc, I'm not claiming some special insight when I say I find religious irrationality unreasonable and indefensible. I don't buy the light at the end of the tunnel that religious conviction is selling, so I'm not getting back into the bubble. From what I have seen and experienced in the army, being on the outside is going to be lonely. That faith bubble is hermetic and permanently sealed for most people."

Doc Solly answered thoughtfully: "Maybe you will become the new Oscar Wilde. He claimed: 'Religion is like a blind man searching in a black room for a black cat that isn't there and finding it.'"

"Wouldn't mind having his intellect, but let's not take the comparison any further!" Mike replied quickly.

34

THE CONSCIENTIOUS OBJECTOR

March 1975

"I've got a confidential case for you. Can we meet in your office tomorrow morning at 9am? I'll be bringing someone with me." It was the first time that Van Niekerk had made a direct request for PI services.

Van Niekerk arrived with Colonel Piet Stander, who was the officer in charge of Western Province Command and stationed at the Castle in Cape Town.

Van Niekerk made the formal introductions and started proceedings.

"Mike, I'll ask Colonel Stander to explain."

"Thank you, Andre. Well, you see Mike, my son, Braam, is missing. I'd like you to find him. It's a sensitive matter. That's why Colonel van Niekerk suggested I use a PI like you."

"What do you mean by sensitive, Colonel?" Mike enquired.

"I have a strong suspicion that he left home because he doesn't see eye-to-eye with South African government policies. He's not an activist, but over the past years we've noticed significant shifts in his attitudes towards politics."

"What shifts?"

"He's been at UCT for the past six years studying medicine, and his friendship circle, particularly over the past two years, included many executive members of NUSAS.[54] Huh, it was a big mistake sending him to University of Cape Town. It should have been Stellenbosch University."

He added in a lighthearted vein: "I blame it on Doctor-bloody Chis Barnard[55] and his heart transplants. Oh, and Braam was also editor of the *Sax Appeal* rag magazine – another receptacle for radicals.

"He got deferment from doing his military training until he'd finished university. He was due to finish this year, but went missing three weeks ago during a diving expedition in Mozambique. We have contacted the Mozambican authorities. They have no idea where he is. There's a record of him entering the country and then the trail's cold. Neither their police nor hospitals have any record of him."

---

54 The National Union of South African Students (NUSAS) was an important student base force for liberalism in South Africa in the latter part of the last century. Their mottos included "non-racialism" and "non-sexism".

55 Dr Christiaan Neethling Barnard was a South African cardiac surgeon who performed the world›s first successful human-to-human heart transplant

"What do you think happened to him?"

"Worst case scenario? He drowned in Mozambique or was murdered.

Best case? He decided he couldn't go to the army because of his new convictions, and it wasn't on to be a conscientious objector, considering his family tree, so I guess he may have appealed to Frelimo[56] to help him. Heavens knows where he would be in that situation."

"Could I have a list of his friends and their contact details in Cape Town?"

"I have it here." Colonel Stander supplied many more details, but Mike had enough to go on.

He promised to give weekly feedback as Stander departed.

"So what do you think, Mike?" Van Niekerk asked curiously.

"Let me investigate first, Colonel."

"While I'm here, Mike, I have agreed to second you to the local bomb disposal squad. They're short of specialists. Incidents of bomb scares are rapidly increasing. You're one of the best in the business and they could do with a helping hand. It won't blow your cover. As you know, a squad member looks like the Michelin Man in his gear. Expect a few calls."

---

56 The Mozambique Liberation Front (FRELIMO) was a liberation movement founded in 1962 to fight for the independence of the Portuguese Overseas Province of Mozambique.

Mike was called out at least once per week. The struggle was hotting up. More angry blacks and more fearful whites were driving up conflict levels.

Braam Stander's friends were helpful, leaving Mike in no doubt that Braam was an ANC sympathiser and that in all likelihood, he had planned an exit strategy from South Africa to escape military service and possibly help the ANC abroad. Mike made enquiries with Mozambique Airlines. With the right financial inducement, he found out that Braam had boarded a flight to London from Lourenço Marques. He informed Colonel Stander at their first feedback session.

"Please find him, Mike. We want to know that he's okay. That's all." Stander was a mature man and realised that the apple did not always fall close to the tree, and that with Braam, his apple, may have politically fallen a great distance away. He still wanted to know that his son was safe so that he could pacify his own concerns and those of his wife.

Mike phoned Van Niekerk to find out if he had any idea of Andile's whereabouts in London.

"As it turns out, Mike, I have every idea. He's on our payroll."

"But, I thought he was ANC."

"He is, because we want him to be."

Van Niekerk supplied Andile's London address.

The following evening Mike boarded the SAA Boeing 747SP from Cape Town to Heathrow. The London Underground and the connecting bus were simple to work out, and by 12 noon, Mike was standing in Fournier Street in front of Andile's Spitalfields apartment. Andile was out. Mike waited in the nearby Ten Bells pub, fascinated by its history, particularly its association with two victims of Jack the Ripper: Annie Chapman and Mary Kelly.

I wonder if they hired PIs in those days. Maybe I could have helped them, he thought, sipping abundant amounts of ale until Andile arrived home around 5pm.

"Mike, this is a surprise. To what do I owe the pleasure? How long are you staying? We must go out and celebrate!"

As Andile caught his breath, Mike answered.

"Slow down, I've come because I think you can help me find someone. I'm only here for two days. But, that can wait. Can I take you to dinner? Then you can show me something interesting about London. Where do you suggest?"

"Should we go for some typical London food, then, maybe a show with a South African flavour?"

"Lead on, Andile!"

Dinner was as distinctively London as it could get – bangers and mash. The conversation was less so, with Mike diving straight into controversy.

"Andile, once again I am confused about you. Who do you really work for? When I saw you in Johannesburg, you gave me a sob story about political oppression. I was impressed when you told me you were escaping the political injustice in South Africa. My latest information informs me you're on BOSS's payroll. To me, you don't give a damn, you don't care. You've become a typical impimpi."

"Stuff you, Mike! How can you call me an impimpi? That's a traitor. Who am I a traitor to? Besides, what am I a traitor to? I'm not an impimpi. I'm a mercenary. To me, it's a job.

"Care? I do care, oh yes I fucking care. It's my dad who died of TB because your kind marginalised him like a third-class piece of shit. It's my mum who had to run off to Maseru to find a place where she could be with the man she loved – a white man, Mike, never forget it was a white man.

"I was the one who couldn't go to a decent high school, I couldn't go to university, I wasn't allowed to buy a house, and I couldn't stay in a decent suburb.

"So, fuck you, Mike. I care for my kind. My comrades are radicalised because of your government's actions. The boere think they can stop us from aspiring to freedom through harsh laws and penalties to restrict our movement. In the short term, they may control our bodies, but they will never rule our minds. We will prevail.

"However, despite my shared commitment to the struggle, I'm not stupid. I know that when the Day of Judgment comes; when the ANC rules South Africa; there will only be a place for one angel on top of the Christmas tree. There's only one person in the world with the gravitas to sit on top of the South African Christmas tree, Mike. Nelson Mandela is our angel. No, not just our angel, he's our saint. He applied long ago and got that position hands down.

"Mike, you watch, when the ANC takes over, most of the comrades and cadres will shout about democracy and liberty while thinking about money. Sure, there will be the ones who will sacrifice themselves and live according to the Freedom Charter, but I would guess that many will not. They will become bitches of the bucks. Oh yes, and its good old greed again. No different from any revolution, the spoils go to the victors, or should I say the leaders of the victors. The masses won't get it.

"You'll see. When the time comes, ANC cronies will head up all state institutions. In most instances, they will rip them off and watch them crumble while pontificating about their hard-fought freedom. They've learned to talk the talk, but very few will walk the walk.

"You will see black entrepreneurs emerge, making money because of their struggle credentials and the colour of their skin. Who do you think will get the tenders? Guess. Finally, who will run the municipalities, the provinces and the national government? Have another guess, and do you know what the priority for the majority of these governments will be? Making money, lots of money, for themselves.

"At the moment there's a black against white struggle. It's about racism. When it's over, the new struggle will be between the rich and the poor. It will be about class. So, cash in while you can, I say, and that's what I decided to do and have been doing for some time. I am paying it forward to myself.

"There's no way when the day of judgement comes that I am going to get the job of angel, entrepreneur or head of a corporation. So, I'll take it now and I am taking it from your stupid tribe. It's never been at the expense of my kind. I am ANC to the core. I give the boere just enough information in the monthly envelope to keep them happy. They hear how the ANC feels about Mandela and Tambo. They're informed about Mbeki's movements. So what? They would never attack him anyway.

"I was never Snake van Niekerk's bitch. He was mine. He is so caught up by the illusion of white supremacy that it makes him easy to outwit. And you, Mike? Are you a traitor? Are you an impimpi? Your tribe looked after you. When are you going to betray them? When will you sell them down the river?

"So far, your government has erected metaphoric walls around white people to protect them. Whether it's their personal safety, jobs or even trading – you have boards for everything – wheat, maize, sugar ... When the ANC assumes power, they will tear those walls down."

Andile slowed down just long enough for Mike to slip in a comment: "Shit, Andile you're giving a helluva speech. Maybe you should become a politician?"

Andile continued: "Oh stuff it, it doesn't matter. Why should we quarrel? Let me show you some of London, like Piccadilly Circus and Soho!"

A tube ride later, they were standing in front of Raymond's Revue Bar. London was in the death throes of winter, embracing the joy of chestnut-roasting vendors and streetside hawkers of winter wear. They looked up at the rotating lights of the billboard that flashed through the lingering London fog.

Now starring: South Africa's sensational stripper, Glenda Kemp, and Oupa

"Who's she?" Mike asked.

"Wait and see. Better still, watch and see."

"And Oupa? That's an old man in South Africa. Is she going to strip with an old man, or for old men?"

"Mike, patience, wait!"

As they passed the tough-looking bouncer, Mike glanced down the road to Ronnie Scott's Jazz club and thanked his lucky stars that he about to enjoy a strip show and not a night of jazz.

They shuffled through the smoky, male-dominated venue and found a table close to the stage. Without them ordering it, the waiter put a bottle of champagne and two glasses on their table. Mike was about to refuse when Andile packed up laughing.

"You're so backward. You can't refuse. They charge a shitload for the champagne, that's the entry fee. Just don't order more."

The lights dimmed as Marvin Gaye's sexy *Let's Get it On* played.

Mike whispered: "Will we see it all? You know … everything? Or does she end up wearing a g-string?"

The man seated behind them answered loudly: "She'd better, or we'll shove the champagne bottle up the manager's arse."

Glenda Kemp, the sexy ex-South African school teacher, made her appearance on stage. Afterwards, Mike commented that the show was good and added that the manager's backside was safe." He did admit to getting a fright when Glenda revealed Oupa, her python. The snake had wrapped around her to the raunchy sound of Diana Ross singing "*Someday we will be together*".

As they walked out, Andile asked: "What's up with you? When Oupa made an entrance, it was as if you saw a ghost."

"I thought I did. It's a private joke. I may have herpeto-phobia," Mike replied.

"Big word for a fear of snakes. Aren't you a South African? We kill snakes. Man up!"

They chatted as they surfed the sex shops. Mike's eyes were on stalks as he noted the casual British approach to sex toys.

"Why are all the big dildos black?" Mike asked.

"You still need to ask? Are you a South African, white boy?"

Mike asked about Braam Stander.

"Yup, he's here, want to meet him? He helps at the AAM." answered Andile.

"Oh hell, that will go down well back home. Army colonel's son leaves country, joins Peter Hain and stops Springbok rugby tour."

The next day, Mike was introduced to Braam.

"I don't want to embarrass my folks. I guess it's fine if you can find a way of telling them without it hurting them.

They're my folks and I love them, but I just don't think like them anymore."

"Your dad's a mature man. I don't think it'll be so hard, and I am sure both your dad and mum would like to hear from you, or at least to hear that you're okay."

As Mike was about to leave, Peter Hain entered and Andile introduced Mike.

"I recognise the accent. Are you here to join us or to infiltrate us, Mike?" Hain said, beaming.

"I won't be doing either at this stage." Mike replied.

He considered seizing the opportunity to ask Hain if he would back off ruining South Africa's rugby tours, but dismissed the thought.

Mike and Andile spent the day and evening together, talking into the wee hours of the morning in Andile's apartment. Mike had a few beers while Andile had maintained his marijuana habit claiming: "It's only about twice a week, besides the shit here's not as good as the stuff grown in the Eastern Cape. However, I occasionally try a few lines of the white stuff. That's high quality. Want to join me?"

Mike politely declined and Andile continued, unperturbed. Outside of the movies, it was the first time he had seen anyone snort cocaine. That's a tad too far for me, he thought.

The following afternoon, Mike caught the tube to Heathrow for his flight back to Cape Town. As he left, Andile warned him: "You must know that if you're working for BOSS, they're watching you. Those guys are scary, and the scariest is Van Niekerk. You have double trouble, though. The ANC's also watching you."

"Why would the ANC be interested in me?"

"What? Grow up. How about because you're one of the best explosives experts in the country? What about: You're the guy that caused mayhem in Angola? These things don't go unnoticed by the ANC."

"How do they know about me and Angola?"

"For a PI, you ask some dumb questions. The ANC put a mole in the psychiatric ward of Wynberg Military Hospital. He's in a perfect position to hear everything. I even think you know him.

Here's my phone number at the apartment in case you need to get hold of me in future. You're the only one in South Africa who will have it. My mum has it, but she lives among a bunch of ANC exiles on the outskirts of Maseru. By the way, did she ever get hold of you?"

"No, I haven't seen her since school days."

"Oh well, she asked about you some time ago, before I left SA. She sounded quite anxious at the time, but it's probably not important anymore if it's waited this long."

It was time to leave.

Mike hoped to have a good sleep on the overnight flight to Cape Town. He didn't. The snippets of slumber were invaded by technicolour dreams. This time, they featured Glenda Kemp stripping with a snake, but it wasn't Oupa. Instead it was the now familiar reptile that haunted Mike. It was apparent in the dream that the sadistic serpent was leading Glenda, and not the other way around.

35

You Have Captivated
My Heart

April 1975

"Doc, is it possible that the world's more random and more chaotic than we'd like to think?"

"You will have to give me more than that to go on."

"Well, if we look around, we see stable structures and cycles, but I have a feeling this may be a false perception. For example, until a few centuries ago, when people looked at their immediate surrounds, they thought the Earth was flat, but as they gained a greater perspective, they worked out that it was round."

"I see what you mean. I agree stability's an illusion created by the shortness of our lives. Even our short lives won't be lived in a straight line. Our reality will be multi-layered, granular and mostly unpredictable. Sudden changes occur for all of us. I like the example of the Christmas turkey. It's got no idea that the farmer has arrived with a machete instead of the meal it has got used to receiving every day of its life. But, what are you leading up to?"

"No, I'm not leading to anything, I'm simply contemplating randomness and wondering if the world has limited or infinite possibilities. So far, I have experienced more ambiguity, confounding variables and paradoxes than I believed possible."

"That's heavy. Do you realise how much you've changed since your stint in hospital?"

"I guess so. I've been trying to reinvent myself since Angola. It's challenging because it means finding new ways of thinking and of letting go of some of the old ways. So far, I've only managed to become more sceptical. Despite what they tried to teach us in army basics, I don't believe in Illuminati-type global conspiracies which supposedly cause events through secret planning. So when things happen, I would rather assign them to randomness or to a perplexing riddle than to a global conspiracy. But paradoxically, on a limited scale, I accept that there are groups, like the Broederbond[57], that conspire and plan."

How would you describe your current philosophy?"

"Oh heck, it's a moving feast. I guess I'm moving towards an existential philosophy at the moment. I currently think

---

57 The Broederbond was a secret, exclusively male,
    Afrikaner Calvinist organisation in South Africa dedicated
    to the advancement of Afrikaner interests. It was largely
    responsible for the metastasizing of apartheid. It was
    founded in 1918 and its influence within South Africa could be
    compared to that of masons in Freemason conspiracy theories.

many aspects of life will always be a mystery. I also believe there is no meaning to life itself. On the other hand, I feel that meaning can be constructed by individuals themselves."

"You certainly have put a question mark on faith and meaning!"

"I guess I have, but there's another question I want to pose that rivals the illogic of religious faith. It's around the whole issue of love. What's the difference between falling in love and loving? In the male context, of course."

"It's about time you answered your own questions. What's your view?"

Mike suggested: "Is it okay to say falling in love is about romantic love, and that's the initial boundaryless attraction we feel for another?"

"That's fair. How about falling in love and its role in a relationship?"

"No, it's your turn again, Doc. You answer it."

Solly continued; "Falling in love starts a relationship on a good footing because you're willing to compromise on so many levels when you're romantically inclined. But, seeing that you wanted a male context, let me warn you about some typical male pitfalls.

"You see, when men fall into romantic love, they try to impress the one they think's the magical other. Part of impressing is giving the other disproportionate psychological power. The main problem, though, is that men assume they have a special contract with the person without checking its veracity. In an attempt to make their one-sided pact come true, they try to convince the other that they are someone they aren't.

"At this stage, the woman possesses power she did not ask for. The man senses the imbalance and applies instinctive possessive behaviour based on a fear of losing her. Sadly, the possessiveness can lead to the female rejecting him. In this case, he feels like a victim and expresses reactive grief in the form of anger and disappointment. Then he avoids her. In summary, men impress, possess and avoid."

"I can relate to that, Doc. Surely not all men are as stupid as I was."

"Not all, only the archetypes. Remember, everything's nuanced, and you weren't stupid."

"Okay, not stupid, just blind?"

Solly carried on "The roots of the old saying: 'Love is blind' are in romantic love, because we're so willing to overlook the obvious."

"Doc, why do we fall in love?"

"You're kidding me."

"Sort of, but I want to hear it from you."

"Fine, we fall in love because we have nostalgia for connection. Of course, we also want a mate and to pro-create."

"And then?"

"Didn't your mum tell you these things?"

"Just carry on."

"We look for and usually find a person who we think is a good match, and then the falling-in-romantic-love part starts."

"What then?"

"Mrs Hanssen, what did you teach your boy?" Solly looked skywards, appealing with his hands outstretched.

"Just keep going. I want to hear your version."

"Okay, very soon in the relationship, we project our emotional baggage on to the other, and them on to us. Now, because there can never be a perfect match, the gaps between what we projected and our reality start to widen, creating inevitable conflict. If these gaps are not brought to the surface and clarified while we're still in romantic love, there will inevitably be some sort of breakdown in the relationship later on not, necessarily a break up."

"I guess if I tried to see Maddy in the light of what you have just said, I imagine she felt I didn't live up to her projection of a stable future provider that was going to become an eminent member of society, like a doctor. Sadly, she's not around to confirm or deny my assumption."

Solly replied: "That must be a possibility. What were your projections on her?"

"Mine were clearer. Maddy failed to live up to my projection of an exclusive lover; faithful to the feeling of romantic love and willing to work through mishaps. When it ended, I felt betrayed, exiled, angry and disappointed."

"What do you think Maddy felt?"

"That's a big ask, She probably felt disappointed in me for behaving like a victim, and relief that she had another option."

"Doc, you know I made a naïve covenant to her many years ago. I think it's time I lifted the burden for me and for her. Not that she feels it anymore!"

"Okay, do you have any suggestions on what a love covenant should be based on?"

"I think I will start with accepting that all aspects of life are competitive, therefore no beating up people that steal my girlfriend!" he volunteered with a smile.

"That's a good start, but life's messy and you might find your suggestion hard to sustain. Remember, relationship behaviours are hardwired in our nature. Everyone projects their emotional baggage on to others, and everyone transfers old relationship wounds on to their new relationships. Awareness of your own and the other person's projections is a good start to a covenant."

Solly continued: "I can assure you there are no magical others. There are only strangers with whom you may or may not have similar connections. That does not rule out developing closer connections. Despite gaps, relationships don't have to implode. We can choose to mind the gaps, fill the gaps and in so doing, grow relationships beyond romantic love."

"Doc, I'm not sure I want to go beyond romantic love. One of my best memories is that oomph that came with romantic love, and how it was stoked by inexhaustible amounts of sex."

"Mmmm, the sex need not stop, but the nature of the relationship will change. When the energy associated with romantic love's depleted or near depleted, it may be too late to create a sustainable love relationship if the gaps are too wide. If the gaps are substantial, sex will fly out of the window anyway.

Mike, be warned: Many people develop a dangerous dependence or obsession with romantic love. As a result, they will, in all likelihood, repeat cycles of dissonance as they discover that the magical other does not fit their projections."

Despite the intellectual authority of Doc Solly's advice, the penny did not drop for Mike. Then again, he did not have his therapist's psychological capital.

"Doc, a lot of your stuff sounds good, and some seems like psycho mumbo-jumbo made up of big university words that do not consider the big feelings of real life. Maybe I don't want to be a clinician with an antiseptic relationship. Perhaps there will be times when I simply want to be struck down by a romantic virus.

"Sure, I didn't get it right with Maddy and now I understand there's no magical other. But, I still look forward to plain old attraction; being captivated by another; going with the crazy edge of passion; showing my cards; wanting the other to be exclusively with me; competing for what I want, trying to outshine opposition and being mesmerised by the excitement of being with the object of my desire even if, sometimes, it's chasing forbidden fruit.

The good doctor sighed, "Once you lose beauty or status, which happens to us all eventually, then you will count on loving relationships, not the excitement of romance.

Oh hell, so much for a doctorate in psychology. Still, we're making progress, but instinct needs to be balanced with reason. Where that balancing point is becomes the next challenge. We will unconsciously put our burdens on others, but reason must surface so that we release them of our baggage."

"Doc, you haven't said much about the female perspective."

"I don't have female clients and you asked me to talk within a male context. I know most men will say you will never understand women. I agree with them. From personal experience, I have learned three important things that are worth sharing. The first is: If the object of your affection starts to make excuses, like she is too tired or too busy to meet, it's time to pack up. The chances are there is someone else in her orbit. Come to think of it, you can throw headaches in there, too. The second is: If you get dumped, and you will; don't indulge the feelings of rejection, anger and disappointment for too long. If she comes back, and that's unlikely, it will be because you got over the self-indulgence and showed composure and grace. It won't hurt if you acquired wealth as well," he added, beaming. "Oh, by the way, if you hitch up again, you won't be able to revert to how you were. The only way it will work is to find a new normal.

The third, especially with your background: Don't fall for a femme fatale."

"Is that some sort of female spider?"

"Sort of, but worse. The femme fatale's a mysterious and seductive woman who charms and ensnares her lovers into dangerous situations. Her strongest feminine wile is her sexual allure."

"Sounds like the kind of girl I'd like to meet." Mike felt like he was in a healthier emotional space and better equipped for new collisions with romantic love.

They came, all filled with promise and highly satisfying. All were ephemeral, and none had the negative conclusion he had experienced with Maddy.

36

THE FORBIDDEN FRUIT

May 1976

Lesley Simson, personal assistant to Tom Roberts, Managing Director of Hudson and Hopkins, called to ask Mike if he would consult with Mr Roberts on a delicate matter of suspected industrial espionage. The appointment was set for Tuesday morning, 10am. Hudson and Hopkins was a global player in the fast-moving consumer goods market.

Mike was, as usual, on time – actually, five minutes early. The army had taught him that arriving at the appointed time was already late. Despite his early arrival, he waited an additional 10 minutes in Robert's reception area with nothing better to do than absorb PA Lesley's presence.

Lesley wasn't the type of woman who turned heads. That didn't mean she wasn't attractive. She was. Her looks weren't just captivating, they were intoxicating. The more one engaged with them, the greater their effect. Her body shape was commonly considered rubenesque; ample breasts and widish hips. In the limited time he had at the reception, she displayed a cheeky, flirtatious disposition.

Roberts was late, but given the circumstances in the reception area, he had arrived too soon.

Hudson and Hopkins made fast-moving consumer goods for supermarkets, ranging from household cleaners to innovative food products. The case hinged around Robert's concern that over the past two years, their competitors had been beating them to market with similar product innovations at slightly better prices.

Roberts exclaimed: "There's no way their research and development could be coming up with this stuff. Something's going on. Someone's selling us down the river. Can you help us?"

Mike replied: "What did you have in mind?"

"That's the problem. It's no good investigating the supermarkets. They won't know. How about snooping around the competitors?"

"That's an idea, but unless I get a job with them, I will have limited access. It's probably best to start here and to try to identify the source – assuming there is a source."

"That sounds fine, but how will you be able to move around here without spooking the staff or the perpetrator?"

"I'll get back to you with a proposal."

That evening's administration session at his office was dedicated to formulating a plan for finding Hudson and Hopkins's spy.

Mike phoned the next morning.

"Miss Simson, could I have an appointment with Mr Roberts, please?"

"I can arrange that for you, please call me Lesley. Can you make Friday morning at 10.30am, after the coffee break?"

"That sounds great," he replied, and then impulsively threw in: "Is the coffee break at 10? Would you like to join me for coffee?"

"I can do that, but you will have to join me in our canteen. Is that okay?"

"It's okay, see you at 10."

Hanssen, what are you doing? he thought.

The coffee was good, and the company was great.

His proposal to Roberts drew immediate approval.

Essentially, Mike would pose as a newly-appointed staff member from the company's Australian office who was visiting their South African agency for two weeks in order to familiarise himself with the South African systems.

He liked the idea of practising his Australian accent. It was even more attractive when he considered the prospect of coffee breaks with Lesley.

Roberts ended the meeting by suggesting that he start the following Monday. He would post a notice on all company noticeboards. Lesley would arrange temporary office accommodation for the duration.

He arrived at Hudson and Hopkins at 8am wearing his only suit. Lesley gave him a tour of the premises and introduced him to the department heads.

Oh my word, she's stunning, he thought as they navigated the building.

For the following two weeks, Mike systematically ruled out options, whittling his list down to two suspects: Patricia Westwood from Research and Development, and Lindsay Nel from Accounts. Patricia worked with the creation of new products, and Lindsay with costing them. Both had opportunity, but which one had motive?

Mike favoured Lindsay. According to Lesley, he had been in the same job for the past 10 years and had twice been overlooked for promotion.

Could Lindsay have set up a lucrative deal with the opposition? If he had, where was the evidence? Mike confided in Roberts about his suspicions. They deliberated and Roberts made the call. Lindsay would be called in and questioned.

It wasn't long before he confessed. Roberts showed no mercy. He was horrified at the treachery and betrayal. The police were summoned and Lindsay had the book thrown at him. He was eventually charged with commercial espionage, and the unlawful acquisition of critical technologies for competitive advantage. Roberts immediately sought an injunction against his competitors to stop any further use of product formulations that reflected the competitive advantages of Hudson and Hopkins.

Over the period of the investigation, daily coffee in the canteen became a much-anticipated event. The few occasions that Lesley had not been there even affected the taste of the coffee.

At the final coffee break before his assignment ended, Lesley spoke about her lack of fitness and expressed the desire to start running again.

"Would you like to accompany me on a run this evening?" she asked Mike.

"Only if we have a glass of wine afterwards," came the knee-jerk reply.

"Of course I would, but it may be awkward."

"What do you mean?"

"After work hours, we won't be under the cover of a company canteen."

"Okay, you're losing me. What's going on?"

"Mike, I'm classified as coloured; you're not allowed to date me!"

"Oh shit, will it be alright if we run at a respectable distance from each other? Mike joked. "Okay, not funny. I'm not giving up easily. Can we run and then have the drink at my apartment in Rondebosch?"

She gave a sassy smile. "That can be done. How about 5:30pm at Rhodes Memorial? Do you have a servant's entrance to your apartment?"

"That's as unfunny as my comment," Mike replied.

The run was pleasant, but only as a prelude to the drink. Mike had a bottle of pinot noir chilled in the fridge, accompanied by salted cashew nuts.

The evening was spent talking. Any advances Mike made were gently set aside with a tempting: "You have to wait."

He did wait, but not for long. That night started a series of secret liaisons scheduled for Thursday nights.

The next Thursday, they had their run and met at the apartment. The plan was to enter separately, a precaution against being arrested in contravention of the Immorality Act. But, the fear of arrest paled into insignificance next to the eagerness for intimacy.

Mike arranged a solitary red rose, chilled pinot noir and a sumptuous spread of cashew nuts and takeaways.

"Oh heavens, she's gorgeous." The words circled in his mind, like wooden horses on a carousel, as he surveyed her during idle conversation.

"You realise you're not my exactly my type. I prefer bigger tits," he ventured mischievously as his mind capitulated to his carnal cravings.

Mike would soon learn she was up to the challenge. She stood up from the sofa to deposit her empty dinner plate into the sink. The plate went down and her top went up. She raised it as if she was flashing at a sport stadium. Her boobs hung free on her naked chest.

"Are these big enough?" she asked with teasing, downcast eyes.

He was floored, speechless. That round belonged to her. They were certainly big enough and they were beautiful.

She pulled her top down.

"Aw no, no not down, up." Mike exclaimed hastily, almost pleading.

The top went up and off as she nestled up to him.

His T-shirt followed her top's journey. Flesh met flesh as she pressed her soft breasts into his chest.

"I still have my period," she volunteered coyly.

"It doesn't bother me, and you?" he asked.

"No, it's nearly over anyway."

As he slowly undressed her, his eyes fixed on her emerging nudity, taking delight in her every detail: Her inviting smoky eyes; luscious lips; a figure that poured into shapely curves; soft, supple back; bounteous breasts; big, brown nipples; v-shaped pubic hair; and ample arse. He traced every inch of her with his fingertips, and then smothered her with kisses upon kisses, indulging parts that moments earlier were privileged by underwear.

His lips found hers.

Their eyes met. She looked intoxicated with longing. Her eyes widened, and then narrowed as she gave a slight gasp at their moment of merging. Her mouth tasted like the wine, and the wine like her mouth, as they continually toasted their carnality.

At times, they were quiet, letting desire deepen with their calm. At times they spoke, sharing their pleasures, perceptions and erogenous zones. He caressed her recently, revealed erotic regions that took him to the edge countless times, only to recede and create a new sensuous series.

Hours later, they fell off of each other, sweating and exhausted. He observed her nakedness. Even in his post-passion melancholy state, as blood started to make its way back to his brain, she still looked desirably erotic yet elegant.

An appealing combination, he thought. No, she wasn't a head turner, but she was perfectly imperfect. Not light, not dark a different colour, like pinot noir.

He wanted more. He wanted her to stay. She had to get back to her family home. At the door, they took hands. He looked deep into her misty eyes: "You realise I can never have coffee with you again without mentally undressing you."

She smiled provocatively, lifting her eyebrows twice in quick succession.

The weekly amorous appointments ticked by and the run was soon excluded from the schedule. Seeing Lesley was like eating forbidden fruit. It was illegal and immoral, as well as exotic and enticing. He gave her the nickname GDL. She was a Gorgeous Dark Lady.

Long, languishing nights were spent in exquisitely enjoyable situations. There were always roses, wine, take-away foods, the odd gift and candle-lit bubble baths, flirtatiously providing the hors d'oeuvres to the main course – her bountiful body.

Her lovemaking was natural, curious and animalistic. She started with a kittenish come-hither smile to lure him. Once he was secured, she progressed to predator mode as hormones hijacked her brain functions. Her mind combined alertness and fuzziness; her need to be touched increased; her heart beat elevated; her breath became a shallow panting; her conversation became erotic and the part that felt empty with desire built up moisture while it swelled and pulsated; and her whole body starting screaming: YES.

The thought of her had him in a state of perpetual desire. Comparing her lovemaking with anyone else was like comparing the Monte Carlo Grand Prix to any other foreseeable Formula One races: It was a better environment; a more exciting unpredictable track that was full of surprises; it needing constant gear changes, acceleration then slowing; and had no repetition of laps.

During recess times, they would talk and tease as he cupped her buttocks, then her breasts. He told her about visiting Soho, seeing Glenda Kemp and about the sex shops.

"I couldn't believe the huge dildos! They don't do much for a guy's self-esteem." Mike volunteered.

"They're useful." Lesley replied.

"Have you tried one?"

"Of course, but I don't like those huge ones. Besides, they're hard to conceal. Do you want to see how they work?"

"Sure, are you going to whip one out of somewhere, like a magician?"

"Sort of"

"She opened her purse and removed a small, white, plastic instrument reminiscent of, but slightly thinner than, a lipstick."

"You want to see how it works?" she asked.

"Okay, I'm game."

"You sure you can handle this? You won't get jealous?"

"Me? Of that? Maybe if it was one of those huge multicoloured ones. No, no ways, go for it."

It gave a slight buzz as she flicked the tiny switch and directed the pointed end to her clitoris.

"This doesn't always result in a climax, but it's more reliable than a man."

"Now I feel great. Thanks for sharing that."

In a few moments, she started writhing. He watched as she lay next to him, not knowing whether to give her tacit support by hugging her, whether to masturbate, or to read a book. Thankfully, it was over in 10 minutes, her climax announced by familiar orgasm sounds. A panting *hhhh, hhhh,* was followed by a moaning *aaaah, aaaah,* and finally a louder *OOOHH, OOOHH.*

She looked at him with that dreamy post-coital look: "You okay?" she asked in low voice.

"I guess so, if okay means feeling a bit like a voyeur and a tad like a spare part, but you seemed fine." he said, bemused.

"Were you faking?" he asked, trying to make light of the situation.

"Afraid not. Now it's your turn. I'm sure you can beat that." She drew him towards her.

"Where do I put it?" he said mischievously, glaring menacingly at her little pale instrument of pleasure."

"I am putting it away. No more gadgets. Now you!"

Enthusiastic for her, as usual, he complied, happy to take on the little white competitor for size, but with nagging doubts about his ability to match its efficacy.

They held meetings between their Thursday assignations. It only took a quick phone call to arrange a rendezvous in a local supermarket during a lunch time, or after work. Their get-togethers were passed off as coincidental while they ambled down aisles filling their baskets. Frivolous double talk disguised their intimacy from legitimate shoppers, while creating suggestion and unspoken possibilities for them. His level of arousal was amplified as his nose picked up hints of her Chanel fragrance wafting behind her. As if her scent wasn't enough, she would deliberately cause a lascivious rush by the sensual way she selected and scrutinised fruit with suggestive hand and eye movements. Mike often wondered if a double penalty would be imposed should he surrender to his desire in the supermarket. He could imagine the magistrate pronouncing his sentence: "You are guilty of immorality and indecent acts in a supermarket. You are sentenced to life in prison!" It may be worth it, he thought wickedly.

The best meetings were at coffee shops, where they would treat the others' presence as a surprise. Mike was very daring, believing that the best disguise was doing things in plain sight. He would attempt to put her on the spot in a matter-of-fact tone, with questions like: "What colour panties are you wearing?" Her responses would invariably more that match his adventurous approach: "I'm not wearing any. I took them off, too damp in the middle."

But, with passing months, the secrecy around their meetings became palpable. They knew they needed to remain anonymous. Her conversation often drifted with concern to the futility of their relationship and the inevitability of a break-up, as she looked toward having a permanent partner, not an illegal lover. A shroud of sadness stifled his soul whenever his mind confronted the prospect of losing exclusivity. Even the idea of her morphing into a friend with benefits was undesirable to Mike.

From then onwards, whenever she mentioned the possibility of another, it had a temporary negative effect on his libido, like having an "off" night. His interest invariably recovered, but his regret didn't. He berated himself for his vulnerability. He had fallen for this woman. He wouldn't share her and didn't want to face the prospect of losing her.

He wondered if their lingering lovemaking was his subconscious attempt to compensate for contributing none of the other benefits of a relationship: No holding hands in the movies, no romantic dinners, no long walks, no surprise outings, and no holidays. The haunting questions persisted: Am I trying too hard? Am I trapping her in a life of clandestine liaison? Was it the transience that was giving the moments with her their exquisite edge?

He tried a change of scenery to modify the momentum. Several Thursdays at the plush Vineyard Hotel were fun, but they didn't materially change what seemed to be an impossible situation.

He concluded that the only light at the end of the tunnel was for them to leave the country. When he called to see her for coffee during the week, she couldn't make the appointment and explained that she was busy. At that moment, he didn't recall Doc Solly's astute advice on women.

He planned to discuss a move to London at their Thursday Vineyard rendezvous. The thought of living in London didn't faze him. Life without her did. He contemplated: Why didn't I think of it before? I have a secret stash. We could see Andile, I could get work as a PI. Who knows, I could be the next Sherlock Holmes, or better still, the first Mike Hanssen!

He checked the calendar. Thursday would be 15 November 1976. They had been seeing each other since May, except for a short stint when he was summoned to the Soweto uprising.

37

THE WALLS OF JERICHO

14ᵗʰ June 1976

Van Niekerk sounded anxious when Mike answered the call. "Mike, I need you to come to Pretoria today. I have arranged a military flight from Ysterplaat Airbase at 12 noon. Shit's going down and we need additional bomb disposal members."

He was waiting for Mike at the Waterkloof Military Airbase. They drove off in a military vehicle to the BOSS headquarters in Pretoria.

Van Niekerk explained: "We're reliably informed that there will be a series of mass action protests[58] led by high

---

58 Black high school students in Soweto protested against the Afrikaans Medium Decree of 1974, which forced all black schools to use Afrikaans and English in a 50-50 mix as languages of instruction. English would be the medium of instruction for general science and practical subjects (homecraft, needlework, woodwork, metalwork, art, agricultural science). Indigenous languages would only be used for religion instruction, music, and physical culture.

school students in Soweto on the 16th. The reason they give is the introduction of Afrikaans as medium of instruction in their schools. You and I know that's crap. These kids are manipulated by other forces that want to overthrow the government.

"We've had one strike at the Orlando West School, which nearly turned ugly. Our concern is that ANC cadres might use the chaos to plant bombs and to start some kind of general insurrection, spreading unrest throughout the country."

Mike stayed at Van Niekerk's house until the early hours of the 16th June, when he joined a unit of the bomb squad. They drove in unmarked cars and parked a few hundred metres from the Orlando Stadium.

A short while later, 20 000 students started their protest walk from their schools to the stadium. The protest was planned by the Soweto Students' Representative Council's Action Committee, with support from the Black Consciousness Movement.

The students had hardly begun their march when they found that the police had barricaded the road along the intended route. The leader of the action committee asked the crowd not to provoke the police, and the march continued on another route, eventually ending up near Orlando High School, where they were confronted by a police patrol. Students sang and waved placards with slogans: "Down with Afrikaans", "Viva Azania" and "If we must do Afrikaans, Vorster must do Zulu".

Some of the children started throwing stones at the patrol. Colonel Kleingeld fired the first shot. He drew his handgun and pulled the trigger, causing panic and chaos. Students started screaming and running. More gunshots were fired. Police unleashed their dogs on the protesters.

The crowds reacted by stoning them. The police in turn shot teargas and live bullets at the children. It was as if a fog had descended around them, reminding Mike of his trip to London, where he had witnessed a London fog for the first time. In this Soweto fog, people were not cloaked in a fine watery mist, but a toxic shroud that attacked mucous membranes and caused their eyes to stream and bronchial tubes to constrict. Those who had them, held handkerchiefs to their mouth and nose. The police had donned gas masks, which made them immune to the deadly gas, while giving them an eerie anonymity. Twenty-three people died on the first day.

Mike watched through gunfire smoke and teargas as a mother carried her dead child away from the carnage across the road. Her daughter could not have been older than 12. She held one of her daughter's shoes in her right hand, the other still hanging loosely from the limp girl's foot.

He sat with his bomb disposal team, thinking and anguishing: What kind of hold does my society have on me that I am immobilised in this vehicle while my fellow human beings are being gased and mowed down in front of me? When did I become this way?

Black anger grew as the news spread and violence increased. Bomb threats poured in. The ratio of hoaxes to actual bombs, usually 5:1, stood at 10:1. The increase was an insurrection tactic to keep the authorities busy and the population scared. The situation was dangerous. Due to the high call-out incidence, many of the bombs had to be detonated at the closest safe spot without causing any harm or injury.

Hospitals and emergency clinics were swamped with injured and bloody children. The police requested that the hospital provide a list of all victims with bullet wounds. The hospital administrator passed on this request to the doctors, but the doctors refused to create the list and recorded bullet wounds as abscesses.

About 1 500 heavily-armed police officers were deployed to Soweto on 17 June. They drove in armoured vehicles while helicopters monitored the area from the sky.

The violence died down on 18 June. By then, 700 people were dead and thousands were wounded.

That final night, Mike and Van Niekerk had a dinner together before Mike's flight back to Cape Town.

"Mike, they're barbarians. They stoned Dr Melville Edelstein to death. That man devoted his life to social welfare among blacks. He was left with a sign around his neck proclaiming: 'Beware Afrikaners' Well I say: 'Beware ANC.'"

Mike replied: "Yes, it's a great pity. Do you know that one of the first students who was killed was 13-year-old Hector Pieterson? That's going to make very bad PR. He will become a martyr. We're going to pay for it."

"No, Mike, they're going to pay, not us," was Van Niekerk's defiant reply.

In the aftermath, the University of Zululand's records and administration buildings were set ablaze, and 33 people died in incidents in Port Elizabeth in August. In Cape Town, 92 people died between August and September.

The ANC printed and distributed leaflets with the slogan: "Free Mandela, hang Vorster".

Van Niekerk was absolutely livid. He blamed the Black Consciousness Movement (BCM) and the ANC for the rebellion and deaths. He swore to make amends.

He ranted: "I know where those fuckers are. They're too shit scared to stay in South Africa. They cause their destruction from the safety of Lusaka, Gaborone and Maseru. They think I can't get them. Well, they'd better think again while they still have a head to think with."

Van Niekerk initiated plans for raids on BCM and ANC cadres in these cities.

* * *

Friday 9th October

The plans for Operation Payback were complete. On 11 October, three groups of 100 men each would simultaneously cross borders into Zambia, Botswana and

Lesotho. Their targets were houses where members of the BCM and ANC were believed to be living or hiding.

The South African combatants were recruited from a special forces unit. These men were trained to operate behind enemy lines. Their creed was: "We fear naught but God and I will succeed with the guidance of my compass, the Word of God."

On the Friday evening, Van Niekerk phoned Mike at the apartment. "Mike, everything's in place to settle the score for the Soweto uprising. I know you would love to be part of the operation, so I have arranged with the officer commanding the Maseru operation for you to be seconded as part of their demolition crew. You can help blow up that bloody ANC cesspit on the outskirts of Maseru. You need to be here tomorrow. How about it? Are you up for it?"

Mike was horrified at the prospect. Think! Think! His mind was in turmoil. The lie came fairly easily: "Oh hell, Colonel, I've got the worst flu ever. I'm in bed as we speak. I'd love to go, but my sneezing will compromise the mission. Shit, I'm sorry." He added a double cough for authenticity. He held back on trying to sneeze, doubting his ability to mimic the sound.

"That's a pity. I know you would have valued a chance to hit back at those criminals. Maybe next time?"

"For sure. I'll be thinking of the lads."

He put down the receiver. "Shit, shit, shit!" he exclaimed.

His mind was racing. Van Niekerk is so in touch. Andile warned me that BOSS would be watching me. Has he seen through my excuse? Oh shit, Maseru. That's where Beauty lives. Sunday morning! I must warn Andile. Where's that number?"

The number rang. Eventually an answering machine kicked in. "Yo, it's Andile. You know the drill, so go for it."

"Andile ... It's Mike. The army's going to hit houses where they suspect ANC people are living in Maseru. I am worried your mum's there. Warn them. It's going to happen very early on Sunday morning. Call me on 021 689 7855."

Mike decided to take a chance to make sure Andile received the message. He called the only other person who could help Beauty.

"Hello, Solly Goldberg here."

"Doc, I need your help, so I am taking a bit of a chance here.'"

"Go for it.'"

"My friend, Andile, in London, told me the ANC has a mole in the psychiatric ward at Wynberg Military. I'm guessing it's you. I frickin' hope it's you."

"Uh huh."

"I can't get through to Andile. Can you use your contacts to warn the ANC about an attack on their homes in the outskirts of Maseru early on Sunday morning?"

"I can try."

That Sunday at 1am in the morning, 30 ANC activists and 12 Basotho were killed in Maseru by the South African Defence Force. The mission was accomplished without loss to the SA forces.

The South African newspapers, at least the ones favourably disposed to the government, hailed it as a victory for the SA Defence Force and a massive blow to ANC operations. It was alleged that the ANC casualties were all members of an active cell that made raids into South Africa. They had allegedly been planning terrorist activities against civilian targets.

Overseas newspapers gave a different account, denouncing the invasion as a "cold-blooded massacre", charging that the people who were killed were political refugees who had fled South Africa, not terrorists. No names were given.

38

FOR I STILL HAVE PLANS FOR YOU

Monday, 12th October

Mike was horrified when he read the papers reporting on the raids on ANC strongholds. He tried to call Andile, but there was no reply, nor was the answering machine on.

He called Solly. "Doc, what happened? Have you read the papers? How come the attack was successful? Shit, I should've gone to Maseru. I could've done something. I might've have been able to save Beauty."

"I'm not sure what happened. I passed on the message, as you asked. Maybe they couldn't get hold of anyone. Or possibly, they did and took a different approach, I can't say. I hope your friend's mother's okay. Let's chat on Thursday."

It was one of the quietest weeks since Mike had started as a PI, but he was just looking forward to seeing Lesley on Thursday to chat about leaving the country.

* * *

Thursday, 15th November 1976.

The ambulance stopped at Groote Schuur's Emergency Unit. Before they could unload their cargo, a senior policeman approached the driver, instructing him to move their patient to Wynberg Military Hospital.

Mike was in a coma, but stable. His wounds were categorised as serious but not critical. Dreams entered his stupor state. They were a mish-mash of serpents interacting with his dad, Maddy, Andile and Lesley. A new, and even more confusing scene had been added to the macabre mix. His mother was giving birth. A healthy baby came out of the birth canal laughing then crying, in a repetitive pattern.

Mike was in the coma for 14 days. Near the end, he could smell the typical medicinal odour and cleaning agent scents in the emergency ward. In the background, he could vaguely hear Van Niekerk asking someone: "How is he?"

Doctor Cilliers, the resident physician, answered: "He's in shock and a bit bashed up, but he'll be fine. This is a tough one, obviously from good stock. Do you know his parents?" The other voice asked.

"Sort of," Van Niekerk replied.

"I need a favour, Doc."

"Sure, Colonel, name it."

Mike couldn't hear the whispered exchange.

"I have three blood vials. I would like the labs to test using that HLA system of tissue typing. They're marked,

'A', 'M' and 'C'. I would like to know which one – 'A' or 'C' is the father of M."

"Okay, Colonel. It will be a few days. Can I guess? Is the young man on the bed 'M'?"

"You're too smart for your own good," replied Van Niekerk.

Van Niekerk stared at the comatose patient. He reflected on his current, frustrating love-hate relationship with the young man. His mind went back to 1962 when they met and had gone on the first hunting trip soon afterwards. Then he thought back to 1950 and the Beacon Island Hotel. Could it be? he wondered.

* * *

10th August 1950

The young Andre van Niekerk was amazed at how gorgeous Edith looked when he first saw her. She had a temporary assignment at the Beacon Island Hotel as housekeeping manager. He was an intern assistant manager doing his apprenticeship in the hospitality industry. He felt fortunate to be assigned to a coastal resort after growing up in the Karoo Desert region of South Africa.

He had admired her from a distance for weeks, before venturing to sit with her at coffee times and meals. He wondered why most Afrikaner boys found English girls intimidating. To Afrikaner boys, they were like aliens, and more liberal than Afrikaans girls.

Was Edith the exception? he wondered.

What was up with the wedding ring? He never saw her husband. Could it be a decoy? She never spoke of a husband.

He remained intimidated, but heard no hint of liberalism from her. She was friendly, but always preoccupied.

When he heard it was the last day of her assignment, he plucked up the courage to make his move.

She was inspecting rooms on the second floor. He knew she was alone. It was lunch time and all the cleaning had been done. He found the English rose in room 215.

"I find you so beautiful," he bumbled through his opening line.

"Why thank you, Mr van Niekerk," she replied.

"Is there any chance we could go to dinner sometime?" he continued.

"Oh dear, Mr van Niekerk, that won't be possible, I am happily married," she said, pointing at her ring finger.

"I see. If you're so happy, why haven't you mentioned your husband before?" His tone changed drastically.

"I don't see what that's got to do with you."

"You know, you English are so arrogant. You think you're better than us Afrikaners, don't you?"

"Mr van Niekerk, I have no idea what you mean. Please leave the room."

"I'll leave, I'll leave, but when I am good and ready," he said as primal lust hijacked his mind.

He crossed the distance between them in a dash, grabbed her arms and pushed her on to the king-sized bed in the centre of the room. Once again, with incredible speed, he pounced on her, pulling her dress up with his left hand while thrusting her panties down with his right, using his weight advantage to immobilise her.

His left elbow slipped under her chin, pressing down on her throat. The pain was excruciating as she struggled to breathe. Simultaneously, he thrust his hips to penetrate her. She had no moisture to assist entry, so he shoved harder and harder until he disappeared into her womanhood, causing cuts and tears. Mercifully, he ejaculated within seconds of entry. His discharge stung the walls of her vagina and also caused sanity to return to his crazed mind, like the flick of a light switch.

As he pulled his underpants over his turgid erection, Van Niekerk's thoughts raced. He knew he had committed a serious crime that carried severe consequences. He looked catatonic as he pleaded repeatedly in a high-pitched voice: "Oh God, I am sorry, oh God, I am sorry. I have sinned. Please forgive me. Forgive me Mrs Hanssen."

"Get out, Mr van Niekerk, GET OUT!" she spat with utter hate and loathing.

She lay on the bed distraught. Tears streamed down her face as blood trickled from the torn walls of her vagina.

The incident wasn't reported. The next time she saw Van Niekerk was when Carl introduced him in 1962.

* * *

Doctor Cilliers dropped the vials with the ward sister, instructing her to arrange the HLA tissue typing tests for Colonel van Niekerk's eyes only.

Nurse van Jaarsveld was in the ward when Mike finally woke up.

Mike tried to make sense of his situation, asking: "How long have I been here?"

"Hello, Mr Hanssen. Welcome to the world of the awake. You have been in a coma for 14 days. Now try to be still. When you feel able, let me know and I'll get you a nice cup of tea. I'm sure you will feel hungry soon. It's not nice surviving on a drip for so long. You can't taste the food, now can you?"

Mike replied: "Thank you. Do you know if a lady named Lesley called or asked for me?"

"Sorry, Mr Hanssen, no one by that name contacted the hospital."

He wondered ruefully why she hadn't visited. Was it because she couldn't, or wouldn't? Either way, it felt like a punch to the solar plexus. Being a part of each other had many pains, but being apart held no pleasures, he concluded.

"Your frequent visitors have been Colonel van Niekerk and Dr Solly Goldberg. They both asked me to let them know when you awake."

"Sure, let them know,"

A short while later, Van Niekerk and Doc Solly entered the ward.

"What happened?" Mike opened the conversation as they gathered around his bed.

"You tell me," Van Niekerk shot back.

Mike scanned his memory. A message on the answer machine ... adrenalin kicked in ... a dash for the door ... a blast hitting him from behind ... tinnitus in his ears ... flying through the air as if he had been shot from a canon in a circus act. Then nothing, not even dreams.

"I think there was a bomb blast at my office?"

"You got that right. Mike, when last did you check your office, or at least your phone, for bugs?"

"I haven't. Are you telling me my office was bugged?"

"I'm afraid so."

"Oh shit, by whom? ANC or BOSS?"

"You're lucky. As far as we can tell, just BOSS."

"And is my apartment bugged?"

"Funnily enough, it isn't.

"We heard about your warning to Andile through other sources. You know you signed Andile's death warrant when you tried to warn him about the Maseru operation? You nearly got away with it, but you made a big mistake."

"But how, who ..." Mike was bewildered.

"Think about it. Who did you tell about Maseru? Who did you tell about trying to warn Andile, Mike, who?"

"No one, except ... No, not you, Doc, not you. Surely it's not you."

The realisation that Solly was in cahoots with BOSS and had betrayed him hit Mike as if he had walked into a glass door.

The mendacious Doc Solly avoided eye contact.

"Solly, you helped to rebuild me. I trusted you, and then you deceived me. Why?"

Solly, his confidante, offered no protestation of innocence.

"I'm afraid he did, Mike. You're going to have to brush up on your investigating skills," continued the condescending Van Niekerk.

"We placed the good doctor with you the moment you moved into the psychiatric ward. Surely you, of all people, know that we have an agreement with the Mossad. Israeli and South African intelligence services work together. We face similar challenges, the Jews and us. They're God's chosen people and we've added ourselves to that list.[59]

"It was fortunate for us you that you called Doc Solly straight after you left the message on Andile's answering machine. Would you like to hear what you told Doc Solly? It's all recorded.

"It wasn't difficult for our doctor to call one of his Mossad agent mates in London to give him the brief. The job was done within two hours. They're nothing if not efficient, our

59 Israeli and South African military gave each other unfettered access to the other's battlefields and military tactics. Israel shared with South Africa highly classified information about its missions which had previously only been reserved for the United States. The South African government's yearbook of 1976 wrote: "Israel and South Africa have one thing above all else in common: They are both situated in a predominantly hostile world inhabited by dark peoples."

Jewish friends. You know that our impimpi, the venerable Andile, enjoyed taking substances for recreation. Pity he died of an overdose. You just can't trust the quality of things like heroin. Awful death … Eventually the overdose victims gag and suffocate in their vomit. It's quite gross."

"But … then why did you try to kill me?"

"No, Mike we didn't try to kill you. If we wanted you dead, you would be. We wanted it to look like we tried to kill you. We planned for you to survive. We know your skills and gave you enough time to make it out of the building. But, that's the past. You may be interested in what we have planned for you now."

Mike didn't reply. He was angry at his own shoddy work and devastated about Doc Solly's betrayal.

"I'll tell you anyway" the unscrupulous Van Niekerk continued smugly.

"Soon you will go to London, because you want to escape the horrible apartheid regime in South Africa. The ANC will trust you now. They think the South African government tried to kill you. Also, they will find your message on Andile's answering machine, warning him about Operation Payback. You see, nothing's stopping you from joining them. Then you can do for us what Andile failed to do.

"And don't even think of double-crossing us, because I will destroy your GDL. Yes, we will throw the Immorality Act at her, and your little half breed will face the full wrath of the law. If you try to escape with her overseas, I will finish her family.

"Of course, the Vineyard Hotel has been very co-operative. Amazing what one will do when one's licence is under threat. And, naturally, we have some great pics. I'm sure you remember the part in your little show where she's on her back and dangles her legs over your shoulders – nice touch. She really liked that position. Think I'll try it sometime.

"Oh yes, I almost forgot. She phoned you last Thursday after we left the warning on your machine. She also left a message. I remember it word perfect."

Van Niekerk recited it as if he were in a stage show: "Something has come up, I need to cancel tonight. I'll explain later," he said, impersonating a female voice with a slight coloured accent.

Van Niekerk quipped: "There you are. Aren't you lucky? You didn't miss much. She stood you up, anyway.

"Oh yes, Doc Solly tells me you abandoned God, not so Doc? I haven't listened to your confession yet, but that's good news, Mike, because from now on the old Snake Van Niekerk's your God. I can't have you confusing your loyalties."

Mike felt as if he were in a trance. As he watched Van Niekerk's face, he realised that he was seeing the face of the serpent from his dreams.

The deceitful duo left his ward to wreak havoc elsewhere, leaving Mike to contemplate his impossible predicament. Van Niekerk gave a parting jibe as he went out the door: "By the way, thanks for the tip-off about the mole in the hospital. We are dealing with it."

An ashen-faced Mike closed his eyes, but was brought back to reality when a green-eyed nursing sister with auburn hair walked into the ward.

"Ahem," she cleared her throat to attract his attention. "Mr Hanssen, are you alright? You look as pale as a ghost. Can I get you something?"

He didn't reply.

"Let me introduce myself. I am your ward sister … ta-da … all the way from Mozambique, Sister Mandy Macadam. My job's to look after you."

About the Author

Dr Steve Harris lives in Cape Town. He is a successful business man, a conference speaker and an academic. His most noteworthy past and present activities are:

- PhD and MBA
- Author of Mental Toughness Mastering your Mind
- CEO of eta College – specializing in sport and exercise science qualifications
- Former mind coach for the Springbok rugby team
- Former team manager for the Springbok rugby team
- Winner Anglo American's national "Build a Business" contest for entrepreneurs
- Former world champion in surf lifesaving
- Former general manager of an international F.M.C.G. company

ALSO FROM STEVE HARRIS

Mental Toughness: Mastering Your Mind

A practical, no-nonsense look at mental toughness

(Kindle Edition)

"An easy reading practical guide to mastering your mind and enhancing performance in life, business or sport. Many books cover these area's but few make practical sense to make it achievable." – Howard Vernon

www.ingramcontent.com/pod-product-compliance
Lightning Source LLC
Chambersburg PA
CBHW031427240626
47154CB00001B/237